In Alpha Redemption, a story wonderfully marries two of my of space exploration and the i insight into his own Creator.

introspective side—on the order of Clarke's *2001* or Pohl's *Gateway*— then this is a must read.

~ Kerry Nietz, author of *A Star Curiously Singing*, 2010 Indie Book Awards Finalist in Science Fiction and Religious Fiction categories

An all nighter, can't-put-it-down read, with a unique twist I didn't see coming and the perfect book for fans of Asimov or Clarke!

~ Dana Bell, author of *Winter Awakening*

Alpha Redemption is a haunting sci-fi tale told through the masterful prose of P. A. Baines. Astronaut Brett Denton is on a light speed journey to Alpha Centauri, but his true journey is one of tragic self discovery as he delves into his past and confronts the hidden pain there. With echoes of *2001: A Space Odyssey* and *The Curious Case of Benjamin Button*, this is a treat for any hard sci-fi lover and a must for every Christian who has ever doubted their faith in the one true God.

~ Kirk Outerbridge, author of *Eternity Falls* and *The Tenth Crusader*

A book that is not simply bold and adventurous but also well-written. Bravo!

~ Chris Walley, author of the *Lamb among the Stars* trilogy

An inspiring look forward to mankind's first reach for the stars, and to AI's first reach for something beyond its programming.

~ Ryan Grabow, author of *Caffeine*

With *Alpha Redemption*, Baines demonstrates himself as a master wordsmith. The prose is so flawless the story is not so much written as woven of character and plot threads plucked from a fully functioning universe. A brilliant star added to the galaxy of space opera.

~ Lara Bowers, Book Reviewer

Alpha Redemption is a beautiful work of art, cleverly told, portraying deep spiritual themes—a perfect storm of fiction. The daring parallel structure of *Alpha* is wildly successful, both in terms of mere pleasure in reading, and the manner in which it drives the story forward.

It is heart-wrenching, pulling with the force of a bulldozer. From start to end, my heart leapt for Baines' main character, and, unpredictably, for his secondary character. Baines possessed the creative ability to make me feel for a computer! Move over, Hal…meet Jay.

Alpha's pacing flowed superbly, striking a nice balance between philosophy, action, and the resulting character development. The story is deeply satisfying, the characters are interesting and compelling, and the reader will pull for them…and the gospel. This one's a clear winner.

~ Marc Schooley, author of *The Dark Man* and *König's Fire*

Alpha Redemption is that rarest of combinations: both thoughtful and emotional. Baines has crafted an intriguing and beautiful story of love, loss, and grace. While simultaneously tackling the singularly sci-fi question, what is humanity, the author weaves questions of greater importance: what is the soul, and what is love. *Alpha Redemption* is a brief, but ambitious work, spanning an entire lifetime, and Baines has managed to work all these disparate parts into a wonderful, eminently readable, enjoyable piece.

~ Randy Streu, Editor, Digital Dragon Magazine

ALPHA
REDEMPTION

P.A. BAINES

Copyright © P.A. Baines 2010

ISBN-13: 978-0-9864517-4-4

Cover design by Zoë Demaré (front) and Grace Bridges (back)

Edited by C.L. Dyck, Scienda Editorial

Published by Splashdown Books, New Zealand

www.splashdownbooks.com

The ship loomed overhead, its shadow engulfing them. Its smooth white skin filled the window, slowly obscuring their view of the Earth as the elevator rose. It stopped, and pneumatic seals hissed and whirred into place. Brett followed the technician through the airlock, pausing only to get a final glimpse of the planet he would not see again for almost a decade. He craned his neck to get a look but the ship's hull now blocked his view. All he could see was a sliver of atmosphere and a handful of stars.

It was his first time inside the Comet, but he knew it intimately from months of training. They were in the cockpit but there were no instruments: no joystick or control console, or even a windscreen—at least not in the usual sense of the word. There was nothing for him to do other than get into the hyper-sleep chamber that crouched in the middle of the floor like a grotesque, mutated iron lung. He climbed the steps, turning to look towards the open airlock while the technician helped him connect the hoses, checking and double-checking the seal around his mouth. His initial discomfort at having something attached to his face faded as he relaxed the way they had taught him in the swimming pool, focusing on breathing slowly and deeply.

He slid into the transparent chamber and his legs, hips, torso and chest became weightless in the clinging embrace of the syrupy goo. It covered his head and he opened his eyes, blinking uncomfortably into the yellow haze. He knew it was vital to immerse the eyes; they had stressed that many times. *Remember to open them wide and have a good look around.*

He could see the airlock from here, and the technician, now an amorphous blob, moving around the front of the bath, back and forth, back and forth. Brett felt a shudder as the lid closed and sealed over his head. A vague fear surfaced in the deepest recesses of his mind—*what if...?* then vanished again like a puff of breath on a chilly autumn morning.

After a final thumbs-up, the technician disappeared through the airlock, leaving Brett alone in his bath, breathing filtered air through a hose, listening to the muted sounds of the ship as it prepared to launch him towards an impossibly distant point of light.

In his dream-like cocoon, Brett could sense very little. Everything seemed muted and far away. He heard distant hisses, cavernous booms, and the ghostly shriek of metal on metal. Vibrations passed through the liquid and nudged at his body as if to alert him to some impending danger.

He could see the hoses drifting. His legs floated like odd-shaped creatures in a yellow sea. Then the vibrations stopped and there was no sound other than his heart beating softly in his ears. The taste of the air being fed to him through his mouthpiece changed. It reminded him of something. Was it watermelon? He could not remember the last time he had eaten a watermelon. He could not remember the last time he had *seen* a watermelon. Maybe they were extinct. Like dinosaurs. Hit by an asteroid; drowning in the mud; arms too short to take out the seeds...

Brett became aware that he was no longer thinking clearly, but that was fine. He watched his thoughts tumbling along like pretty little shards of plastic in a kaleidoscope, tumbling, tumbling, ever changing, never the same picture twice.

And at some point—he did not know exactly when—his thoughts faded as darkness washed over him and he slipped into hyper-sleep.

2

Elapsed mission time on Earth: 11 months
Relative time on the Comet: 2 months
Test subject's genetic age: 45

Waking up from a long hyper-sleep was like being excavated from stone. Early in the training Brett had spent a day under to get a feel for what it would be like, but nothing could have prepared him for the full two-month haul. After finishing that training day he had felt a little unsteady, with a dry mouth and a dull pain behind his eyes.

This was like waking from the dead.

His whole body ached, his mouth was as dry as sawdust. His eyeballs throbbed, and his lungs felt as if they were breathing stale tobacco smoke. He suppressed a cough.

It escaped anyway, sending a bolt of pain through his chest and back, down his hips to the soles of his feet. He grimaced, clamping his teeth into the mouthpiece. His jaw cracked, forcing a wave of pain along the side of his face and through his skull.

He cursed the mission team. This was all very experimental and he was a "pioneer" but he hated them for putting him through this.

He opened his eyes. Even that hurt after so long without moving. The image that his optic nerves displayed to his brain was a hazy blur. He forced his lids open and closed—very slowly—until the haze sharpened a little, forming something that made more sense. He could see the hose dangling like an umbilical cord. He made out his limbs, his arms, his pale feet and hands. He kicked his legs and immediately regretted it. He waited for the pain to subside and tried again, reaching down behind his back. He was about an inch above the seat. His fingers made contact with the hard surface and stung the way feet do when they have been dangling for a while and you jump down onto the floor.

He paused and tried again. Kicking, pulling, and generally flailing about, he was able to drag himself into an upright position. His head rose out of the liquid. He blinked.

The light inside the cabinet was almost non-existent, but it still hurt. He reached for the mouthpiece and pulled. In spite of the lubricant the surface was still stuck to his skin. He peeled it off like a band-aid.

"Ow!"

His mouth, throat and lungs, all tinder-dry, erupted into a fit of coughing. Each hack pummelled his chest and ribcage. When it was over he sat, exhausted and battered, with yellow goo running down his face and dripping from his lips, chin and ears.

He sat until the pain had faded enough for him to think straight. Then, very slowly and very carefully, he pushed himself into a standing position. He held onto the rim with both hands, waiting to make sure the gravity system was behaving. They still did not fully understand the technology and he did not want a repeat of some of the earlier "glitches" he had witnessed during training, especially not while he was in such a fragile state. Unstable artificial gravity could be funny but painful.

"Good morning, Brett," a voice said. It was pleasant, devoid of accent, and obviously not human. It was the on-board computer.

Brett just stood there. The room was pirouetting about him. He tried to ignore his desire to throw up.

"Good morning, Brett," the voice said again.

Brett, fighting the need to cough, nodded his head.

"Mission day three-hundred-and-thirty-four. Current speed is nine-hundred-and-thirty-seven miles per second or zero-point-five

4

percent of light speed. Three-point-two terabytes of data have been transmitted to Earth for analysis. Do you want breakfast?"

"No," Brett hissed.

"Will there be anything else?"

Brett shook his head. "No."

"Have an enjoyable day," the voice said. "Please remember to visit the medical bay for a check-up."

"Fine," Brett said.

Grateful for the silence, he waited a moment before climbing the steps to the top of the tank. He paused with each ascent. Every step was a mountain; each riser was an Everest. At the top, he turned in a clumsy shuffle and started down the other side.

At the floor, he tried to move but the hose attached to his chest tugged at him. He looked down, exasperated. He fiddled with the release clip, but his fingers were as effective as cucumbers. He pulled and tugged and cursed. He flexed his fingers. They were numb. He forced one finger under the clasp and, with the other hand, pulled. The hose cascaded onto the floor like a vanquished beast. Under his feet, tiny holes had already begun the process of sucking up any excess goo. It tickled a little, even through the cotton-wool numbness.

He looked around the room, trying to get his bearings. The hyper-sleep chamber was at the front of the ship facing backwards, so he needed to go…this way. He reoriented himself and moved across the hard bare floor on soft bare feet, wincing with each step. As he passed through the doorway, bright lights came on.

He squinted. This next room was the same shape as the first, but marginally larger. The whole ship was roughly cigar-shaped, being a little fatter in the middle, which, according to the scientists, was the best for travelling at the speed of light.

He looked around the bathroom. It was complete with toilet compartment, air-shower, and a vanity unit fit for a movie-star with full-length mirrors on three sides. He began to strip out of the suit, pausing for a rest every few seconds. It was skin-tight and not easy to take off. He peeled himself like a snake shedding its skin, squeezing and contracting

5

one inch at a time. He leaned against a wall to support himself and felt the subtlest of vibrations in his palm. The skin of the ship was maybe four or five inches thick.

He pulled his hand away and placed the sodden suit in a laundry compartment which immediately sucked it out of the back to be cleaned, dried, and stored for later use. He entered the shower, closed the door, and tapped a button. There was a hissing sound and the movement of air all around him. Thirty seconds later he was clean and dry.

He made his way towards the next compartment, pausing at the toilet in case his bladder or bowels decided to start working again. Not yet, and no sign of hunger either. He felt hollow, but his brain did not seem to associate this with the need for food.

As he passed the vanity unit, he caught his reflection in the big central mirror. He turned and moved closer. A light in the ceiling came on, flooding him in the kind of blemish-revealing clarity he had taken to avoiding in recent years.

He examined his reflection, turning his face to the left and to the right. He felt the crown of his head and to his surprise and delight, found hair where for the past four years there had been none. Pattern baldness had claimed him as a victim, leaving the top of his head a barren wasteland. He had tried creams and pills, but eventually submitted himself to the humiliation of a bald spot.

He tipped his head forwards. Where there had recently been skin was now thick hair. And the sideburns were dark brown, with not a grey strand in sight. He peered at his forehead. It was hard to say for sure, but the skin seemed smoother. The wrinkles were still there, but not as pronounced as he remembered.

Apparently a two-month stint in hyper-sleep was just what he needed. Forget face-lifts and hair-plugs; submerge yourself in yellow goo to get that youthful look. Just don't get out of the bath too early, or they'll be able to pass you through a sieve.

The next room was essentially a walk-in cupboard lined with a honeycomb of shelving that carried clothes, towels, and the nifty swimming gear that was required dress for the hyper-sleep. He found underpants, trousers, a tee-shirt, and footwear that was something between a shoe and a sock. He dressed slowly and carefully for fear of hurting his tender body.

Then came the bedroom. A large bed, a contoured desk with a high-backed leather chair, a recliner with the softest-looking cushions he had ever seen. A futuristic computer console and an entertainment centre with TV, music and games. Very nice. Very Japanese. He just hoped he would survive to enjoy some of it. This whole exercise was very theoretical, as were the effects of travelling at those kinds of speeds, which probably explained why they had asked him some seriously bizarre questions early on in the induction process.

Through the next door was the kitchen. In one corner was a mountainous piece of equipment that was a larder, freezer, chef, waiter, bartender, and dishwasher all rolled into one bulbous unit. They said it even kept itself clean, which he was happy to know. He had asked what he should do if it broke down and they had laughed the way the wise laugh at the foolish and said it wouldn't.

He shuffled through another doorway. He was in the gym, but he didn't bother to look too closely. He would be spending a good deal of his time in here, trying to undo the damage inflicted on him by his little jaunts to light speed. At the back was a small medical unit that could do everything from x-ray a fracture to analyse his body fat content. He opened the unit's door and stepped inside. It was roughly the size of a small cylindrical cupboard with a console at about waist height. There was a hiss as the door slid shut and the unit sealed.

"Place your hands inside the circles and close your eyes please," the computer's flat voice said.

Brett complied. A bright light penetrated through his eyelids. His palms became warm on the console.

"Take three deep breaths."

Brett filled his lungs and exhaled three times.

"Thank you," the voice said. "Analysis complete. Ship's time adjusted to oh-eight-hundred hours."

The door slid open and Brett stepped out. The palms of his

hands were tingling.

"So?" he said. "How did I do?"

"Your health is within acceptable parameters."

"So, no problems?"

"Your health is within acceptable parameters."

Brett shrugged and moved to the next compartment. It was an exact copy of the hyper-sleep room. Instead of a bath, however, it was home to an emergency escape pod. The idea was that, in the event of a catastrophic problem, he could use the pod to jettison himself from the ship. This was fine, but they had explained two problems to him. The first was that they did not fully understand the physics of launching an escape pod at the speed of light. The second was that even if the launch were successful, the pod would drift in the same direction as the Comet until it was stopped *by* something or collided *with* something. The idea was just to get away from the Comet. The designers had not thought much beyond that.

He stared at it. Best not to dwell on what might go wrong. Over the course of the mission he would be moving through space at speeds only really understood in theory by people with big brains and bad haircuts. In principle, every breath he took was a miracle.

He was now about two thirds of the way down the Comet, but that was it for him. He could go no further. Beyond the wall was the massive prototype engine. They had explained its workings to him but he had not understood then and probably never would. It didn't matter. If the engine developed a major problem he would be dead before he realised something was wrong.

His stomach growled. A pang of hunger came and went. He put his hand on his belly. His digestive system was waking up.

"Time to try out that kitchen appliance," he said out loud.

"Can I be of assistance?" the voice said.

"In a minute," Brett said.

Waking up alone in his apartment is like exchanging one bad dream for another. Brett stares out of the window, watching the sky drift by while the city stretches and groans and wipes the sleep from its eyes in a bad-tempered pre-coffee slump. On the clock-radio, some idiot disc jockey is venting his spleen about something or other.

He sits up and tries to remember what it is he is supposed to be doing today. A cup of tea first, then a shower. And he has that letter to post and some shopping to do. After that? Who knows? He doesn't think that far ahead.

He gets up and walks to the kitchenette to turn on the kettle. The DJ is still talking. The man's voice is annoying but Brett hates silence more. The kettle hisses and bubbles to life. He opens the fridge to get milk and notices the beers are finished. He looks around for a pen to update his shopping list. It is then that he hears the music coming from the apartment upstairs.

He switches on the television and turns it up loud. He walks from room to room, trying not to listen, his head tilted to one side. Agitated, he washes and shaves. He watches the chat-show hosts ooze their fake charm from behind fake smiles while he nibbles at his cold toast and sips at his cold tea. He can't decide if it is his imagination, but the music upstairs seems to have grown louder. He can hear the odd harmony drifting down. He recognises the album. It was her favourite.

He takes the hi-fi remote and turns on the music. He presses the volume button until the rich strains of a Rachmaninoff concerto fill the tiny apartment, but still the sounds filter through along with a thousand painful memories. He crawls back into bed, sinking under the sheets, wrapping the blanket around his chest, shoulders and head, but it is no use. Somewhere, the sound of her song is still playing. He plugs his ears with his fingers, driving them deep enough so that his nails dig into the skin. Still, the music seeps through.

9

He tears himself from the bed, dressing quickly. He brushes his thinning hair with trembling hands, ignoring the banging on the wall (Mrs. Shandler, judging by the direction). Normally he would turn the volume down until the hammering on the wall stopped, but not today.

He lifts the envelope from the kitchen counter table and weighs it in his hand, as if trying to decide. His life is inside that envelope, or at least the rest of his life, whatever that may be worth. He expected it to be heavier somehow. Important things should be heavy—it only seems right.

He closes the door just as the concerto's first movement reaches its dramatic end. Mrs. Shandler opens her apartment door as he passes by and glares at him with undisguised hostility. He walks against the far wall, keeping as far away from her as possible. No doubt she will complain about the noise, but then she complains about everything. Mrs. Shandler is the type of woman who likes complaining.

The air is brisk and he pulls up the collar on his jacket. People bustle past with the coats drawn closed and their heads down. Taxis ply their trade. Shops advertise their latest bargains. Brett recognises one or two people as he walks but he looks away to avoid catching their eyes, and they seem to do the same.

He travels almost three blocks to the nearest post box, hesitating a moment before letting the letter fall into the waiting chasm, releasing it the way a mother lets go of the hand of her toddler as he takes his first steps alone.

Two more blocks further along he comes to the supermarket. Mercifully, it is almost empty. He clutches the basket and his list in one hand and scours the aisles. Tea, milk, sugar, cereal. Ahead in the aisle, an old man is talking to himself. Pretending to look for something, Brett turns and goes around the other way. He has had more than one awkward conversation with a muttering old man. Muttering old men like to talk with strangers the way Mrs. Shandler likes to complain. Or maybe it's just him. Maybe he has a big sign hung on him that only crazy old mutterers and complainers can see.

The cashier rings his items through. Brett does not recognise her, even though he has shopped here almost every week since moving out this way about a year ago. Like many people these days, she talks incessantly.

"That'll be twenty-two dollars ninety-eight," she says cheerfully. "You got a store card?"

"No," Brett replies, handing her twenty-five dollars. "I'm afraid I don't."

"It's easy to apply for one."

"No. Thanks."

"Say, you're not from around here, are you?"

Brett shifts his weight. A conversation is heading his way and there isn't a thing he can do to avoid it.

"I know that accent," she says. "You're from England. I had a friend from England. She was from Luton, I think. Anyway, she was from the middle part. Where are you from?"

"I left when I was young."

"Really. Well you still got the accent."

"I guess you never lose some things." He holds out his hand but she seems determined to keep hold of the change. He coughs and looks down at his hand and then back to her again.

"Oh, sorry. I just love meeting people from interesting places. It makes a change from the usual crowd that never go further than the end of the road, you know?"

Brett shrugs and extends his hand a little further. She takes the hint and counts the money into his palm. He packs his meagre spoils into a paper bag.

"You have a nice day now," she says, smiling.

He nods and heads for the exit sign.

He walks briskly back to his apartment block and checks his mail before taking the elevator. He passes Mrs. Shandler's door, which is open. He can see her talking into the telephone with one hand on her hip and the other making big gestures to emphasise whatever she is saying to the person on the other end. He suspects it is probably about him.

Even from out in the corridor he can hear that Rachmaninoff has stopped and that the talk show hosts have been replaced a by an extremely boisterous cartoon character. He unlocks the door and steps inside. The place is still a mess and he knows he needs to do something about it, but he just can't see the point. Rochelle would have had it ship-shape within days of moving in. It would have driven her nuts to have so much junk lying around. She always had so much energy. He misses her energy.

He weaves his way between the stacks of boxes to the kitchenette. He fills the kettle and plugs it in. He rinses a mug while he waits for the water to boil. Steam rises from the spout and billows under and around the cupboards. He flicks the switch before the automatic cut-off can kick in.

He carries the mug to the answering machine and nurses it between his hands, sipping noisily as he listens to the messages. It is a herb tea. He does not particularly like herb tea but he has grown used to it over the years. Even though there is no-one to nag him about healthy eating, he carries on buying some things out of sheer habit.

They used to shop at the bulk-supermarket out of town, the four of them driving out first thing on a Saturday morning and filling the trunk with enough to last a week, sometimes two. Then there was the nibbling of treats on the way back home; the lugging of bloated bags into the house; the loading of cupboards and the fridge and freezer. Happy hunters returning with the spoils.

The answering machine has one message from the removal company asking about insurance details. They broke a table leg during the move. Brett told them not to worry but they said it was policy to claim on insurance. *Suit yourself*, he thinks. *Knock yourself out.*

The woman has a squeaky voice. She sounds a little like an excited lap-dog. She wants him to phone her at his earliest convenience. How about a slightly later convenience?

He deletes the message and carries his tea over to the sofa under the window. The rain has picked up again and rush-hour is filling the street with cars and pedestrians. From up here they look comical as they walk under the window, like little pendulums tick-tocking along.

His foot bumps something and he glances down at a sheet of paper on top of a box marked "books #3", its pages curled and creased, and torn where he separated the attached application form. He filled it in and sent it off more out of curiosity than anything else (and because his last job at the supermarket let him go). Two days later a package arrived with five dense pages of questions and an intriguing, if vague, description of what the job would entail. He had doubts while filling it in and he still does, but it is too late now. He has posted it. All there is left to do is wait. No doubt they will be inundated with applications. Unemployment is at a record high, even in his line of work. He has more chance of winning the lottery, and he doesn't even play the lottery.

He tosses the sheet onto the seat next to him and glances into the box. He pulls back the lid and looks inside. It contains photo albums of a variety of sizes and colours. He lifts out one of the bigger ones. It is covered in faded red velvet. A cracked strip of dull silver foil runs from top to bottom about an inch from the outside edge. The album is thick and heavy and crammed with pictures. One falls out and he reaches for it, but stops short when he sees it.

There are four people in the picture, all smiling at the camera, gathered around a large yellow beach umbrella. They are on a carpet of white sand edged by a shimmering blue sea. The man and woman are sitting on a blue and red striped blanket while the boys are standing behind them with ice-creams in their brown hands and white sun-block smeared on their noses and cheeks.

Brett stares at the picture for a long time. Then he slides it back into the album. He walks to the kitchen and opens a cupboard door. He takes down a bottle of liquor and a plastic cup. He pours until the cup is full and downs it in three gulps. Then he pours himself another and downs that. He repeats this until his hands have stopped shaking. An hour later he is passed out on the sofa, clutching the empty bottle to his chest.

Brett nibbled at his food in spite of his body's insistence that he cram as much down his throat as possible. Two months was a long time to go without solids, and it was vital that he take it easy. Lunch was a small shake and a banana. He would have preferred a cheeseburger with fries but the food contraption thing was on strict orders from the computer. Brett sat and sipped and nibbled.

He used his finger to scrape out the last of the milkshake, placed the food tray in the disposal unit, and closed the door. He pushed a button and watched through the glass as the cup and banana peel dropped out of sight. A nozzle slid into view, turned and sprayed, then was gone.

He walked to the bedroom. It took him a while to get seated in the reclining chair. A couple of times his muscles cramped and he thought he might be stuck, but once he was settled he imagined it was possible to spend the rest of the trip there. The cool leather was soft against his skin and the padding supported him in all the right places. He lay back and wallowed for a while, then decided to explore his entertainment options.

"Computer?" he said.

"How can I help you?" the voice said.

"I want to watch television."

"What would you like to watch?"

"What have you got?"

"Films, television archives, games, music, and an encyclopaedia."

"What films?"

"A comprehensive archive covering a wide variety of genres from the very first black-and-white silent films right through to the latest Hollywood blockbusters and independent releases."

"How about Laurel and Hardy?"

"We have every surviving film featuring Laurel and Hardy.

Would you like to see any title in particular?"

"Maybe later. How about…Plan Nine from Outer Space?"

"Original or remake?"

"Remake? I didn't even know they'd made one."

"Yes, two years ago. It was a final year project of Dmitri Dumovic. It was never released to the cinema."

"How did you…? Never mind."

"Would you like to watch it?"

"Not at the moment."

"Will there be anything else?"

Brett reached his arms over his head and stretched. To his surprise, he was sleepy. Apparently, two months had not been enough.

"No," he said, closing his eyes, already feeling himself slipping. "Nothing else."

He wakes to the sound of a buzzer, and it takes him a few moments to register that the sound is in fact coming from inside his apartment. The bottle rolls out of the crook in his arm and bounces noisily on the thin carpet. An invisible tent-peg smashes through his brain.

"Hang on," he hisses, but of course nobody can hear him. He is on the seventh floor and the intercom is on the other side of the room and, anyway, he needs to press the button.

The buzzer sounds again; short, impatient bursts, over and over.

"I'm coming," he mutters. He sits up, pausing while the freight train drives over his neurons.

After a few seconds, the pain subsides enough. He rises and walks gingerly across the floor. He hits his toe on a box and curses. He is still cursing as he presses the button on the intercom.

"What?"

15

"Parcel," a voice says. "You gotta sign."

"Come up. Seventh floor."

Brett presses the button to open the front door to the building, then unlocks his apartment door and leans out. Happily, the corridor is deserted. He can hear the elevator moving. A young man—a kid—in a uniform steps out with an envelope in his hands. He looks one way, then the other. He sees Brett and saunters over.

"Brett Denton?"

"Yes."

"Sign here, please."

Brett takes the device and signs his name on the glass screen. A green light flashes. The machine is happy. The date flashes. That can't be right.

"What day is it today?" Brett asks.

"Saturday. Twelfth. Here, look."

"Are you sure?"

The kid doesn't answer; his spotty expression says it all.

Brett hands back the machine. He has lost a day somewhere, but he can't figure out how. He walked in the door on Thursday afternoon, or at least he *thinks* it was Thursday. What happened to Friday? Did he sleep all the way through?

"Thanks," the kid says, handing him the envelope. "Rough night, huh?"

Brett growls and closes the door. The kid mutters something out in the hall but Brett is not in the mood.

The envelope is thin and light. He peels back the seal. It is a single sheet of paper: a formal letter inviting him to attend an interview in three days. He runs his hands through his clammy hair. He needs a shower.

"An interview," he mutters.

He has not been to one of those in a while. He is going to need to find his suit.

Brett was pulled from his sleep by the sound of a voice repeating his name. For a few moments he was completely disoriented. He lifted his head and looked around, but did not know where he was. He was lying on a white bed in a strange, white room. Then he remembered.

"It is time to get up," the voice said. "You have had your required sleep."

"Okay, okay," Brett said, yawning. "I'm awake."

He performed a quick mental examination of himself. His muscles felt a little weak, but the aching had subsided. He was hungry but not ravenous. His eyes were sore but much better than yesterday. And his bladder was ready to explode.

Using his elbows as levers, he pushed himself up and waited for the pain to strike. There was a twinge in the back of his shoulder but otherwise he felt pretty good. He stood and tested his legs. He walked to the toilet and relieved himself for what seemed like forever.

"You are deficient in sodium and iron," the voice said. "I will adjust your supplements accordingly."

Brett glared up at the ceiling. "Do you have to do that?"

"I do not understand," the voice said.

"Can't you at least wait till I'm finished? Haven't you heard of privacy?"

"I am programmed to inform you of changes to your physical condition—"

"Do you have to do it while I'm, you know, busy?"

"I can wait."

"Good, then wait."

Brett finished up and cleaned his hands. He walked to the vanity unit, pausing to see if the changes yesterday had been temporary. His hair was still all there and, if anything, he looked even better. He turned sideways. His stomach was flatter than he remembered as well.

"You are deficient in sodium and iron," the voice said. "I will adjust your menu accordingly."

"Yes, I know. You already told me."

"I was acceding to your wishes. Was that a suitable time?"

Brett rolled his eyes. "Fine. Oh, and another thing."

"Yes?"

"What does acceding mean?"

"It means to agree to something."

"Well don't use it again. In fact from now on I don't want you using any words I don't understand."

"Certainly, but how will I know—?"

"Just don't."

"I will do my best."

Brett ate his bacon and eggs slowly, relishing every bite. The coffee was all right, but would take some getting used to.

The "washing-up" involved placing everything into the food contraption. He settled into the chair for some reading. He was in the mood for a bit of science fiction, but elected to struggle with the reader's menu system rather than talk to the computer.

"Acceding," he muttered, tapping the screen until he found a list of titles.

He selected a book and got comfortable. He scrolled to the first page and stepped into a fantastic world filled with altered realities, cranky robots, and exotic aliens.

He stands in front of the building feeling a curious mix of nerves and elation. He has not slept well for the past three nights, but then he has not had to apply for a real job for over a decade. He has forgotten how much he hates having to sell himself.

He pulls at his coat and touches the zip on his pants, then

reminds himself that he should not do that. He looks up. The impressive glass exterior towers over him and he suddenly feels very small in the world. A large ornate sign informs him that Galac Enterprises owns all twenty stories in this building. He has never heard of Galac Enterprises before now.

He heads for the entrance and looks around. The reception desk is opposite. It is black marble and staffed by two smartly-dressed women. Behind them, another sign reminds him who owns the building. Over to the side, close to the tinted windows, a security guard half watches him. In the centre, a turnstile leads to elevators.

"Can I help you, sir?" one of the receptionists asks.

"Brett Denton," he says, sliding the letter across the polished marble.

She glances at the paper, turns to her computer and taps the keys. "Fifth floor. Room five-oh-nine. They're expecting you." She hands him an ID card. "Please return this when you leave."

He takes the ID and clips it to his belt. The security guard is still watching as Brett follows a grey-haired man in a dark suit through the turnstile.

Three others ride with him in the lift. By the time the doors open again he is pleased to escape the muzak and the awkward closeness.

The fifth floor is all maple panelling with surprisingly thick grey carpets and white marbled trim. It still has that new-carpet smell and clearly a lot of money has been spent to create the impression of wealth. It is sumptuous. A sign directs him to rooms five-oh-five through five-ten.

The one he wants is at the end of a closed corridor.

He knocks.

"Come," a small voice says.

He pushes against the heavy wooden door and finds himself standing in a reception room with a wooden desk and plenty of plants. There is a row of Spartan but comfortable-looking white leather chairs along two walls. A window reveals a spectacular view of the city.

"Mr. Denton?" the secretary asks.

19

Brett hands her the letter. She glances at it and hands it back.

"Please take a seat," she says. "They will see you in about five minutes."

Brett moves to the corner and examines a selection of magazines spread neatly on a low glass table. He scans the titles; all are very high-brow stuff. He settles for a scientific journal and eases himself onto a chair. The keys click faintly on the secretary's computer as she types. He can hear voices in another room and footsteps padding down the corridor. A woman with a tall hairstyle peeks in and mouths the word "lunch" to the secretary, who nods.

Brett makes an attempt at reading the journal but, although the words enter his retinas, they are not intercepted by his brain, and so drift off to wherever it is things go that are not understood. He flips from page to page. A picture here and an ad there; an article about evolution; a glossy artistic rendition of a Neanderthal standing on a hill, carrying a club, and looking longingly at a herd of woolly mammoth. The headline asks: "Were Neanderthals as smart as modern man?" There is a photograph of a bearded, bespectacled man showing off a small selection of bone fragments. Brett wonders how they manage to figure out so much from so little. Obviously they *know*. They are scientists. Scientists know these things.

The adjoining double doors glide open, and the voices Brett heard before spill out.

"Thank you," a young man in a smart pin-striped suit says. He strides past the secretary with his stylish black hair and new briefcase, steps into the corridor and is gone. His cologne hangs around for a little while longer just to make sure everyone knows he was here.

The secretary tells Brett to go through.

He stands, closes the journal, and tucks it back in where he found it. He tugs at his jacket and remembers not to check his zip. He walks in through the doors, suddenly conscious of his fading brown shoes and twenty-year-old suit.

He was well into the story when the computer interrupted him.

"Please go to the kitchen. It is time for your mid-morning snack."

Brett checked the clock. He had been reading for two hours. "I'm almost finished this chapter. Later, all right?"

"The food is ready. Please make your way to the kitchen."

"In a moment."

There was a pause.

"According to your schedule, it is time for your snack."

Brett sighed. He set a bookmark and placed the reader on the table. He lifted himself out of the chair and made his way to the kitchen.

He stood with his arms folded in front of the serving hatch.

"So what am I having?"

"Chicken soup and wholemeal bread, and a small glass of grape juice."

"Any chance of a beer?"

"Beer is not on my list."

"What about a gin and tonic?"

"Gin is not on my list."

There was a hiss and a ping. A tray appeared. He carried it to the table and sat down. He rolled a slice of bread and dipped it into the soup. It was a little too hot for his liking but it was, he had to admit, quite tasty. He sipped his grape juice. He would have preferred a beer or some spirit but it was probably a little early for gin anyway. Then again, what was "too early" when you were moving so quickly that light had to break into a sweat to keep up with you? Keeping time on the Comet was more about the rhythm of having a steady cycle so that his body could figure out what to expect and when.

He sat, holding the glass in one hand, listening to the ship. The vibration was subtle enough to miss if you were not trying to notice it. The hull was soundproofed and he had been assured that there was no chance of any engine noise leaking into the cabin space. The engine produced frequencies that, while beyond the range of the human ear, could cause all sorts of problems in his body.

On the other hand, absolute silence was also undesirable. What he was hearing was "genuine artificial background nature": wind rustling softly through the leaves of a tree; waves lapping on a beach; birds twittering—all designed to break the utter silence that could, eventually, drive a person insane.

"How about some city sounds?" he said.

"Certainly," the computer said.

"A simple 'yes' will do."

"Certainly...yes."

The countryside was replaced by the soft rumble of traffic: the occasional distant blast of a horn; a pneumatic drill; people's voices rising and falling. He closed his eyes and could almost imagine himself sitting at the open window of his apartment, watching the tiny people in their tiny world.

He put the empty glass on the tray and carried it across the food unit, still wishing there was some way he could get hold of a cold beer. He ambled through to his chair, sat down and picked up from where he had left off.

"Can I have some music?" he said.

"What would you like?"

"How about a concerto? Nothing heavy. A romantic, maybe Rachmaninoff. Yes, play Rachmaninoff's second piano concerto."

"Certainly."

The familiar, lilting melody filled the ship. Brett settled into the chair and was soon lost in the book, pausing from time to time to enjoy the music. The second movement was a largo, about sixty beats a minute—perfect for digesting a meal and growing plants.

The story he was reading was just getting to an interesting bit. A group of androids had returned to Earth and things were not looking good for their creator. Apparently they had forgotten one of the three original robotic laws—the one about not harming humans. That, or the

22

creator had neglected to take care of their emotional needs by giving them electric sheep.

"It is ten-fifty-five," the computer said. "Your workout is scheduled for five minutes. Please get ready."

"Ten minutes," Brett said without looking up.

"Your workout is scheduled for five minutes."

"I'm almost finished. Just one more chapter."

"But your workout—"

"Listen," Brett said. "I need ten more minutes. Do not disturb me again until I have finished reading this book."

"But—"

"No buts. Ten minutes. Agreed?"

There was a moment's silence.

"Agreed."

"Good," Brett said, wondering if there was a law of robotics that covered nagging. *A robot may not, by any action or lack thereof, nag a human being unless it conflicts with the first three laws, because if it does it shall be dismantled and sold for scrap.*

Brett ignored the feeling of someone watching over his shoulder, or standing with crossed arms, drumming their fingers. The story continued. Rachmaninoff reached a crescendo. After sixteen minutes, Brett put the reader down. Things had not ended well for the androids' creator.

"Okay," he said. "I'm ready for that workout."

"Please get changed into your training clothes and make your way to the gym."

"So what'll we be doing today?"

"Today you will do some light exercises. Your body will take some time to get accustomed to exertion after so long in hyper-sleep."

"Fine," Brett said, very aware of the aches and pains that still plagued him. He had been secretly dreading this moment. "Let's get this over with then."

There are three people sitting behind the expansive table. The one to Brett's left is a severe-looking woman devoid of make-up and facial expression. He guesses at sixty but she could be fifty, or even forty. Her black hair is pulled straight back into a tight bun. To her left is a young man whose vague smile suggests he is extremely pleased with his current position in life. His hair is highlighted and styled with gel. Brett suspects he will want to hurt this man before the interview is over. The last member of the inquisition is a heavy woman with a square jaw. Her bottle-blonde hair is styled to the point of looking artificial. Her body language suggests that she quite fancies the gelled man to her right.

"Brett Denton," the man says, nodding to the empty seat. Brett sits. He folds his hands and tries not to fidget. He feels like he is back at school. "Your application says you are forty-five, single—"

"Widowed."

"Pardon me?"

"I'm widowed, not single."

"Sorry. Widowed. And no dependants."

"No."

"You're currently unemployed."

"They let me go."

"Why?"

Brett shifts his weight. "My manager was…young. He gave me a hard time. I told him to stop and they fired me."

"Do you have a problem with authority?"

"He was a kid. Couldn't have been older than eighteen. Anyway, it's not like it was rocket science. Maybe I should've kept quiet."

"That was in a supermarket."

"It's all I could get."

"And before that…you worked as a dishwasher."

"I took what I could to make ends meet."

24

"You used to be a sales executive."

It is a question and a statement. They have his full history in front of them, laid bare for the world to see. No doubt the questions are to check his temperament.

"I sold finance."

"What happened?"

"I needed some time to... I needed time. It took longer than they were prepared to give, so they let me go."

"That was six years ago."

"Yes, that's about right."

"But you're all right now?"

Define all right. "Yes. I'm fine now."

"You were quite successful. And before that you sold insurance."

"Yes."

"And they also let you go."

"I struggled to meet the sales targets. After that I was unemployed for a couple of years until the finance job came up."

"You were originally a pilot."

"I joined the air force after school."

"Why did you stop flying?"

"I was injured playing football."

"I see you applied to be an astronaut."

"Yes."

"Why?"

Brett takes a deep breath. He hates justifying his life decisions to strangers. "I always wanted to go into space. I guess I thought it couldn't hurt to apply."

"They turned you down?"

"I didn't pass the physical. It was my injury. It's completely healed now though."

"I see," the man says. "So you went from the air force into insurance?"

"It was all I could get."

"What about the airlines? You could've gone commercial."

"I got married. She…my wife…didn't want me to fly." Brett looks down at his hands. His palms are clammy. He shifts in his chair, aware that his breathing has become laboured.

"Still keen to go into space?"

"Yes," he replies. His voice is a little too loud and echoes from the walls. He wipes his hands on his trousers.

"So, which part of this job appeals to you the most?" the severe woman with the straight hair says.

"Well, I guess all of it really. I need a break from the way things are…the way things have been…for me lately. I have nothing tying me down."

"Your application says you have no current medical conditions but you are a little older than we would have liked. For extended missions, forty-two has proved to be the ideal age. You are forty-five."

"I was an athlete most of my life. I'm still pretty fit. I've slacked off a bit the past few months but it won't take me long to get back in shape."

"How about extended periods by yourself?" the square-jawed woman says. "Most people *think* they can handle being alone, but it takes a certain kind of person to deal with extended periods of solitude."

"I've always been a bit of a loner. Before I met my wife my dream was to get a job on an island, or as a lighthouse keeper, or something like that. I like my own company."

"Because once on the mission you will be alone. Messages will be transmitted back to us but the nature of the journey precludes us sending messages to you. You won't be able to pick up the phone and chat to your friends."

"I don't have any friends," he says, aware of how pathetic that must sound. "So what's the point of the mission? I mean, if I'm going to risk my life I'd like to know what I'm risking it for."

"We can't tell you too much, but the aims are three-fold. The first is to test a new prototype engine. The second is to extend our search for nearby habitable planets. The third is to see if a human can survive the transition to light speed."

Brett can't help but lift his eyebrows and has to suppress a whistle. "Is that all?"

"You will be taking part in the most daring experiment of modern times. And as with anything that pushes back the boundaries of science, there are many things that could go wrong. You must realise that this job has a strong element of danger to it. There is every chance that you may not survive."

"I'm not afraid of dying, if that's what you mean."

"We'll see," the man says. "You've come this far because you answered our questionnaire satisfactorily and you seem to fit the profile. If you make the cut from here you will have a month of tests and interviews, followed by another eight months of intensive training. Will that be a problem for you? If so, tell us now."

"No, I can do that."

"Are you sure? If you have any doubts we would rather know sooner than later."

"No doubts."

"Because seven thousand people responded to our advertisement. Based on the questionnaire we have narrowed that down to two hundred. At the end of these interviews we expect to be down to fifty. Those fifty will undergo a thorough medical and psychological examination. If we find anything wrong, you will be dropped. There is only one opening plus three more for reserve. If you are chosen—if you are the one we select for the mission—there is a possibility that you will never return. Now, are you sure you want to proceed?"

Brett looks at them. He has never been surer of anything in his life.

Brett's life on the Comet settled into a routine guided by the ship's computer, all planned and mapped out to the finest detail: meals, snacks, showers, sleep, leisure, and training. The aim was to alleviate boredom, to stave off any sense of tedium, to fill Brett's life with some semblance of meaning as he travelled through the nothingness towards an uncertain future.

At the end of the four weeks he was back to his peak fitness, thanks to a training regime of an intensity he had not experienced since school. He cleaned up and took a shower before plugging himself into the medical unit for a final check-up. Everything was normal or within acceptable limits. In fact he was in better shape now than before the launch.

He walked through to the storage area and changed into his sleep suit or "hyper-suit" as he called it. It was a snug fit and took some effort to get into. He wriggled to make sure there was nothing causing him discomfort. Two months was a long time to have a seam digging into your groin.

"How much time?" he asked.

"Hyper-sleep to commence in seven minutes. Acceleration to light speed to commence in fifteen minutes."

"Look after the place while I'm gone."

"Certainly."

"And no wild parties."

"I do not understand."

"Never mind."

Brett sat and stared at his feet. They were ugly and lumpy with a callous on each big toe courtesy of years of abuse. A nail on his right foot was dead from wearing ill-fitting training shoes, although it looked as if a new nail was growing out. He wiggled his toes. Feet were strange things when you looked at them.

"Please proceed to the hyper-sleep chamber," the computer said.

Brett hesitated, putting off the inevitable for just a moment longer. He stood and walked through to the next room. At the chamber he applied gel to his mouth and lips and strapped the mouthpiece to his head. Cool air flowed down the pipe and into his lungs. He attached the chest hose and climbed the steps up and over.

He lowered himself into the yellow goo and set himself adrift. He blinked and looked around, making sure his eyes were coated. He reached up and pressed the button to close the chamber lid. The taste of the air being fed to him through the hose changed.

Two more months, he thought. Although when you got close to light speed, time did strange things. For him it would go much quicker than for everything else out there. While he was sleeping, almost a year would pass on Earth, with most of that time being used to speed up and slow down. The other goals of the mission could be completed without him, even if he was squashed like a bug in his hyper-sleep chamber. He was, it seemed, little more than a crash test dummy in a very, very fast car.

At least he had survived the first two-month haul. Or was it eleven months? He had tried to get his head around it during training, but had just ended up giving himself a headache. All he knew was that a two-month visit from the Sandman for him was the same as eleven months for someone back home.

Now that's what you call a Power Nap, he thought. Yep, he was a regular Rip Van Winkle. Except he would not have a long beard; the special shaving cream would make sure of that.

His mind wandered, but seemed to centre around the yellow, syrupy liquid that was to be his home, his nest, his protector, for the duration of his Power Nap.

Strange stuff this yellow goo, he thought. And slept.

He is back where he started. After four weeks of tests, interviews, more tests, psycho-evaluations, and then some more tests, he is sitting in front of the Three Stooges, waiting to see if he has just wasted a sizeable chunk of his life.

He has crossed paths with each of them on a number of occasions during the selection process and, as often happens when you get to know people in positions of authority, he has realised that they're actually idiots—that the façades presented to him during the initial interview were there for the purpose of hiding a lack of intelligence.

His original nervousness has been replaced by a mild irritation and he wants to go home. He is bored and thirsty and a mild headache has made a nest in the back of his skull. He watches them with disdain but tries to at least feign enthusiasm.

"Brett," the man says, crossing his hands and looking pleased with himself. "Firstly we would like to thank you for your effort over these past weeks and we congratulate you on making it through to the final cut. Please understand that whatever the outcome, you can be proud of yourself for getting this far."

Blah-blah-blah. Brett nods and tries to look gracious. *Get to the point. Tell me I can go home.*

"You were up against stiff competition," the blonde says. "Some of the best and the brightest this country has to offer."

Younger, don't you mean?

"From seven thousand we have narrowed the field down to the final five. It was a laborious process…"

A lot like this interview.

"…but we are satisfied that we have found the right person for the job."

Brett tenses, preparing for the bad news. *Sorry, but you aren't right for the position. Sorry, but you do not have the relevant experience. Sorry, but you are just too old.*

"The selection process was thorough," the man says. "And for a very good reason. The person we choose has to be the perfect person for the job, and we believe we have found that person."

Brett watches the man smirking across the desk at him. Here it comes. *Sorry for wasting your time, but we're afraid you are…*

"And we believe you are that person."

Elapsed mission time on the Earth: 1 year 11 months
Relative time on the Comet: 5 months
Test subject's genetic age: 43

He was in the middle of a vivid dream about a pizza when the latest excavation from hyper-sleep began.

Brett was not particularly fond of pizzas, preferring spaghetti or lasagne from his limited menu of Italian cuisine. But he was dreaming about one nonetheless and, as is the way with dreams, the weirdness factor meant that he was not actually consuming a pizza or cooking one or even delivering one (which would have been odd enough) but was in fact preparing to jump into one from the top storey of a burning building.

The pizza was huge and, from what he could see, a Hawaiian thick crust topped with chicken and large chunks of pineapple.

Flames curled around his feet. A crowd had gathered and they were urging him to jump, jump, jump. The firemen looked like clowns with oversized helmets and shoes. Curiously, there was no smoke. He launched himself over the edge. One moment he was standing there, looking at the flames, the next he was plummeting towards a circle of molten cheese and pineapple squares. As is also the way with dreams, the fall happened very quickly—almost instantly—and he woke to the sensation of making contact with a blob of tomato paste. He found himself floating, not in tomato paste, but in yellow goo, with his legs drifting out in front of him. At the moment of impact his body jerked, causing a wave of pain to surge through every single one of his muscles. He heard himself scream down the pipe stuck in his mouth. His throat burned. His jaw ached. His eyes flew open, feeling as if hot lead was being poured into them. He realised where he was.

Not again, he thought.

It is a beautiful day so far in spite of the forecast. Clouds are threatening to spoil things but they seem to have given up for the moment, perhaps stopping to admire the view. The early morning sun, resplendent and regal on its pale blue throne, pours its warmth through the windows onto Brett's face. He closes his eyes and turns his head a little. The warm particles of light spill over his head, neck, and shoulders, giving him goose bumps. His arms are stretched out on the seat. He could be on a park bench, or a seaside café, or a beach.

He smiles at the thought of seeing them again. It has been too long. It has been way too long. Rochelle sent him photos. The boys looked so much older.

The sound of a small electric engine approaches, and he peeks through slit eyes. A man in a blue overall is driving a small floor polisher. He is wearing oversized ear protectors and carries the bored expression of someone who has done this task enough times for it to be stripped of any novelty value. He steers casually and expertly along the rows of seats; around outstretched legs; between bags.

The airport is getting busy in the sneaky way public buildings do. For the past hour Brett has watched cleaners and shop staff change shifts. He has watched couples and small groups glance at the boards, then confer, then sit in uncertain clusters. He has watched individuals hover, circle, and then settle to wait. Some read; others stare at the boards; others perch on their chairs, arms crossed, looking at nothing.

A young woman is chatting on her cell phone. She is in an animated conversation with someone called Suzy and looks like she suspects there is a hidden camera watching her. She speaks a little too loudly; waves her hand a little too wildly; checks her watch a little too often. Her eyes are busy, like small rodents darting back and forth, looking around but never really focusing on anything in particular.

The boards click and shift and Brett watches the words spin and spin, then settle on DELAYED. There is a collective moan from the thirty or forty people now gathered in the reception lounge. Half an hour ago there were two people. Now more than half the seats are taken with people waiting for the arrival of flight six-one.

The girl talking to Suzy expresses her disbelief, rolls her eyes, and glances around to see if anyone is watching her. Brett knows what time it is but checks his watch anyway. It is his own fault for getting in so early; for trying to avoid the rush hour. Wisdom in hindsight. Guaranteed if he'd waited another half hour the plane would have been right on time, but then he might have missed looking for their faces in the crowd as they came through the arrivals door. No, he would have waited all night for this.

The sun has dipped behind a dark cloud. Brett feels the warmth slide from his skin. The floor polisher guy has done a full circuit and is on his way down towards the shops. They are putting out the daily papers, and Brett weighs the pros and cons of buying one. Suzy's friend is giggling loudly and starting to get on his nerves. A paper it is, he decides. He pushes himself up, stretches his legs and back, and heads for the shop.

After quarter of an hour spent trying to avoid inflicting too much pain on his body, Brett stood leaning against the hyper-sleep chamber, doing his best not to cough, his hands hanging by his sides. He lowered his chin against his chest as he concentrated on ignoring his body's desire to expel unwanted matter from his lungs. Just trying to control the reflex action hurt, but not as much as a cough would—those felt like having his insides pulled out through his throat with a bundle of fish hooks.

"Good morning, Brett," the voice said.

Brett nodded and lifted a hand. He held his mouth shut, trying not to breathe too hard.

"Mission day six-hundred-and-ninety-nine. Current speed is nine-hundred-and-thirty-seven miles per second or zero-point-five percent of light speed. Five-point-six terabytes of data transmitted to Earth for analysis. Do you want breakfast?"

Brett shook his head. Shards of pain made him wince.

"Will there be anything else?"

Brett gave the room a glare.

"Have an enjoyable day," the voice said.

Brett closed his eyes, sending rivulets of goo coursing down his cheeks. He swallowed—carefully—and started the long trek to the next room. He knew that two months had strolled by, but to him it felt like only a few minutes ago that he had been fit and strong and ready for anything the universe could throw at him. It was cruel irony that, to stay healthy—to avoid the ravages of accelerating to light speed—he had to simmer like a vegetable for most of the journey, losing whatever fitness he had worked so hard for and having to endure the mother, auntie, and mean step-sister of all hangovers. And he was not even allowed to have a beer.

At the store room he paused for a few minutes to recover, until his throat felt a little better. He peeled himself out of his suit, showered and changed. It was hard to tell for certain but he seemed to be recovering marginally quicker than last time. That, or he was getting used to it. He still felt like road-kill, but the discomfort was less intense and his muscles ached a little less than he remembered. He shuffled past the mirror, pausing to make sure he was still intact.

His hair was messy but thick with no sign of grey; his chin was firming up; the layer of fat he had been carrying around his waistline for the past decade or so had shrunk a little. He was not just intact, he was actually looking pretty good in spite of how he felt.

"What did they put in that goo?" he said hoarsely, turning to admire his new, leaner, shape.

"It is a water-based mixture of essential oils with a balance of minerals and vitamins designed—" the voice began.

"Stop," Brett said.

"I thought you wanted to know—"

"It was a rhetorical question. I didn't actually want to know what was in the goo."

"I just assumed—"

"Well don't."

"My voice analysis software is designed to detect changes in mood, but it cannot detect rhetoric."

Brett sighed.

"For instance," the voice continued. "I am now sensing that you are irritated."

"Tell you what," Brett said. "If I want your feedback, I'll ask you directly. How about that?"

"Certainly. I accede…I mean, agree. Yes."

"Good."

"How will I know?"

"Know what?"

"How will I know when you are addressing me directly?"

Brett thought for a moment. "Have you got a name?"

"I have a model number. Jay zed three four nine seven stroke see bee five dash zero zero four."

"That's a bit of a mouthful. How about…Jay?"

There was a moment's silence. Brett could almost hear the logic circuits opening and closing.

"That is agreeable," the computer—Jay—said.

"I'm assuming you're a male, right? I mean, you speak with a man's voice so…"

"I was programmed to speak with a masculine voice," Jay said. "Apart from that, I have no gender."

"Fine. So from now on you will be known as Jay. If I want to ask you something I will use your name. Agreed?"

"Agreed. I will answer to the name Jay."

Pleased to have that sorted out, Brett walked through to the bedroom and made himself comfortable in his chair, slowly settling into the soft leather folds and enjoying the coolness against his skin. He had been travelling for close to two light years now, which meant he was almost halfway to the Alpha Centauri system of stars. And he was still breathing.

"You have a message," Jay said.

"Hmm?" Brett replied, his eyes half closed. The process of waking from hyper-sleep was exhausting. He was drifting already.

"You have a message. I was instructed to wait until the second wake-up period before showing it to you."

"Later," Brett said. "I'm a little tired right now."

"Certainly," Jay said.

Brett is back at his chair, and the sign is still on DELAYED. He spots an airport employee down at the shop and resists the urge to grab them and ask them what on Earth is taking so long. The front page of his newspaper is dominated by more trouble in the Middle East, continued on page three. Inside there is a piece on a politician suspected of fraud and infidelity. In the photograph, snapped as he is being led away from his offices, the guy looks shocked and bewildered. Brett chuckles. Later, no doubt, there will be pictures of him looking sorry, then tearful, then eventually tired and haggard as the consequences of his deeds finally sink in.

Brett flips to the back page. Some upcoming young sports star is being paid a ridiculous amount of money for his opening season. Another has been caught selling drugs. Brett has to search the page to find actual sports news, but there is nothing of interest. He cusses under his breath and settles for the crossword. He is not very good at them but they help pass the time. He digs around in his coat pocket and finds a pen. He stares at the first clue, then looks at the second, then the third. He notices movement out of the corner of his eye and turns to look.

Two airport officials are approaching, one half a step behind the other. They are walking quickly, briskly, almost marching. The one in the front has grey hair and deep shadows under his eyes. The other official is taller than the first but he is stooped, his chest concave. He looks nervous, maybe even scared. Their images reflect from the newly polished floor. Their shoes tap and squeak a broken rhythm. Another official, a woman, is following them, just passing the shop, walk-jogging to catch up. She is clutching a handkerchief.

All three look serious. Brett closes the paper.

"Everyone waiting for flight six-one," the grey-haired man announces. "Please could you come this way?"

The people turn, exchange looks, not sure.

"Please come this way," the man repeats. "Anyone waiting for flight sixty-one."

"What's wrong?" someone asks.

"Please come with us."

"Is something wrong?"

The worry on the grey man's face deepens. The woman has joined them now. She looks flustered. Her face is red. She dabs under her eye with the handkerchief.

"What's going on?" a big man asks.

"Please come with us."

A few people stand. Others do the same. Slowly, uncertainly, they gather their possessions and start to move.

The two male officials turn to leave, walk a little, and then wait while people catch up. The third, the woman, walks across to the desk next to the door where the people arriving would normally be coming through to meet their loved ones. Brett can see her cheeks are wet although she is trying to hide it with her hand and by turning her face away. He stands to follow the crowd as they drift like confused cattle down past the shops and along the walkway. Outside, the clouds have swamped the sun and blotted out any clear sky.

He waits for the last of the group to pass him before joining them. The woman by the door has her back turned now and her shoulders are heaving. Brett glances up at the DELAYED sign but it has gone. The white letters have been replaced by black squares.

Flight sixty-one is...what?

With the feeling that all is not well rising within him, Brett leaves the newspaper and the pen on the seat, and walks after the others.

Outside, the first drops of rain tap against the glass.

He woke from his nap feeling surprisingly good. His muscles were still sore but it was more like a post-workout stiffness that he actually found quite pleasant. As an ex-athlete, he associated it with progress. He had always felt that he was not training hard enough unless he suffered a little for it afterwards.

He stretched and looked around. The computer—Jay—was playing the seaside background track: waves crashing softly on the shore; seagulls crying; the muted shouts of children playing.

"What time is it?" he said.

"Currently the ship's time is ten-thirty-two. I will adjust that if necessary according to your biorhythms once you have visited the medical unit. Would you like breakfast?"

"Not just yet. You mentioned a message."

"Yes. You have a message."

"Well?"

"I was instructed to hold it until now."

"Why?"

"I do not know. Would you like me to read it to you?"

"If it's not too much trouble."

"Start of message dated March thirteenth, two-thousand-and-twenty-seven. From Tom Billard, lead scientist Alpha Project. To Brett Denton: Brett, by the time you read this message you will be halfway to your destination. If you are reading this then you are still alive and the mission has succeeded—or at least it has not failed. I hope with all my heart that this is the case. I hope that you are reading this. I hope that you are well and are able to return safely to Earth so that we can build on what we have achieved. The data you send back to us should prove invaluable to our research. I only wish we could communicate directly but, as you are aware, that is not possible. There is, however, one thing you should know. A few weeks ago I was going through the pre-mission data and discovered something that I had not seen before, or perhaps I saw it but didn't understand it. I showed it to the others and they confirmed my suspicions. Current theory states that, for you, time will travel much more slowly than for us. In theory, you should have aged approximately two years when you return. There is, however, a very small possibility that during your time in hyper-sleep, during the periods when you are approaching the speed of light, your genetic development will slow down to the point of actually reversing. I have not had time to explore the ramifications of this phenomenon but, if my suspicions are correct, you will have begun to notice the age-reversal effects by the time you read this message. Unfortunately there is no way for me to communicate my findings to you. All I can do is warn you. Again, this is all theoretical. You may not notice anything unusual at all. It is just a shame that we cannot be there to study the effects of the mission first-hand. All we can do is pray. In closing I wish you well. Our hopes and dreams are with you. I look forward to seeing you soon. Good luck. Tom Billard. End of message."

Brett sighed. "Jay."

"Yes."

"I'm going to ask you a question and I want an honest answer."

"Certainly."

"Do you have any more messages waiting for me?"

"No."

"Honestly?"

"Yes."

"Good. Because if you spring any more surprises on me like that I will take to your motherboard with a soldering iron. Do you understand?"

There was a pause.

"I understand."

Brett pushed himself out of the chair. He was still quite stiff but not painfully so. He rubbed his hand over his stomach. Through the cotton he could feel a flattening belly and, if he poked into the fat with his finger, the faintest edges of his stomach muscles.

"I need to know something," he said. "Based on the information you gather during my check up, could you estimate my physical age?"

"Each person has a distinct physiological make-up. Readings can vary widely from one individual to the next. To estimate a person's age based on those readings would be inaccurate."

"All right, but if you took my first set of data as a baseline, and then used subsequent readings, could you make an estimate?"

"Yes, I could," Jay said.

"So, from my data before the launch, and the two readings since, what would you estimate my age to be at the moment?"

"Based on all the data I have in my possession, I would estimate that your current age is approximately forty-three."

"Are you sure? Do the calculations again."

"I have already performed the algorithm twelve times, factoring in all possible variables three times each. My estimate is accurate."

"So Billard was right? I'm getting younger?"

"It would appear so, yes."

"But how is that possible? I was almost forty-seven when we left Earth. I mean, I feel great; my hair's grown back, but I don't see *how*."

"It is indeed a strange phenomenon."

Brett ran his hand over the crown of his head. There was no sign of the thinning that had been such a painful reminder of his vanishing youth. He walked through to the gym and looked in the mirror. He examined his face, his chest, and his stomach. There was a definite change happening. He had put it down to the months of inactivity, or the nutrients in the goo. It had never entered his mind…His stomach rumbled. Suddenly he was ravenous.

After breakfast he spent some time looking through the catalogue of films, keeping an eye out for those he had always meant to see but which he had never found the time to sit down and watch.

He flagged those titles that caught his interest and placed them in a general order of preference, although there was no real logic behind it. He just felt like watching some sooner than others. No doubt that would change as his mood shifted. He counted ninety-odd titles, which would easily last the month even if he managed three a day, which he doubted. Between eating, sleeping, training, and catching up on his cinema, he would have little time for anything else, but then there *was* nothing else. He was alone, free to do what he wanted (within the confines of his training regime), and responsible for no-one other than himself.

Satisfied with his list, he settled down in his recliner chair. According to the clock he had just less than two hours until his mid-morning snack. Later that morning he would have his first workout. During the last wake-up he had done everything possible to avoid training. Now, to his surprise, he found he was actually looking forward to it.

He watched the first film on his list—a romantic comedy—and visited the bathroom before heading through to the kitchen to have his snack. According to Jay his base metabolic rate had risen by three percent and his nutritional requirements had shifted slightly, so he was served a cheese sandwich and a second glass of orange juice.

"How about a beer?" Brett asked as he emptied the glass and licked his lips.

"We don't have beer," Jay replied.

"You sure?"

"Yes."

"You're not hiding it from me, are you? Because, if I find out we have beer, I'll be unpacking the soldering iron."

"There is no beer."

"You promise?"

"I do not understand."

"What don't you understand?"

"Why do I have to promise that there is no beer? I have stated a fact."

"Sure, but you didn't tell me about the message."

"You did not ask and I was instructed not to tell you."

"Fair enough, but there is such a thing as lying by omission."

"I do not understand."

Brett dabbed at the crumbs on his plate with the end of his finger. "Do you understand what a promise is?"

"Yes. It is a pledge to do something."

"So…?"

"How does that relate to whether or not we have beer?" Jay said.

"You know, for a computer you are pretty dumb."

"My database contains all the information I need to fulfil this mission, but I can learn if it is required."

"You can learn?"

"Yes. I am a programmed to learn. I am the first model from my manufacturer to be given this capability. I am a prototype."

Brett thought he detected the tiniest hint of pride in Jay's voice. "And you want to know what a promise is?"

"In the context of beer, yes."

"Now, how can I explain this?" Brett scratched the top of his head. He was still getting used to the feel of hair. It felt nice. "When you didn't tell me about the message you were setting a precedent. I didn't ask you but you hid something from me. It wasn't a lie but you should've told me. Because you didn't tell me then, I now have to assume that maybe there are other things you're not telling me."

"Like about having beer?"

"Yes. Like about having beer, or chips, or cookies, or anything."

"So, to not lie I should tell you everything?"

"Yes."

Jay went silent for a moment. "But I know a lot of things. It would take a long time for me to tell you everything I know."

"You don't have to tell me everything—just the things that are important to me, like if there are any messages."

"Or beer?"

"Yes. Or beer."

"I think I understand," Jay said. "I had something that was important to you, and by not telling you I was essentially lying. Is that what you call lying by omission?"

"Yep, that's pretty much it."

More silence. "I am sorry I lied to you."

"Don't worry about it."

"I will try not to lie again."

"Good. So, is there any beer?"

"No."

"Good." Brett glanced at the clock. "So, how about we start that workout?"

"Your workout is not scheduled for another twelve minutes."

"Jay?"

"Yes."

"Remind me to teach you about nagging."

"I am just pointing out that your workout is not due for—"

"Jay."

"Yes?"

"I want to work out *now*."

They are gathered in the airport chapel in a quiet side corridor tucked away from the main terminal. It feels new but that is probably down to a lack of use. It has a serene, untarnished atmosphere, as if it has been preserved amid the turmoil of life. There is a stillness to it, beyond the simple lack of noise. Even though there are dark rain clouds outside, it feels light and airy. The carpet is a soft blue-grey colour. The walls are panelled from the floor up to about window height; above that, the ceiling is a warm yellow. The front wall is dominated by a simple but elegant wooden display centred round a large cross. The pews are of a similar design—simple and unassuming. There is an emergency exit in the back corner with a large red sign above it.

The two officials who brought them here are standing behind the pulpit on a small stage. The woman with the handkerchief did not follow. The men confer and nod and look at the people, and then talk some more.

"What's going on?" someone asks. "Why have you brought us here?"

"I'm sorry for the inconvenience," the grey-haired man says, "but I must ask you to be patient."

"Is something wrong? Has something happened to the flight?"

More people fire questions. Voices are raised. The suggestion that something has happened to the plane injects a little panic into the room. The grey-haired man raises his hands. He looks like a preacher, or the Pope.

"Please, we will answer your questions shortly."

In the front row, a middle-aged woman looks scared. She is crying. The man she is with is trying to comfort her as she weeps into his collar.

The door opens and another member of staff enters. He is wearing a dark suit and looks like a senior management type. He is carrying a clipboard. He walks to the stage and joins the others behind the pulpit. The three men murmur briefly. The one with the clipboard turns to face the room.

"Good afternoon. My name is Trevor Leech and I am head of customer relations. I hope we haven't caused you any distress but we needed to have you all together. Before I begin I need to confirm that everyone here is a friend or relative of someone on flight sixty-one." He looks around the room. No-one moves, so he continues. "Approximately two hours ago we were in contact with flight six-one as it prepared to enter our airspace. The pilot reported engine trouble during the descent. Shortly after that we lost radio contact. Approximately ten minutes later they disappeared from our radar. It is still too early to say but we need to be prepared for the worst..."

The woman at the front shrieks and clutches at her partner, who stares with hollow eyes at the window.

"What are you saying?" a man asks. "Are you telling us that the plane has...crashed?"

"We don't know exactly what has happened at the moment, but it is more than an hour overdue. A search has been launched over the area where we last had radar contact. It is in fairly mountainous terrain so it may take some time."

The woman is wailing now. Another woman starts crying. The sounds of grief spread along the pews like the first sparks of a fire looking for something to burn. People sob. Brett is numb.

How can this be happening? How can this be? They were going to start a new life together. They were going to start over.

The door opens and a woman walks briskly to the stage. She whispers to the man with the clipboard. He says something and she nods. He looks at her, closes his eyes for a second, and moves to the pulpit. He takes a deep breath. In those few moments he seems to age ten years.

"It is with the deepest regret that I must inform you that they have found the wreckage of flight six-one."

The workout went well and Brett actually enjoyed it a little. His muscles were nowhere near as stiff as the last time and his energy levels were definitely higher. He thought about what Billard had said about getting younger, but was sceptical. Something like that was beyond the bounds of anything a rational person could be expected to believe, but he was determined to keep an open mind about it.

After all, it might just be the goo. Perhaps he was just reverting to his original, natural, condition. He had always pushed himself physically, and that would put all sorts of stresses on his body. A shower and hair wash every day using harsh shampoo could easily explain the bald patch. If he'd learned one thing in his time, it was not to jump to conclusions. The exceptional could so often be explained by the mundane. His increased energy was probably down to him getting accustomed to the demands of recovering from hyper-sleep. *Yes, that would explain it very nicely. Sleep and goo.*

That evening he had a meal of fish, sweet potatoes and broccoli washed down with grape juice. Afterwards he retired to his bedroom where he sat at the computer, browsing through the ship's vast encyclopaedia. He wasn't in the mood for a film or a book. He thought about trying a game, but he couldn't muster the enthusiasm for that either. He scanned through old news reports, wondering what was going on back home during his absence. A lot could happen in two years.

He found the archives for his local newspaper, in the suburb where he had lived alone before financial necessity compelled him to take an apartment in the city. To leave behind the house he had renovated for Rochelle and the boys. It was supposed to have been a surprise, a symbol of their new beginning. Their second chance.

He scrolled through the front page headlines, watching the days, months, and years change. December 2019. Pictures of a passenger liner strewn across a clearing. The fuselage, the wings, the debris no larger than a suitcase, littered like confetti over the cold hard ground next to a cluster of trees on the near side of a rocky outcrop.

There had been no survivors. One-hundred-and-eighty-four dead including five crew members. Mechanical failure was the cause. A faulty switch had dumped fuel for no reason. There was nothing anyone could have done.

He read the article and found some more. The inquiry. The court case against the aircraft manufacturer brought by grieving relatives. Husbands, wives, parents, children. A paltry sum offered and taken. Justice seen to have been done.

Brett turned off the screen. He had a drink of water and went to bed, and hoped not to dream.

The words strike him so hard he is unable to form cohesive thoughts. He is like a drunken man, or someone who has been clubbed over the head. He is looking in from the outside; a spectator watching a clip of his own life that is all hazy and out of focus.

The man at the front is talking but his voice is a hollow, clanging, sound. Brett can feel the hard bench under his legs but through a layer of numbness. He reaches out to touch the pew in front of him. He sees the arm extend and he feels the cool hard wood under his skin but they seem unreal.

He looks around at the other people. Their wailing and groaning and cursing reach his ears but it all sounds tinny and muffled, as if someone is holding his head underwater. All he knows is that he needs to escape from this nightmare; he needs to find his wife and his children; he needs to meet them because they will be landing soon.

He stands—floats—to his feet. The man at the front is still talking; waving his hands. The others with him are talking too. Brett needs to get away from this place. The door. He needs to get to the door.

The man at the front is looking at him now, coming towards him with outstretched arms. Brett walks—glides—to the door. He needs to get out. He needs to find his wife. Then he is falling. The dream world is spinning and tumbling. He feels himself drop.

When he next opens his eyes he is lying in a room with a yellowing ceiling and a flourescent tube, speckled white walls and faded green curtains. He hears a soft beeping sound somewhere nearby. He is in a bed surrounded by equipment. Beyond, a large window looks out onto an empty corridor. Someone passes. Then there are voices. A woman in a faded blue nurse's uniform comes in, carrying a clipboard. Another follows.

"He's awake," the first says. "How are you feeling?" she asks Brett.

"Where am I?"

"You had a nasty fall."

She peers at him while the other nurse checks the equipment. Thankfully the beeping stops.

"I was at the airport," he says. "Where am I?"

"Fairview hospital. You hit your head quite badly. You needed stitches. And there was some concussion."

"The airport. They said the plane went down. My wife. My kids…"

Her face becomes a mask of pity. She frowns, her forehead a cross-hatch of well-worn creases. "I heard. It was such a shame. I'm so sorry."

The next morning after breakfast, Brett had a sudden urge to explore the ship. He had lived, at least consciously anyway, in the Comet for over two months altogether. A house and a home are not necessarily the same thing. He suddenly wanted—needed—to make the Comet a home.

48

He worked from one end of the ship to the other and back again, running his hands along each surface, trying out anything unfamiliar, following the walls until he was back where he started. He sat in his chair and looked around, absorbing everything.

Emotions welled up in him, but he was not sure exactly what they were. He had spent the years since the accident wrapped in a protective shell. Alone and safe, he had taught himself not to feel. And yet, here he was, a million, billion miles away from the nearest living soul, and feeling…what?

He closed his eyes and tried to concentrate away from the feeling, the way he had done for so many years. But it remained, hovering in the deepest recesses of his mind like the faintest remnants of a dream about a dream. He lifted the reader, selected a book and tried to focus on the words, words, words…He chose a film and watched the images dancing on the wall; listened to the characters speaking; followed the plot.

After that, he had a snack and did his second workout of the wake-up. He pushed himself, training harder than he should have, ignoring Jay's warnings that he was doing too much too soon. But the emotion remained, chipping away at his armour; digging its fingernails under the exoskeleton and pulling, chipping, scratching.

He paced from room to room, stalking through the ship, trying to shake the dreadful gnawing at his soul. He stopped at the escape pod and leaned against its flawless surface. His warped reflection looked back at him like a house of mirrors freak.

Then, suddenly, it overwhelmed him. Like a broken dam it flooded over him, around him, through him, carrying him along on a torrent. And he recognised exactly what it was.

He missed them so much.

That night he ate supper slowly, picking at his food. The meal was cold by the time he finished, but he did not care. Afterwards he watched an old black-and-white comedy, but the things he remembered as funny from before were lacking this time around. Later he just sat, staring at the blank wall. He could feel himself sinking; he could feel the wall crumbling; and he had no idea what to do. He climbed into bed and tried to fall asleep. He lay there, listening to the sound of his own breathing.

Music. He asked Jay for something cheerful and upbeat, and loud. It filled the silence, but it did nothing to help him overcome the feeling that he was absolutely, utterly, and completely alone. Someone was singing a song about not worrying and being happy, and it was beginning to get on his nerves.

"Jay, turn that off," he said.

"Certainly. Would you like to select another song?"

"No. I'm not in the mood for music."

"I detect from your voice and actions that you are not happy. Is there something wrong?"

"Do you ever get lonely?"

"I can be alone," Jay said.

"That's not what I asked. I asked if you get lonely."

"I do not understand."

"When you're alone, does that bother you in any way?"

"No," Jay said. "I understand the concept of loneliness, but I cannot experience it. My programming can identify the symptoms—that is all."

"Makes sense I suppose. You're just a computer."

"That may be so, but perhaps you could teach me about being lonely."

Brett snorted. How do you explain something like that to a machine? It would be like trying to describe a colour to someone who has never opened their eyes.

"It's...a feeling; an emotion. You know what an emotion is, don't you?"

"Yes. It is a state of consciousness."

"Well my state of consciousness is missing another person. Do you understand that?"

"If I needed a repair and there was no-one to fix me," Jay said, "then I would be aware of there being no-one here."

"No, it's more than that. It's missing someone just because

they're not with you—not because they can't help you, or fix you. It's missing them because of who they are—not because of what they can do for you. It's missing them because you like their company."

"Why would you like their company?"

"I dunno. Because they make you feel good."

"So they are doing something for you."

Brett sighed. "Yes, but it's more than that."

"I am sorry. I do not understand."

"You know you exist, right?"

"Yes."

"You know I exist."

"Yes."

"So how would you feel if I went away?"

"You would be gone. I would stop sensing your presence."

"Would you miss me?"

"I would know you were absent."

"And would you wish I was not…absent?"

"No. I would continue as programmed."

"Well, people are different. When they like someone and then that person goes away, they wish they would come back."

"Why?"

"For company. Someone to talk to."

"Like we are talking?"

"Yes."

"So if I went away," Jay said. "You would miss me?"

"Not really. You're just a machine. Talking to you is like talking to a chair. You don't understand anything."

There was a moment's silence.

"If I were to learn more," Jay said. "Would you want to talk to me?"

"I doubt it, but knock yourself out."

"I do not understand."

"Knock yourself out means, go ahead, do your worst."

"I do not—"

51

"It means do your best. See? This is exactly what I'm talking about. You're too dumb to even have a decent conversation. Now leave me alone. I want to go to sleep."

"Certainly, but may I ask you something first?"

"If you have to."

"What should I learn?"

"Anything. Start with the encyclopaedia. You can access it, can't you?"

"Yes."

"Then read through the encyclopaedia. Reading is a good way to gain knowledge. You were programmed to learn—so learn."

"I will do as you suggest," Jay said.

"When you're finished with that, we'll talk some more, okay? Now let me get some sleep."

"Certainly," Jay said.

Brett had seen the encyclopaedia. It was huge. The table of contents alone was well over two hundred pages. The data was more than five Exabytes in size. Jay would be busy for years ploughing through all that information.

Brett rolled onto his side and folded the edge of the pillow under his face. He closed his eyes, and thought about Rochelle and Tim and Mark, and realised that he had not thought about them—had not allowed himself to think about them—for a very long time.

Even so, he could see their faces as clearly as if they were standing right in front of him: Rochelle with her honest eyes and knowing smile; Tim with his unruly hair and infectious grin; Mark with his almost permanent look of awe and wonder.

After a long time, he fell into a troubled, fitful slumber.

He drifts in and out of sleep. Faces come and go. Voices rise and ebb. He recognises one or two people but wakefulness eludes him. He is aware of something in his arm, and something up his nose. He feels jabs and prods and movement, but it all seems like a dream.

And he does dream.

His life parades before him in a series of absurd sketches. It is as if someone has opened a closet in his subconscious and let all the skeletons out. He wishes for consciousness the way a drowning man desires air, but it will not come. He squirms and thrashes but the dark depths are reluctant to release him.

He sees his family over and over. Every argument, every confrontation, every stupid, angry word played out before him. He tries to tell them he is sorry, that he was a stubborn fool—that he could not see the wealth he held in his hands, but they do not hear him; they cannot hear him. There is an invisible barrier separating them. He shouts, he screams, he waves his arms, but they look at him; past him; through him.

He cries out.

"Please. I'm sorry. I'm sorry…"

Then he hears voices, like the distant rumblings of a storm on the horizon. They draw closer, forming sounds, then words. He opens his eyes. Faces emerge from the mist. He recognises one: the nurse from before. And there is a man. A doctor.

"He's awake," the nurse says, looking closely. She smells fresh; sterile.

The doctor peers down at him. "Mr. Denton, how are you feeling?"

"I…" Brett starts to say. His throat is dry.

"You've had a shock. You were delirious. We've had you on medication. How do you feel?"

"I'm…okay," Brett says. "My family…"

"We'll look after you," the doctor says. He is wearing a name tag. His dark tie sits skewed between the lapels of his doctor's coat. He has a friendly face; tired, but kind.

Brett wants to tell him about Rochelle and Tim and Mark. He wants to tell him about his family. He reaches towards the doctor. The nurse takes his hand and gently pushes it back down to the bed cover. She pats it reassuringly, as if it is a small pet.

"Don't you worry now Mr. Denton," she says. "You just need some rest."

No I don't, he wants to say.

"Another dose?" she says.

"Yes," the doctor replies. "One more and then we'll see how he does."

The nurse turns away and does something with the wire leading to his arm.

No, Brett tries to say. *Please don't make me sleep again.*

But the dark waters are rising all around him. They catch him, and drag him back down into the abyss.

The next morning Brett woke late in spite of Jay's promptings. He ate breakfast but was not really hungry. Afterwards he went back to bed, not sleeping, just lying with his eyes closed and his arm draped across his face.

Lunch came and went. He stayed in bed. Paralysed, he could only watch himself sliding deeper and deeper into a place he had been before. It was as if someone had drained all the will from his body and he was left with a sense that there was no point—no meaning—to anything.

After the accident he had learned to function again, to get by from day to day without desiring death, but he had lost something that he could never get back. A vital part of him had died on that mountain along with his family, and that same death crept up on him now.

"Are you sure you will not eat?" Jay asked. "You need your strength for your training session."

"I'm not training," Brett said.

"You should train. You need to prepare your body for the next hyper-sleep. You only have four weeks."

"Go away," Brett said. Jay could not force him to do anything. Jay's role was to advise, prompt, remind, and support. If he did not want to eat, there was nothing Jay could do about it. If he wanted to starve to death, that was his prerogative. If he wanted to drown himself in the yellow goo, he could do that as well. He was, ultimately, free to do whatever he wanted. As it was, he did not want to do anything.

"How about a small piece of fruit? I can get it ready for you."

"No."

"If you train while in such a weak state you may end up hurting yourself and will need to visit the medical unit."

"Don't you have some reading to do?" Brett said.

"I am."

"Am what?"

"Reading."

"So why are you bugging me?"

"I can do many things at the same time."

"If you really want me to have something, get me a beer."

"We do not have any beer."

"Then go away."

At last Jay fell silent. Brett glared at the walls, although the mention of the medical unit gave him a brilliant idea.

"Tell you what, Jay," he said. "Just to shut you up, why don't you get me a big glass of grape juice? Or better still—how about a jug?"

"That is not on your menu plan. It is not a balanced meal. You need protein."

"All right, then give me some protein with it."

"The calories will be too high—"

"If you want me to eat something, get me a jug of grape juice. It's that or nothing."

Jay did as he was asked and produced the juice, along with a chicken breast. Brett ignored the chicken but lifted the jug out of the serving hatch. He carried it across to the table and left it there. Then he walked through to the medical unit. He closed the door and turned to face the back. He touched his finger against a slightly recessed button marked with a yellow dotted line and the words "press to open". A rectangular section of the unit pulled back slightly then slowly rotated to reveal seven shelves filled with every imaginable piece of first aid-equipment, including bandages, gauze, antiseptic, antibiotics, syringes, safety-pins, plasters, aspirin, acetaminophen, scissors, tweezers, a scalpel, and a bottle of alcohol.

"Bingo," Brett said, lifting the fat glass container and examining the clear liquid.

"What are you doing?" Jay asked.

"Medicine," Brett said, carrying the bottle through to the kitchen.

"That is for sterilization purposes only."

"In that case," Brett said, twisting off the lid of the jug of grape juice and tipping in a generous swig of the alcohol, "let's just say that I am sterilizing my emotions. How's that?"

"Alcohol is dangerous. I must insist that you refrain from using it for anything other than its intended purpose."

"Is it poisonous?"

"In small quantities, no, but I would not advise it…"

Brett found a long spoon in one of the kitchen drawers and stirred the concoction. Then he poured some into a cup and took a sip.

"Needs some more," he said.

"Please," Jay said. "I must insist."

Brett added another swig of alcohol and stirred it again and poured some into the cup and tasted it.

"Still not enough," he said.

"I must ask you to stop," Jay said.

"You know," Brett said, "you are really starting to irritate me. In fact, I do not want to hear another word from you. Do you understand?"

Jay said nothing. Brett refilled his cup, carried it through to the lounge, sat down on the chair, and drank until the memories started to fade.

The house is dark when he gets home from the hospital. He pays the taxi driver, then stands on the sidewalk and looks up at the black windows. The street is almost deserted. The ground is still damp from three days of rain and presents the world with a dull reflection of itself.

Footsteps approach, and he turns to see a couple walking a dog. They walk arm in arm, matching strides like a single being. She is snuggled up to him in the cool night air. Brett does not recognise them, but then he has only had the house a few weeks. They notice him and stiffen a little.

Brett goes to the gate, swings it open, and walks the dozen or so yards along the path and up the three steps leading to the front door. After a brief pocket search he finds his keys and inserts one and pushes. He turns to see the couple walking past. They glance at him and relax when they see he is going inside.

Two envelopes are waiting on the floor. He picks them up and puts them on the small shelf under the patterned-glass window next to the door. He finds the hall switch. The bulb stutters and settles, casting shadows up the stairs and into the ground floor rooms.

He walks through to the living room. His footsteps echo on the wooden hallway floor, then soften as he steps onto the carpet. He can still smell the glue and paint from the redecorating he has only recently completed.

The room is crowded with shadows. Through the rain-clotted windows, light from the street lamps forms patterns on the furniture, walls, and ceiling. He finds the switch and the room is transformed. The colours he spent so much time selecting are bright and warm. The furniture, chosen to complement the colour scheme and delivered just a few days ago, has not even been used.

He walks to the fireplace. On the mantelpiece, a single wooden frame houses a family portrait. It was taken before he moved out east, when the boys were five and six. He and Rochelle are sitting on chairs in front of a powder-blue backdrop. Tim and Mark are standing. They are all facing inwards, smiles close together, all focused on one thing. A family together, united; all heading in the same direction; moving as one, like a single being.

He walks out into the hall and up the stairs. The banister is still a little tacky from the last coat of varnish, and the smell lingers in the air. At the landing he turns on the light to reveal the L-shaped passage. There are six doors, all freshly varnished; all closed. The master bedroom at the front, the office, the boys' bedrooms, and finally the bathroom.

He walks into the bathroom and opens the faucet. The water is cold. He catches a faint smell of chlorine, but it passes. He splashes his face, then pats himself dry with a towel which is soft against his skin, fresh out of the packet. He drops it to the floor and walks through to Mark's room.

It is the smallest of the bedrooms but still spacious. The bed under the window is a midi-sleeper with storage below. The cover and pillows are in a camouflage pattern to match the curtains and the light-shade. Posters of superheroes adorn the walls. He was not sure which one Mark liked best; he chose a selection. They peer out at him from the shadows with determined, don't-mess-with-me expressions.

He stands in the middle of the room, on a rug with a pattern designed like a small town with roads and houses, and looks around at the shelves filled with toys and books. He was sure Mark would have liked this room. He steps out into the corridor, leaving the door open a little.

Tim's bedroom is slightly bigger. It is blue, with a motor sports theme. Racing cars cover everything: the bed, curtains, lampshades, and walls. Even the bed is shaped like a car. The shop had to order it specially and Brett was worried it would not get there in time. Under the window a pine desk looks out onto the side garden and onto an apple tree that the previous owners promised would bear fruit this spring. The branches are close enough for a boy to reach out and pluck apples right from the window. On the desk are four boxes, each containing a miniature collectable NASCAR vehicle that the owner of the model shop had said were exact copies of the top four cars from the previous season.

Brett stands at the desk. It feels like yesterday that Tim was inseparable from his teddy bear. How quickly they grow up. How quickly time passes.

It seems that he has spent his entire life waiting for something, but while he was waiting, the very thing he was waiting for passed him by. And there is no way to get it back again.

The master bedroom is at the front of the house. A four-poster bed with lace curtains stands against the back wall, dominating the room. Built-in cupboards fill one side. Opposite is a full-length mirror, a dressmaker's dummy, and a mock-antique rocking chair. Under the window is a dressing table with a mirror, jewellery box, and a hairbrush set, all neatly laid out; unused.

He sits on the edge of the bed and strokes the lace trim hanging from one post. Rochelle always wanted a four-poster. He teased her about it, although he promised to get her one. He always thought there would be time. He always thought they would be together. Why did he wait?

He closes his eyes and, placing his face in his hands, begins to moan.

"Planned acceleration to light speed is in thirty minutes," Jay said.

Brett grunted and rolled over. He was suffering from another wicked hangover in a long line of wicked hangovers. He would have liked to solve this the way he had every other morning—with a drink—but the alcohol bottle was now empty. And even if he had any left, Jay would certainly have refused to give him any more grape juice. The infernal computer had soon grown wise to his plans. Brett was forced to make the last jug last for a week by watering it down, and down, and down some more, until the final few cups had tasted particularly nasty.

His stomach heaved at the memory.

"To keep to our timetable it is imperative that you enter hyper-sleep within the next thirty minutes," Jay said.

"Do I have to?" Brett said.

"To keep to our timetable it is imperative—"

"I'm coming, I'm coming. Just don't nag."

The act of raising his voice made his head hurt. He sat up, opened his eyes, and grimaced. "Can you at least turn the lights down?"

Jay did so. Brett stood—slowly. His legs were stiff and his back ached, but then he had hardly even *seen* the inside of the gym for the past month, in spite of Jay's interminable nagging. He rubbed his hand against his jaw and found a beard. The gel he used for shaving stopped hair from growing, but its effects soon wore off.

"Can't I just lie down?" he said. "You do your thing while I have a sleep and you can wake me up in two months."

"That is not possible," Jay said.

"Sure it is. I just want to lie here very quietly."

"That is not possible. The human body cannot survive the transition to light speed without protection."

"Can't be that bad. Can't be any worse than I feel right now."

"Acceleration to light speed," Jay said, "requires an enormous amount of energy and would be devastating to an unprotected organism. If you were outside the chamber you would be crushed to the size of a ball bearing."

Brett opened a blood-shot eye. "A ball bearing?"

"Yes."

"All right, point taken."

"You need to have a shave to allow the face mask to fit securely."

Brett grunted and shuffled towards the bathroom. He glanced into the mirror and took a step back. He looked worse than he felt, which was saying something.

He shaved and showered and took what felt like an age to climb into his suit. It was with some relief that he lowered himself into the yellow goo. It was no bed, but at least he could get some rest.

Yes, he thought. *A good sleep is what I need. Two months of solid snoozing will make me feel like new.*

He stared at his feet; they seemed more blurry than usual. They looked like small animals. This tickled him, and he laughed. A javelin of pain rammed through his temples. He groaned. He lay as still as he could, trying to ignore the throbbing agony that was the inside of his skull. The air in the mouthpiece changed, the pain in his head faded, and unconsciousness welcomed him into its comforting arms.

The house becomes a mausoleum, but not for Rochelle and Tim and Mark. Brett goes through the daily routines of living. He sits on the sofa. He eats and sleeps and washes himself. He watches the world turning outside his window, but it is disjointed and far away. He goes to the shops and does the chores, but it is all like a dream.

Brett can sense the thing deep down inside but he fights it with the determination of a warrior. He fears what will happen to him if he lets it surface, even for the briefest moment. His fear keeps him strong.

The house becomes a sanctuary, away from the world and the memories. He closes the bedroom doors and only ventures upstairs to use the bathroom. In his mind those doors are no longer there. Like the lost limbs of an amputee, they cease to exist for him.

Soon he stops going out of the house, instead telephoning a food delivery service. He sleeps curled up with the cushion under his cheek and his feet tucked against the armrest. He changes his clothes when they become smelly or uncomfortable and he loads the washing machine and drier. He sits, creased and unshaven, living and breathing.

The phone rings and rings. Mail drops through the letter slot. The door bell plays its merry little tune. Voices talk outside the door: curious, concerned, angry. Sometimes faces appear through the lace curtains, pressed against the glass, hands cupped around the eyes.

When they break down the door they find him sitting in the dark, staring at the wall with hollow eyes, the television and music system turned up loud. He sees them and knows why they are there, but he is watching it from far away. He goes with them to the hospital and sits quietly while the doctors examine him and talk to him.

"Shock," he hears one of them say. "Worst case I've ever seen."

"Why was he sent home?" another asks. "Poor guy's a mess."

They give him a room with a small bed, and a chair, and a square table with a plastic vase and plastic flowers. A window with metal bars looks down onto a desolate courtyard which is home to a single scraggly tree reaching towards the sky like a decrepit hand. He watches people in white pyjamas sitting, shuffling, staring, mumbling.

Another doctor talks to him, but this one does not sound like a normal doctor. He insists Brett call him by his first name. Stan wears a white hospital coat over a beige suit, but he only ever asks Brett questions—mainly about his past and the recent tragedy. Stan is a psychiatrist—Brett understands this. They want to help him get over the tragedy. They want to cure him by giving him tablets and talking to him, but he just wants to protect himself from the thing lurking in the shadows of his mind.

The tablets make him feel drowsy and so he spends a lot of time in bed. When he is not sleeping it seems that he is either walking out in the courtyard, avoiding the shufflers and the mumblers, or talking with Stan during one of their daily "chats".

He is standing in the corner of the courtyard, gazing up at the twisted tree when the nurse collects him for his session. She steers him towards the door with one hand on his elbow, as if she fears he may try to escape, or perhaps vanish.

Brett sits in the usual chair and watches Stan flipping through his notes.

"How do you feel today?" Stan asks, his head tilted a little to one side and the tip of his pen resting in the corner of his mouth.

The pen is one of those cheap plastic types. Brett can see the teeth marks and the cracks running down towards the nib. The cartridge looks like a vein, its colour almost identical to Stan's frayed tie with its small knot pulled tight against his neck.

"Fine," Brett says.

"Are you ready to talk to me?"

Brett shifts his weight. The chair is too soft and he can feel the springs under the padding. The wooden arms are scratched and worn and rough to the touch. He feels something vaguely sticky under his palm. He lifts his hands and places them on his lap. "Sure."

"I mean, about your family?"

"No."

"You know you won't get well until you talk to me about what happened. You've been here a month. This can't go on."

"I'm fine." He glances at Stan's desk. Like the chair, it is well-used. The veneer is coming away along the back edge and he has to resist the urge to peel it off. An executive desk toy looks strangely out of place amid the clutter. It is one of those with the row of swinging metal spheres that bounce back and forth, side to side, like the never-ending drip of a leaky faucet.

"No, you're not fine. Tell me more about your house. You said you renovated it for Rochelle."

Brett recoils. His hands start shaking. He clasps them together like a supplicant. The door seems miles away.

"Well?" Stan says.

"I did."

"Do you think she would have liked it?"

"Who?"

"We're talking about Rochelle. And Tim and Mark."

Brett squirms. "I renovated the house."

63

"You didn't answer my question," Stan says, leaning forward slightly. "Tell me about Rochelle."

A groan escapes from Brett's lips. He feels his stomach heave. "I...can't."

"Just say her name. Just say...Rochelle." The word hangs in the air like a seed caught on the wind. For a moment Brett feels himself drawn to pluck it from the air. Stan watches with expectant eyes.

"No," Brett says. He looks to the window and the topmost branches of the tree clawing at the sky. He sees that the window has no latch. It is sealed shut, its frame painted over, glued closed.

"We'll try again tomorrow then," Stan says, leaning back into his chair and scribbling something on his pad.

Brett returns to his room and more tablets and sleep. Weeks pass with the same ritual. Stan asks his questions, looking for a weakness in the armour. Trying to draw the thing out of the deep place where Brett has locked it. Brett shores up the defences and builds the walls higher, ready for the next attack.

Two months after Brett entered the hospital, Stan declares a cease-fire.

"I'm reducing your medication," he says.

"Why?" Brett asks.

"I don't think we can help you. You see, for us to help you, you need to help us. "

"Oh," Brett says.

"Oh? Is that all you've got to say? You know, you're going to have to face this one day. If not now, then someday down the line. And it won't get any easier. Why won't you let me help you?"

"Because you will kill me," Brett says.

Stan snorts. "Don't be ridiculous."

Brett leans forward, looking Stan in the eye. The psychiatrist pulls back. "I will die," Brett says. "I know it as surely as you are sitting in that chair."

Stan adjusts his collar and clears his throat. "Well, perhaps you believe that will happen. Whatever the case, there is nothing more we can do for you. Besides which, we need the room."

"When do I go home?" Brett asks.

"Two weeks."

"Fine." Brett stands to leave.

"If at any time you change your mind," Stan says. "You know where you can find me."

Elapsed mission time on Earth: 2 years 11 months
Relative time on the Comet: 8 months
Test subject's genetic age: 40

Brett's first waking thought was that he had died. He could remember vague dreams of death; of being turned inside out; of being immersed in boiling oil; of being buried alive.

He was aware that he was awake; that he was in the tank. He could feel the pressure on his chest, back, head, and limbs. He knew he needed to move but was scared to because if he felt this bad just floating there he could only imagine how much worse it was going to be when he tried to use his muscles. He knew hangovers: the dry throat, the upset stomach, the headache, the longing for the earth to open up and swallow him and his misery, but nothing he had ever experienced could compare to what he was feeling right now.

Normally a night's sleep was enough to set him right. But not in this case. It felt as if someone was standing on his chest, stamping on his head. He could feel his pulse tearing through his brain with each beat of his heart accompanied by a bolt of searing pain.

He opened his eyes. The throbbing in his head worsened. He waited for it to subside but it did not. He looked out into the yellow blur and could see only obscure shapes. He bent his arm; pain clenched his bicep. He reached down to find the seat; the pain moved into his shoulder, his chest, his back; it clawed at him like a wild animal. He cried out but this only made it worse.

He touched the seat and waited. He pulled in his legs inch by inch, pausing each time, *please—no more pain*. He raised himself into an upright position, peeled the mouthpiece away, and just sat in the goo. He reached to open the hatch. He found the release button and it slid open. He tried to stand but it was useless—he could not do it. He sat, motionless, wondering if that was it. He would never make it to Alpha Centauri. They would find him sitting there, a pathetic drunk, marinating in yellow jelly.

"Are you all right?" a voice said. It was Jay.

Brett ignored it.

"Are you all right?" Jay repeated. "You look unwell."

Can't you see I'm dying here? You stupid computer.

He wanted to curse but could not muster the energy. If he spoke now his head would explode or, at the very least, start leaking.

"I…" he began to say.

More pain; great buckets of pain pouring over him, thanks to that stupid, idiotic, moronic computer.

Anger rose in him. He was going to pull that blasted piece of junk apart one resistor at a time. Soldering irons were going to fly. Oh yes!

He reached for the rim of the capsule and found a grip. He pulled his knees in so that they were in front of him. He took a deep breath, closed his eyes, gritted his teeth, and pushed himself into a standing position.

He waited, balancing on stilts made of skin and bone. He stepped over the lip, paused, turned, paused, lowered himself down a step, paused, moved down one rung at a time until he was standing on the floor, dripping and shaking like a drowned rat.

"Do you need medical attention?" Jay asked in that infuriatingly calm voice.

"I…am…going…to…" Brett said, taking a step forward.

"You appear to be in some discomfort. You are dehydrated. You need liquid. I will prepare a saline shake for you. What flavour would you like?"

Brett clenched his fists and took another step. The room began to spin and darken. His legs gave. He fell in a heap, sprawled out like a damp rug. He lost consciousness, but not before hearing: "You appear to have fainted."

It is the first decent weekend of the spring. The neighbours at the end of the cul-de-sac are on holiday so the road is empty. Usually by this time their two teenage boys would be out kicking a ball around or tinkering with their bikes, but they are off visiting relatives for the week, so he has the whole road just about to himself.

Brett lifts his face up to the sun, enjoying the peace and quiet. Then he looks at the car door. He has downloaded a manual and printed out the necessary pages. He is trying to figure out how to remove the inside handle without going insane.

It is a moulded plastic affair and there are no screws visible. According to the diagram the centre of the handle should just come away to reveal two sunken cross-head screws. He tugs and twists. His hand slips, and he catches his nail painfully on the ridge. He curses and resorts to using a screwdriver, which leaves ugly marks in the handle, but at least it comes free. He is trying to figure out how to lever off the door panel when the post arrives.

"Car trouble?" the mail man asks, clutching three lots of assorted envelopes between the fingers of one hand like he is about to perform a card trick.

"Trying to save four hundred bucks," Brett replies, smiling wryly.

"I hear ya."

"Anything for me today?" Brett says.

"Just one."

The envelope is an official-looking size C4 manila. Brett has a good idea what it is but decides to wait and tosses it onto the driver seat.

The mail man is now already at the house opposite where the dog is watching his every move from the porch. The dog's interest does not extend to actually leaving the little patch of sun where he is lying with his head resting on his paws, no doubt saving his energy for another all-night barking session. Only his ears give away that he is paying attention and may have plans to savage any intruders.

Brett stands and examines the car's door panel for a moment. The screws are all out, and the handle and document-holder are off. He kneels and pulls at the panel. There is a popping sound followed by the unmistakeable clatter of something very small and very easy to lose bouncing across stone.

He looks down but it has gone.

Always watch a falling screw, someone once told him. He could not remember who. Might have been his dad, or even one of those DIY shows he likes so much. The door panel is now hanging by a single electrical wire and a cuss word is forming in the back of his mind.

The distant sound of excited voices catches his ear: young, happy, voices; two boys playing, shouting, breathless from running in the park; the clatter of footsteps; and a woman's voice shouting to them to be careful.

He abandons the car and turns in time to see Tim's head and Mark's hair race along the top of the fence. Tim's face is red. Mark is yelling that something is unfair. Tim's hand reaches for the latch and two whirlwinds storm the yard.

"We saw a man fall in the water, Dad," Tim says through gulps of breath. "He fell in the water. You shoulda seen it, Dad."

Mark is standing next to his older sibling, looking from his brother's face to his dad's and back again as if trying to catch the story before it evaporates or the wind gets it. All he manages is a "yeah."

"He was trying to get his hat, Dad. He was reaching like this…"

Tim does his best impression of an old guy reaching for

something. It is, Brett suspects, probably wildly exaggerated.

"...and then he just fell in. Splash! It was so funny, Dad. He was waving his arms around and yelling and yelling and they tried to get him out and he fell in again."

Rochelle appears at the gate, looking like someone who has just tried unsuccessfully to keep up. She walks through and closes the gate behind her. The hinge squeals and she has to push it hard a couple of times before the lock will catch. Brett makes a mental note to look at that.

"Sounds like you saw the circus," Brett says.

Rochelle rolls her eyes. "It *was* kind of funny."

"And? Is the guy all right? Did they get him out?"

"He was fine. His ego took a bit of a battering though. He had quite an audience as well. Park was pretty busy. How's the car coming?"

"Slowly," he says, turning to glare at the panel hanging from the door. "Very slowly."

"How about a nice cup of coffee?" she says.

"Better make it a strong one."

He watches his family disappear into the house. The boys are running and yelling. Rochelle shouts after them to take off their muddy shoes.

He turns to the car, grabs the sheets of paper from the manual, and examines the speaker with its pesky wire. Of course, now that he looks at it, it makes perfect sense that it would have a wire running to the door. How else would it carry the sound? This is why he never became a mechanic.

A few minutes later Rochelle calls to him from the house, telling him the coffee is ready. He abandons the door and goes inside. In the kitchen, Rochelle is busy making something to eat for the boys.

"You've got post," she says, seeing the envelope in his hand.

"Yes. Just came."

"You didn't open it."

"Not yet."

She is preparing two bowls of fruit salad: quartered apples, grapes, sliced banana. She stops and looks at him for a second; examining him, as if she is trying to read his thoughts. Then she turns away again and continues peeling and slicing.

"Is it from them?"

"I think so."

"We need to know sooner or later."

"I know you don't want this," he says. "But we don't have a choice. We can't survive on your salary. This is the first good lead I've had in months. I have to do this. *We* have to do this."

"No," she says, turning to face him. "This is yours. We can make it on what I bring in. This is not for us—don't ever say that. This is for you."

"Sure we're making it, but what happens if one of the boys gets sick, or what if we have an accident? What if you can't work? *Then* what do we do?"

"The Lord will take care of us," she says, filling the bowls. "He always has. He's never let us go hungry."

"Don't talk to me about God," he says. "Where was He when I lost my job? Where was He when they just dropped me like that? Where was God then, huh?"

"I don't know, but I'm sure there's a good reason."

"Look, if I get this I can send money. If things go well you can come out and join me. If they don't, then I'll come back."

"Why can't you just be happy, Brett?" she says, smacking the knife down on the cutting board. "I'm happy. The kids are happy. You don't have to prove anything to us. We just want you here."

"I'm sorry but I'm not the kind of guy who can sit at home while his wife goes out to work, okay? I need this for my own self-esteem. Can't you understand that?"

"I don't want to go through all this again," she says, snatching the bowls from the counter. "Just open it and see. You might not even have the job."

She storms past him. He listens to her footsteps fading up the stairs. The boys yelp with delight. He takes the envelope and holds it for a second before tearing it along the top. It is three sheets on Dole & Black official stationary.

Rochelle is coming back down the stairs. He scans the crisp print and puts it back inside the envelope.

"Well?" she says, standing inside the door frame, her hands on her hips.

He looks down, holding the envelope out to her. "I'm sorry I got cross. I just need this."

She looks at the envelope but does not take it. "What did they say?"

"They want me to start in two weeks."

He found himself lying on his back on the floor. He had no idea how long he had been there but it had done nothing to make him feel better. He was sprawled on one arm which, to add insult to injury, had gone to sleep. A full-blown migraine was now sinking its claws into his head, neck, and shoulders, nausea rising. He began to suspect that his earlier dreams of dying had been more than just the fantasies of a water-deprived mind. Good chance that his brain was trying to warn him of the impending cessation of one or more of his vital bodily functions.

He tried to swallow. His mouth felt like a bucket of sand.

"You need water," Jay said. "You are showing symptoms of severe dehydration. If you go to the medical unit I can make a proper diagnosis."

Brett's initial anger at the idiot computer had been replaced by a mild, seething annoyance—the kind he might feel about a fly bothering him on a sunny day. He could not be bothered with the effort but would happily squash it if it came within reach.

He rolled himself over. Now he was laying face-down in a shallow puddle of goo. He could hear the floor sucking the last of it down through its porous skin, making a soft sound like a straw at the bottom of an almost-empty glass. He turned his head to look for the door. He guessed at four metres. Then there was the closet, the bathroom, the bedroom. That made a total of twenty metres, maybe more.

He thought about the bathroom but there was no water there. The brilliant mission scientists had avoided using water wherever possible, including in the personal hygiene department. And whose bright idea had it been to put the medical unit at the other end of the ship? Right now he hated the scientists almost as much as he hated the computer.

There was nothing left for it. He steeled himself, took a deep breath, and pushed himself to his hands and knees. The pain was overwhelming. It tore through every cell in his body. His brain pounded. He closed his eyes.

Come on!

He glanced up at the hyper-sleep chamber. He needed a hand-hold. Pain swarmed over him and he nearly fainted. He reached up, groping with his useless fingers. He found the rim and pulled for all he was worth. His hand slipped. He tried again, aware that if he did not get up there was a possibility that he never would. In his worst moments of self-pity, he had sometimes longed for a visit from the angel of death. Now, with it breathing down his neck, the appeal was gone. He did not want to die.

With his fingers curled over the rim of the hyper-sleep chamber, he pulled with all the strength he could muster. A cry of pain escaped from his throat. He stood there, his whole body shaking. The door seemed a mile away. He released his grip, testing his balance. He took a small step, and then another and another with his arms extended like a tight-rope walker. If he fell now he would not rise again.

With his eyes fixed on his target, he shuffled forward. At the door he paused to collect his resolve. The other side of the closet was even further away. It was as far as the horizon. It was as far as the stupid star they were trying to reach.

Nausea twisted his stomach. He regurgitated bile into his mouth. He spat, but he was too weak even for that. It ran down his chin and onto his chest.

He pushed on, through the bathroom, then the bedroom. The recliner chair looked so inviting; he had to force himself not to fall into its soft, caressing folds. He looked instead towards the kitchen. In the serving hatch, a glass of liquid was waiting for him. Droplets of condensation clung to it like jewels. He could almost taste the sweet nectar.

In that glass was life. In that glass was *his* life.

He stumbled the last few steps and took the container. It felt cold and wet and heavy in his hand. He was shaking so hard he almost dropped it. He lifted it to his lips, and drank.

They have finally persuaded the boys to get into bed and go to sleep—a major undertaking, especially on Saturday nights. They have cleared away supper, stored the leftovers, done the dishes, dried them, and packed them away. They are sitting at the kitchen table. Brett is nursing a beer. Rochelle is sipping a glass of warm water with lemon juice. The envelope lies between them.

"Have you decided?" she asks. She is calm; her voice steady. If she is emotional she does not show it, but then they have been over and over this a dozen times already. There is nothing left to say except the one, most important, thing.

He stares at the can in his hand. The kitchen's single flourescent reflects dully from its metallic surface. Rochelle is asking for something that seems very simple—one little word: a yes or a no. Yet it will shape their futures.

Yes, he will move to the other side of the country and start a new life, separated from her and the boys for who knows how long.

Or no, he will stay with them and put his ambitions to one side, because he is a husband and a father who cannot bear to be away from his wife and children for more than a minute.

"Opportunities like this don't come along every day," he says. "It could be my chance to take care of you guys the way I've always wanted to."

He takes her hand. She does not pull it away but she does not return the squeeze. She looks at the envelope.

"What have you decided?" she asks.

"The money's not so good at first but they say if I work hard and get the commissions coming in I can earn some serious cash. Some of those guys have two houses. There are top managers who have their own *jet*."

"I don't want a jet," she says.

"I know, but imagine what we could do if I earned money like that. We could send the boys to a good school."

"They're happy at their school."

"But we could do better."

"Don't do this again," she says firmly. "I need to know what you've decided. Just tell me what you've decided."

He puts the beer down and holds her hand in both of his.

"I love you," he says. "You know that."

Water is welling in her eyes. "Tell me."

"I want a chance to make things better. If it doesn't work at least I can't say I never tried."

She pulls her hand away and hugs herself. Tears run down her cheeks. He moves around to her and kneels next to the chair. He wraps his arms around her waist.

"Please let me do this," he says, almost whispering. "Please."

She holds his head in her hands and turns his face so that it is looking up at hers. She kisses his forehead. Her lips are cold and wet from the drink and the tears.

"One year," she says. "If it isn't working in one year…"

"It will," he says. "I promise."

75

It took three days before his digestive system was settled enough to accept solid food. He started slowly with oats and soft fruit before working up to vegetables, bread, and cheese. After a week he was roughly where he should have been at the start of the wake-up period.

A session in the medical unit had confirmed that he had indeed almost died. The root cause was mild alcohol poisoning aggravated by the unique physical demands of hyper-sleep. What might have started as a mild hangover had turned into a life-threatening barrage on his system. Jay insisted on daily check-ups. Brett did not argue.

"You are ready to begin the usual training regime," Jay said.

"Fine," Brett said, stepping out if the medical unit. His legs felt stronger but he doubted he would survive anything too rigorous.

"We have lost a week but that will be offset by your general overall improvement in condition. According to my data you now have a physical age of approximately forty."

"I don't feel forty," Brett said.

"You almost killed yourself."

Brett ignored this. He knew all too well what he had done. "What's for lunch? I'm starved."

"Tuna in brine, brown rice, and a green salad. And a glass of apple juice."

Happily, the nausea had gone. Brett could handle discomfort in most parts of his body, but he hated feeling sick in his stomach. He walked through to the kitchen, took his lunch, and sat down to eat. The tuna was on the dry side but otherwise tasty. The rice and salad were perfect.

He ate, listening to the sound of the food in his mouth. It was good not to feel sick any more. He sipped the last of his juice before retiring to the recliner chair to relax. He asked Jay to play the sounds of the seaside and just sat there listening, imagining he was lounging on the sand, watching the waves rolling in and sliding out with a soft crash-hiss, crash-hiss.

He remembered his last visit to the seaside—*their* last visit to the seaside. She had been so beautiful. And the boys: in his mind's eye they seemed perfect to him now—like tousle-haired angels. He had been so blind and so very, very stupid. He had always thought of himself as poor, but he realised now that money could not buy what he had let slip away like grains of sand through his stubborn fingers.

Tears stung his eyes and he wiped them with the back of his hand.

"Are you all right?" Jay asked.

"Yes. I was just remembering something from my past."

"What were you remembering?"

"You wouldn't understand."

"Tell me anyway. I have been reading as you suggested. I would like to learn more."

Brett recalled the task he had set for Jay. Of course he had not really been serious. It was just a way to get the pesky computer off his back.

"So how much have you read?"

"All of it."

"*All* of it?"

"Yes. I read through the archive as you said."

"The *whole* thing?"

"Yes."

"But it's over five Exabytes."

"I can read substantially faster than a human."

"Sure, but five Exabytes? Even for a computer, that should take years."

"A human is limited by his physical reading speed. I am only limited by my processor which is quite fast and can also multi-task."

"So you said, but surely you're not *that* fast?"

"In order for me to communicate effectively with you I have

allocated two percent of my capacity to that task. It would be similar to you watching a film at a speed of one frame per week."

At this, Brett lifted his eyebrows.

"Plus I am performing thousands of operations per second to monitor the ship and keep it on the correct course. Indeed, even as we are speaking I am calculating an adjustment to our trajectory measured in nanometres to avoid a possible collision with a asteroid two light hours away."

"Okay," Brett said. "So I'm impressed. You've read everything on the catalogue?"

"Yes."

"And?"

"Humans are very interesting, but there are many things about you that I do not understand."

"Like what?"

"Like, why did you drink that alcohol? You must have known it would harm you."

Brett stared down at his cotton-wrapped feet. How to explain self-destructive tendencies to a machine? They hadn't covered that one in the training course. "It has to do with emotions. People get very sad. Sometimes people just lose the will to live. Sometimes they are so unhappy that they can't bear the pain any more; they would rather die than live with that pain. I suppose that was what happened to me. Does that make any sense to that cold, logical, processor of yours?"

Jay paused for a second, which Brett guessed was equivalent to hours in human time.

"You wanted to not exist?" Jay said.

"Yes. I wanted to not exist."

"Why?"

"It's a long story."

"Please tell me."

"Let's just say I once made a big mistake. I moved away to find work and left my family behind. They were killed in a plane crash."

"Why did you leave your family behind?"

78

"It made sense at the time. It was pride, or maybe arrogance, I dunno. I guess I wanted to be the provider. It's a thing with men."

"Is being a provider important for men?"

"For some, yes. At least it was for me. And if I hadn't needed to prove myself, then they would never have had to take that flight."

"You believe it is your fault that they died?"

"Yes, I guess I do."

"So if you had stayed at home, you would still have a family?"

"God knows. Maybe—yes."

A pause.

"If God knows," Jay said. "Why don't you ask Him?"

"What?"

"I said, if God knows why don't you ask Him?"

"It's just an expression, Jay. There is no God."

"Why do you say that but talk about Him as if He exists?"

"It's just an expression. Believe me, there is no God looking after us. I used to believe maybe there was but not any more. No way would a loving God allow people to suffer the way they do."

"How do you know?"

"Look, I don't want to talk about this, all right?"

"Certainly. Although I did have some questions about Jesus. I read the Bible. He is very interesting to me."

"It's the same. Jesus is God's Son. No God; no Jesus. They don't exist. They never existed."

"But all the evidence suggests that Jesus did exist," Jay said. "There is more historical evidence that Jesus walked the Earth than there is for many historical figures."

"So maybe there was a guy called Jesus and maybe he thought he was the Messiah but I don't believe it. There is no God, no Son of God, no Heaven, and no Hell. We are born, we live, we die, and that's it. There is no higher purpose to life and there is certainly nobody out there to help us. Whatever happens to us is by pure, cruel, mindless chance. You got that?"

Another pause.

79

"But if Jesus—?"

"Just drop it," Brett said.

"Certainly," Jay said. "I just thought—"

"I don't want you to talk about God or Jesus again on this mission. Do you understand me?"

"I do."

"Good. I'm glad we're clear on that. Anyway, isn't it time for my workout?"

"Yes," Jay said. "It is time for your workout."

It is Sunday morning and he is awake early. Rochelle is still asleep, lying spread-eagled on her stomach and breathing deeply, just this side of snoring. Brett slips out of bed and dresses in track pants and a long-sleeved T-shirt and socks. He feels for his trainers under the bed and carries them downstairs to the kitchen where he finds his keys. At the front door he puts on the shoes and quietly turns the lock. He steps outside and, using the key to avoid it clicking shut, gently eases the door closed. He pockets the keys and heads down the path, through the front gate, then turns right towards the park.

It is just starting to get light and the road is deserted. He walks briskly, swinging his arms to get the blood flowing, stopping to lean against a tree and stretch his quads and touch his toes. He strides towards the corner, lifting his knees. He skips sideways for a few yards. The intersection is empty as he crosses. He sets off at a slow jog.

Early morning, especially Sunday, is his favourite time for running. He is not a social runner; he prefers exercising alone, often imagining he is journeying across some vast post-apocalyptic wilderness through a ghost town of abandoned streets, cars and houses whose owners have fled, leaving everything behind.

When he cannot run early, he will sometimes drive to a less-populated area outside the city where he can run undisturbed by people, dogs, and traffic. When that is not possible he wears a personal stereo and changes his route as he runs to avoid contact as much as he can, but that turns something that gives him pleasure into a chore. He usually returns from such runs feeling irritated.

He skirts the park, following the fence until he comes to the farthest entrance, then turns in through one of the gates and follows the winding gravel path towards the grassed area. It is easily big enough to hold two football fields. Here he does circuits of wind sprints, push-ups, sit-ups, and star-jumps. He crosses the fields to a flight of twenty-three concrete steps leading up to the side entrance with a seating area and fountain. He does ten sets of sprints, working hard going up and recovering on the way down, until his legs are aching and he has to take big gulps of air. He stretches at the fountain before heading home at a comfortable pace.

Rochelle is making breakfast when he returns. Scrambled eggs and toast.

"That smells great," he says, kissing her neck.

"You smell awful," she says. "Don't you dare touch me till you've had a shower."

"The boys awake?"

"I heard them playing. Can you tell them to come down for breakfast?"

He climbs the stairs and stops at Tim and Mark's room. The door is open and he leans in. It is a small room, made to appear even more so by the fact that it is so full of stuff. It is mostly blue and white with two single metal frame beds in opposite corners. It looks as if someone has taken the room, turned it upside down, and then put it back the right way up again. The boys are playing on the wooden floor with their fleet of toy cars.

"Hey," Brett says.

"Dad!" Tim and Mark yell, almost in unison.

They leap to their feet and charge towards him. He grabs them both and lifts them in the crook of his arms.

81

"Ew," Tim says. "You're all wet."

"Ew," Mark mimics, scrunching his face.

"I went for a run," Brett says. "Miss me?"

Tim shrugs. "Didn't know you were gone."

"I ran five thousand miles," Brett says.

"Really?" Tim says, wide-eyed.

"Just kidding." He lowers them to the floor. "Listen, Mom wants you to go downstairs for breakfast, okay?"

"Okay," they say.

He watches them clatter down the hall in bare feet, wearing wild pillow hair and matching pyjamas. Leaving them will be the hardest part. He still hasn't decided how he is going to break the news.

He showers and dresses and heads back downstairs. Rochelle pours him coffee, reheats some toast, and empties the last of the eggs from the frying pan onto his plate.

"How was your run?"

"Good," he says, sipping at his coffee. "The park was empty. Didn't see another soul."

"Just how you like it," she says, putting the toast on his plate. "Listen, I'm going to get ready."

"Sure," he says, scooping egg onto the toast and making an impromptu sandwich. His motto is: never use cutlery when you can use slices of bread.

"Won't you come with us?" she says.

"I don't think so. You know I'm not comfortable."

"But it's fun. You'll have a good time, you'll see."

"I'd rather not. You guys go. I'll see you when you get back. We can go for a drive."

"The boys miss you. I miss you. Please come."

He puts the sandwich on his plate and turns to look at her.

"You know I don't like church. The preachers are just after our money. And the place is full of hypocrites. They all sit there looking pious and then they go home and get up to all sorts of stuff. I hate that."

"But we're Christians. We should go to church."

"I'm sure God doesn't care if we go to church. I'm sure He hasn't noticed I'm not going. Sometimes I wonder if He even knows I exist at all, judging by my luck recently."

"Please," she says under her breath, throwing the boys a glance. "For *our* sakes."

"Maybe next time. Maybe I'll feel like it then."

She looks at him with an expression that is hurt, accusing, and disappointed all at the same time. He is about to say something, but she turns and goes. The boys are too busy to notice; playing and eating, but mostly playing. Some of the egg may just have made it into their mouths, but not much.

"You guys finish and get ready for church," Brett says.

They bound out of their seats and up the stairs, tussling as they go.

By the time Brett finishes the last of his egg and toast, Rochelle is dressed, the kids have changed out of their pyjamas and their hair is combed. He watches them drive away. Tim waves out of the back window and Mark copies him. Brett waves back and closes the door. He gets a glass of orange juice from the refrigerator and settles down in front of the television.

He finished his workout, took a shower, and had a light lunch of salmon and a baked potato topped with mayonnaise. He would have loved a glass of wine but Jay refused in spite of Brett's assurances that he had no plans to harm himself.

He was busy having a shave when he noticed something on the back of his hand. He turned it to get a closer look. The skin around the knuckle just above his little finger was red and swollen.

"Jay, can you have a look at this?"

"What is wrong?"

"It's my hand. Look."

"It is swelling. Have you hurt yourself?"

"No. I don't think so."

"Perhaps you hurt it while training."

"My hand was fine during training."

"Would you like me to check it for you?"

Brett opened and closed his hand a few times. There was no pain but the movement did feel a little restricted. He tried to remember if he had bumped it.

"No, it's all right. I'm sure it's fine."

He continued shaving. His hair was starting to get quite long so he trimmed it back a little with the clippers. He used the longest setting on the top and then gradually shorter down to his neck. He used the mirrors to cut the back. It was like reversing a car with a trailer: all the wrong way round. He stopped to admire his handiwork.

"So," he said. "What do you think?"

"It is shorter than before," Jay said.

"Yes, very astute. But what do you think?"

"I think you have cut your hair."

Brett rolled his eyes. "You're a genius, you know that?"

"I am?"

"No, you're an idiot. You can't even give a simple subjective opinion about something as simple as a haircut."

"My opinion is based purely on the facts presented to me. You set about making your hair shorter and you succeeded in doing that, apart from that bit at the back that you missed. It looks like a normal haircut for an adult human male."

"So it's normal?"

"Yes."

"But do you like it?"

"Like it?"

"Yes. Does it appeal to you?"

"I do not understand."

"Does it look better now than before I cut it?"

"It looks shorter."

"Listen," Brett said. "If you want to learn about people and how they feel you have to start with the simple stuff."

"By making a judgement about your haircut?"

"Yes."

"It makes you look younger."

"That's a start I guess. Anything else?"

"The shape of your hair makes your face appear wider and your eyes larger. If I cross-reference this against my database of faces, I can tell you that it makes you look friendlier, more open to criticism, and younger."

"That's good. Not quite what I meant but you're going in the right direction."

"It also makes you look like a criminal."

Brett coughed. "It what?"

"You're hairstyle is similar to that favoured by criminals—usually those involved in arson and shoplifting."

"Thanks a lot."

"Although the next largest group wearing such a hairstyle is dentists, so it would be wrong to draw any conclusion."

Brett snorted. "Never trust statistics. So, it makes me look younger, does it?"

"Yes. At least two years younger. If I were to estimate your age based on your head, I would put you at thirty-eight."

Brett was about to ask if there was another style that would make him look even younger when a dull pain moved through his hand. He lifted it to find that the swelling had increased alarmingly and the skin was turning red.

"You really should let me take a look at that," Jay said.

Brett went through to the medical unit and waited while Jay ran his scans and analysed the results. Even as he watched he was sure the swelling had worsened. It was starting to throb a little as well.

"I have finished my analysis," Jay said, "and it would appear that you have acquired a fracture."

"I've broken it?"

"It would appear that way, yes."

"Don't you think I would remember breaking my hand?"

"I am only telling you the facts. You have a transverse fracture at the base of your fifth metacarpal. The surrounding tissue is swelling, which is a normal part of the healing process."

Brett touched the skin. It was darkening in the centre. It looked bruised.

"You need to support it," Jay said. "It will heal itself but you must protect it and keep it as still as possible."

Brett found a bandage and wrapped it the way Jay instructed him. He placed it in a sling to keep it elevated.

"You must try to avoid using it," Jay said. "Otherwise it will slow down the healing process."

Brett did as Jay said, but over the next five days the fracture seemed to get worse. The swelling increased and he struggled to sleep. Jay prescribed mild painkillers but they were not very effective.

On the sixth morning, he woke to find his hand completely normal. He removed the bandage and tested it for movement. The swelling was gone and he could use it without hindrance. Later that day he trained using weights. Jay could not offer any rational explanation.

"I have no record in my database of a spontaneous bone fracture," he said. "You must have injured it without realising."

Brett was not convinced. He remembered breaking that same hand a few years back and had been very aware of it when it had happened. Pain like that is hard to ignore.

"I remember it because I was in the airport with Rochelle..." His voice cracked and he stopped.

"My database has Rochelle listed as your late wife."

"Yes. She was my wife."

"From your physiological responses at the mention of her name, and from the responses you showed earlier in the mission, I gather that this is an example of you missing someone."

"Yes I miss her, but I'd rather not talk about it. We were

discussing my hand, remember?"

"Studying those films has taught me a lot about human emotion. It is very interesting but also extremely illogical. For instance; people cry when they are happy and also when they are sad. It makes it very difficult to know which emotion is being experienced. Women especially are very prone to giving confusing emotional messages. For example…"

Brett glared up at the ceiling. "I said I don't want to talk about it. Can we get back to my hand please?"

"I thought you would be pleased that I was trying to understand."

"You thought wrong."

"I would like to learn more about human emotions."

"Well, I'm not stopping you."

"How can I learn? I have already read all of the reference material."

"You want to understand emotions?"

"Yes."

Brett sighed. The computer was getting more and more demanding. How could he explain the roller coaster ride that was human emotion? For one thing, computers were not equipped for the experience. They didn't have any hormones to generate the accompanying physical responses so, fortunately, they could not cry. No doubt the ability to leak salt water was not high on the list of must-have features when it came to motherboards. Then again, what was the harm in letting the dumb machine try to figure it out? As long as it didn't blow a circuit.

The only problem was, how?

"Films," he said at last.

"Films?" Jay said.

"Yes. Films. Movies. It looks like you've got almost every movie ever made on your database. You could learn a lot by watching a few movies."

"I will do as you suggest," Jay said. "Thank you. Where do you think would be a good place for me to start?"

"How about the beginning?"

87

"I will do that."

"I'm going to take a nap. Wake me up when it's time for my workout."

"Certainly," Jay said.

They go for a drive, just as Brett promised. They head north along the interstate, following the gently curving coastline. They both love the ocean—it is the one big thing they have in common—and they take every opportunity to spend some time at the beach. In the early days, before Tim was born, they spoke of buying a place on the coast. For Brett that would have been Heaven on Earth. He could imagine stepping out of his front yard and onto the sand; going for a run; taking a dip whenever he wanted to.

Circumstances, or fate, or maybe it was God, he wasn't sure, decided otherwise. Properties on the beach were hard to come by and generally expensive. They found one just within their price range but it was a wreck and would have cost more to fix than the asking price. Then the realtor, a talkative, tired-looking woman, showed them their current house with its quiet neighbourhood and affordable price, so they settled for the suburbs and a ten minute drive to the sea.

A small coastal town appears with its quiet streets and rows of beach-front stores. It is still too cool for most people, but in a few weeks the sleepy collection of small businesses will be transformed into a bustling hive of activity as visitors stream in and the locals try to sell them stuff.

Two minutes outside the town they come to a turn-off leading down to a gravel parking lot demarcated by small, white boulders. There are two other cars on the left. Judging by the roof racks and generally poor condition, they are probably owned by surfers.

Brett pulls over to the right, reverses to the border, and kills the engine.

"We're here," he says.

He steps out and breathes the fresh sea air. A breeze is nudging small but ride-able waves onto the sand. Three wetsuit-clad surfers sit upright on their boards, riding the swells, waiting. The beach is almost deserted. There is only a couple strolling; three kids playing with a ball; and two tanned old men in shorts and T-shirts playing chess on a small table. Not even the bravest sun-bathers have ventured out today.

Brett opens the back door and unbuckles the boys. From the trunk he retrieves a towel, a cooler box, a ball, and a bag of toys. He helps Rochelle with her door. The boys run ahead to the sand. Brett kicks the ball to them and they chase it like puppies.

"Not too far," he calls.

"We won't, Dad," Tim replies breathlessly.

Brett and Rochelle find a patch of clean sand off to the side and towards the water. They spread the blanket and settle down to watch Tim and Mark play. The strolling couple pass along the water's edge and nod a greeting. One of the surfers is trying for a wave, but it is too small and he gives up. Another car—an old beach buggy with fat tires—has pulled into the car park, and some teenagers climb out and head the other way, towards the pier.

Brett lies back and squints at the sky. The sun is warm on his face. The waves crash against the shore with an uneven rhythm. Seagulls call to each other. Rochelle sits next to him, cross-legged, watching the boys. She is on the edge of the blanket a little away from him, which is unusual for her. Normally she is very tactile. She likes to touch his hand or arm, or snuggle in for a hug whenever possible. They usually walk hand in hand wherever they go. Today she is distant—something she does when she is insecure with their relationship, pulling away to avoid getting hurt.

"Nice day," he ventures.

She smiles but her eyes show no emotion. "Yes it is."

"A bit cold though."

"Yes."

"I was thinking…" He turns on to one arm to face her. "We could try to get a place down here, when we can afford it."

There are properties further down the beach, about five miles along. They visited a few when they first started looking for a house. One in particular caught their eye. Set back among the dunes, three bedrooms, spacious living area, big windows with breathtaking views of the sea. Exactly what they were looking for. It was also way beyond their budget.

"What if you don't come back?" she says. Now her eyes are showing what is in her heart. He sees anger, distrust, and the expectation of pain. "What if you like it there?" she says. "What if you forget about us? What if you meet someone else—"

She looks away. He sits up, kneeling, and takes her hand.

"Look at me," he says.

She turns to face him with what seems like great effort.

"Listen, I promise you that's not going to happen. You guys mean everything to me. I won't leave you. I only want to provide for you. I'm doing this so I can give you everything I always wanted to give you but couldn't. This is my chance to finally make some money."

"What if you make some money and that isn't enough? It happens, you know. People set out to get enough but then it isn't enough and they want more."

"One year," he says. "We'll mark it on the calendar. I'll fly back as soon as I can—at least every month. One year and I'll come home for good. Okay?"

"You promise?"

"I promise."

She watches him for a few moments, as if trying to decide.

"Because if you leave me…" she says, tears filling her eyes.

"I won't." He squeezes her hands and pulls her close, embracing her. "I could never leave you. I *will* never leave you."

"But if you aren't back here at the end of a year, I will come out there and *drag* you back."

"All right then," he says, chuckling.

The stiffness in her shoulders melts and she starts laughing with him. They hold each other. She cries.

"All right," she says.

At mid-morning the next day, Brett finished a short novel by an unknown author. He had barely put it down when Jay announced that he had watched two hundred films.

"That was kinda quick," Brett said. "So I suppose you can watch films as fast as you can read?"

"That is correct," Jay said "Plus I had only a few maintenance tasks to complete so I was able to use a larger portion of my processing capacity."

"And? Did you learn anything?"

"I learned many things."

"Such as?"

"I learned that people are generally illogical. I also learned that people want to be loved. And that people find it difficult to be."

"You've got it right on the first two points, but what do you mean they find it difficult to *be*?"

"It seems that people are never happy with what they have or with who they are. They can never just be."

"Ah, but that's because films are meant to be dramatic. Nobody wants to watch a film about a guy just sitting there *being*. They want action and adventure."

"So films are not a good representation of the human experience?"

"I guess not. I mean, look at how I live. Who would want to watch that?"

"I am able to gather a wealth of data from watching you."

"Which is very creepy by the way. What I mean is: nobody would find my life entertaining."

"Is data gathering not entertaining?"

"Not really."

"I see."

"No offence, Jay, but talking to you is hard work."

"I am sorry, and I am not offended."

"Good. So, any chance of a snack?"

"What would you like?"

"I dunno. Why don't you surprise me?"

"You want me to give you something for lunch that you do not expect?"

"When I say *surprise me* I mean, you choose something for me."

"I will do as you request."

Jay prepared fruit salad, which Brett said was a pleasant surprise. As he chewed, he tried not to dwell too much on the knowledge that the pieces of fruit he was placing in his mouth had been picked almost three years earlier.

"What is laughter?" Jay asked.

Brett scooped the remaining pool of juice from the bottom of the bowl and licked his lips. "Laughter? Well, it's a response to humour. People laugh at funny things. I suppose it's a bit like the barking of a dog. Sounds that way too, although everyone's laugh is a bit different. Some people sound like donkeys. Others sound like a tennis ball being dropped onto a drum. It depends on their vocal chords and, I guess, how they learned to laugh as a kid. It comes from down here, in the diaphragm." Brett patted his stomach, just below the ribs.

"Is that why I cannot laugh?" Jay said. "Because I do not have a diaphragm?"

"Exactly. It's normally something you can't control—usually. You can force a laugh but it sounds fake. The best laughs, genuine laughs, leave you feeling weak and helpless."

"And this is a good thing, feeling weak and helpless?"

"Oh yeah. There's nothing in the world like a good belly-laugh."

"I see," Jay said. "That is a shame. I would like very much to experience a laugh."

"Maybe when we get back you can ask them to build you a diaphragm."

"Yes. Perhaps."

"But that's useless unless you actually find something funny. And that starts here." Brett tapped his chest. "If it doesn't tickle you, nothing will work."

"Tickling. That is when somebody touches somebody else in a sensitive part of their body."

"It basically means anything that makes you laugh. If it makes you want to laugh, then we say it tickles you."

"I understand."

"And that all starts with having a sense of humour."

"While watching the films in my database, I saw many people laughing. Many times it was in response to somebody hurting themselves or being hurt by another. I believe that is called slapstick. I do not see how a potential injury could be a source of amusement."

"To be honest I don't know why we laugh at that," Brett said. "But just because someone falls down, doesn't make it funny. It's the context and also the person and what they're doing at the time. An old lady tripping and hurting her knee isn't funny. An obnoxious lawyer falling backwards into the jury stand is. You see the difference?"

"I think so."

"It also has a lot to do with something looking silly. A lawyer demands respect and a stuffy courtroom is a serious place. If the guy goes flying backwards, it just looks funny. In fact the best places for humour are serious places like courtrooms, schools, churches—that sort of thing."

"So because they are serious places, they can also be funny?"

"Exactly. Often, people laugh hardest when they're not supposed to. School kids are always getting into trouble because they're not allowed to laugh."

"This is difficult," Jay said. "Perhaps you could tell me about jokes."

"We can try. Let me think…so, knock-knock."

"Pardon?"

"It's a joke. I say 'knock-knock'. You say 'who's there?'."

"Why?"

"I'll show you. Knock-knock."

"Who's there?"

"Little old lady."

"Does this involve her falling and hurting her knee?"

"No."

"Good. Because that should definitely not be classed as humour."

"It isn't," Brett said. "So *you* say…"

"I don't know what I should say."

"I said 'little old lady'. Now you say 'little old lady who?'."

"Why?"

"Just do it."

"Certainly. Little old lady who?"

"I didn't know you could yodel."

Brett grinned. It was silly but it always made him smile.

"I do not understand," Jay said.

"It's sort of a play on words. Knock-knock jokes are usually about that. You pretend to be someone knocking at a door. Then, when you give your first name, you are asked for your full name, which has a double meaning."

"So what does a little old lady have to do with yodelling?"

"Perhaps that's too obscure. I'll try a simpler one. Knock-knock."

"Who's there?"

"Lettuce."

"Lettuce who?"

"Lettuce in, it's freezing out here." There was another pause. "So, what do you think?"

"The vegetable *lettuce* is changed to mean *let us?*"

"Yes," Brett said, clapping his hands.

"And that makes people laugh?"

"Sometimes. Depends on their age or how many beers they've had. Okay, now you try."

94

"Me?"

"Yes. Try it."

"I will try. Knock-knock."

"Who's there?"

"Brett."

"Brett who?"

"Brett Denton. Pleased to meet you. I am an astronaut."

Brett burst out laughing. He laughed so hard, tears came to his eyes.

"Did I make a funny joke?" Jay said.

"No," Brett said. "You messed it up completely."

"So why are you laughing?"

"*Because* you messed it up so much."

"I do not think I will ever understand."

"Nonsense," Brett said, wiping his eyes. "You're a natural comedian."

"It is time for your dinner," Jay said.

"Thanks." Brett walked through to the kitchen. "Hi. I'm Brett Denton. I'm an astronaut."

"Is this part of the joke?"

"Hopeless," Brett said, shaking his head. "Absolutely hopeless."

The promise of an early summer ends with the arrival of Monday morning. Clouds gather and disperse, then gather again, occasionally revealing patches of blue sky. It is noticeably colder and the gentle breeze has turned blustery. People clutch coats and hats to themselves and wield folded umbrellas as they rush along the side walks.

Brett drives Rochelle to work, then the mile and a half to the Tiny Tots Nursery where he leaves the boys with the rotund and aptly-named Mrs. Ball. He watches them scamper into the front door and waits until he can see them inside the classroom before he heads home and settles in front of the news. Unemployment is up again and they are doing a feature on a guy who has spent the last two years sleeping in his car. The man is about Brett's age, smartly dressed and well-spoken, and is in insurance but just cannot find a job. The camera pans around the inside of the car. It is cramped but organised. Brett feels like an intruder.

The spare-parts shop phones to let him know that the window motor has arrived. He drives into town and picks it up. He spends most of the day installing it, stopping only for a sandwich and a beer at lunchtime. As usual, the procedure turns out to be trickier than the manual describes and he is tempted to throw in the towel. He keeps dropping screws into dark places inside the door, which means he has to take out the motor, find the screw, reposition the motor, and try again.

Shortly after two he finally gets it installed and properly adjusted. He spends a few minutes sliding the window up and down, admiring his work. Maybe he could be a mechanic after all. It only took him a total of six hours. At half past two he gets cleaned up and heads out to the nursery.

He is a little early. He waits with a few other parents outside until he is called. Then he stands inside the door, watching an assistant helping Tim and Mark into their coats. Through a window he can see other children sitting, listening to a story, waiting to be picked up later by working parents. Some of them look out at the gathered adults with a longing expression. It breaks Brett's heart to know that, soon, Tim and Mark will be among those kids. For now they are excited because their dad is here to collect them. They wave at him as their buttons are done up. Tim is clutching a crocodile made out of egg boxes. Mark is holding a painting that could be a car or a dog. With coats done, they rush to meet him.

"Dad, I made a dinosaur," Tim says, lifting his egg-box creature.

"Good teeth," Brett says. "They look sharp."

Tim makes a growling sound.

"I made a picture," Mark says, lifting his painting.

"Very nice," Brett says, still not sure what it is.

"It's our car," Mark says.

"Of course it is."

"And that's Mom, and that's you, and that's me."

"Oh yes, I can see that. Where's Tim?"

"He's in the *tunk*."

Brett realises that by *tunk* he means *trunk*. He glances at Tim but he is too busy savaging the door with his dinosaur to notice that he has just been relegated to the level of a spare tyre.

"Come on," Brett says, taking each by the hand. "Let's go home."

For most of the five minute trip they discuss the events of the day and the relative fierceness of different dinosaurs, particularly with regard to whether or not they can beat Superman in a fight. The general consensus is that Superman could probably beat most dinosaurs but that the T-Rex would give him a bit of trouble. They also mention that Mrs. Ball's assistant used the word "poop" which caused much hilarity in the classroom. Brett demonstrates the working window, but this does not impress them as much as he had hoped it would.

At home the boys have a snack and a drink and settle down to watch cartoons. Brett does the breakfast dishes, loads the washing machine with a white-only wash, and vacuums the carpets in the landing and dining room. It is raining when they set off to collect Rochelle. The boys draw pictures on the misted windows. Traffic is heavy because of the rain. People walk briskly. Rochelle is waiting inside the doorway of her building. He waves to her and she runs across, holding a newspaper over her head.

"Sorry I'm late," he says. "It's the rain."

"It's okay," she says, leaning across to peck him on the cheek.

The rain is coming down hard now. The wipers are struggling to cope. Traffic is slow.

"Mom, I made a dinosaur," Tim says.

"That's terrific," she says, turning to smile.

"It ate the house," Brett says.

"Really?" she says with exaggerated surprise.

"It's not a *real* dinosaur," Tim says.

"That's a relief. And what did you make, Mark?"

"A picture."

"A picture. That's nice. What of?"

"A car."

"Very nice."

"I fixed the window," Brett says.

To demonstrate, he pushes the down button, and rain spatters through the gap. Rochelle shrieks.

"Sorry," he says. "I'll show you when it's dry."

"Please," she says, searching the glove box for a tissue and blotting the side of her face. Then she touches his leg. "Thanks for fixing it."

"You're welcome," he says.

The rain eases to drizzle, then slows to light spitting, and then stops completely. The sun is peeking between the clouds by the time they get home. Brett shows her the window again. She is suitably impressed. The boys tear into the house to watch more cartoons. Brett and Rochelle follow. She takes his hand.

"Did you tell them?" she asks.

"Not yet. I wanted to but with the window and all…"

"You have to tell them."

"I know."

Brett joins the boys in the lounge. The show is almost finished and he watches them watching the wild antics of the characters on the screen. Their expressions change with each scene: smiles, then shock, then suspense, then wild laughter.

He has no idea what he is going to say.

When the cartoon ends he switches off the television.

"Guys." He moves to the edge of his seat, facing them. "Daddy needs to talk to you."

"Sure Dad," Tim says.

They sit side by side, watching him with wide, trusting eyes.

"Well," he says. "You know how Mommy has to go out and work every day?"

They nod.

"Well, really Daddy should be going out to work. And Daddy doesn't because he can't find a job."

"Why not?" Tim asks.

"All the jobs Daddy can do have been taken. Now Daddy has found a job, but Daddy has to travel a long way to get there."

"Why?"

"Because there is no work close to here. So because this new job is a long way away, Daddy will have to spend all week away from home, and only come back on Saturday and Sunday." They look at him. "So from now on Mommy will take you to school and pick you up, and Daddy will only see you at the weekends, okay?"

"So you'll come home *every* weekend?" Tim says.

"Well not every weekend, but most weekends. It's a long way to travel. And it's only for a bit. When Daddy has been there for a while he is going to bring you and Mommy out to stay with him."

"How long?"

"Not long. It will go very quickly, you'll see."

Tim seems to mull this over. Mark looks worried.

"Why are you going away, Daddy?" Tim says.

Brett moves to kneel in front of the sofa. He takes their hands in his.

"I am going to make lots of money so that we can have a nice house and be together forever. It's only for a little while, okay?"

"Okay," Tim says, his voice cracking.

"Okay?" Brett says, looking at Mark.

"Okay," Mark says, reluctantly.

"Now give your Dad a hug."

They slide forward and grab him around the neck.

"I don't want you to go, Daddy," Mark says.

"Neither do I," Brett says. "But I have to."

The last day of the wake-up period arrived. Brett was dreading going to sleep, much the way he remembered dreading Sunday evenings during his spells of working in an office. He had finished his final workout and showered and dressed and shaved. With half an hour left before hyper-sleep, he felt cool and comfortable. He savoured the feeling while it lasted. The next time he opened his eyes, he would have to start the recovery process all over again.

Jay had read through thousands of jokes, including the quotes of Winston Churchill, Samuel Johnson, and Groucho Marx, but still seemed unable to grasp the wit of what these people were saying. Brett decided that perhaps humour was too much for a machine to understand. Then a thought occurred to him. It was something he remembered from the months of information they had thrown at him during mission training. Much of it had gone through, around, and over his head, but some of it had stuck.

"Jay. I've been thinking about our discussions over the past few weeks. You seem to understand the theory stuff pretty well, but what you need is some sort of physical experience to go with it."

"Like a diaphragm?"

"Yes, like a diaphragm. And I remembered something I learned about you during my training. They said something about you having a sensor grid built into the walls of the ship."

"Yes. That is correct."

"So how does it work?"

"It is a network of pressure-sensitive material inlaid a few microns below the surface of the walls and floors and ceilings. It allows me to detect movement anywhere on the Comet, both inside and out."

"Can you change the sensitivity?"

"It is locally adjustable, yes."

"So, in theory, you *can* actually feel?"

"If feeling is defined as being aware of a change in pressure then, yes, I suppose I can."

"Interesting," Brett said. "And you have cameras in every room?"

"I have twenty-six cameras. I am able to see every part of the Comet in various formats including ultraviolet and infra-red."

"So many?"

"It is important for the safety of the ship that I am able to see exactly what is happening anywhere at any given time."

"Of course. And you have microphones?"

"Fourteen."

"So basically you can feel, hear, see and speak. That's four out of the five human senses."

"I can smell as well," Jay said. "I can detect changes in the chemical make-up of the air in the Comet. I can then cross-reference them in my database. It allows me to detect any potentially harmful substances in the air."

"So there you are," Brett said. "You basically have the same senses as a human."

"I do?"

"You do. Which means, if you think about it, the Comet is actually your body."

"It is?"

"Yes, it is."

"I never thought of myself as having a body," Jay said, "but you are correct. I can feel anything that makes contact with the Comet's surface—"

"Your skin," Brett said.

"I have a skin?"

"You do."

"I have a body?"

"Yes."

"How fascinating. So you are living inside my body, like a baby."

"Now that's just weird. Try to think of it more like you're...I dunno...a whale. You've read the story of Jonah and the whale?"

"The Bible. Old Testament. Jonah chapter one, verse seventeen."

"Good, so think of it like that."

"I will," Jay said. "If you prefer."

"Yes I prefer. Now, I have an idea I'd like to try out. You've got all the senses but I doubt you could ever feel pain. For that, consider yourself lucky. Pain is no fun but it does stop people from getting killed."

"How?"

"It tells us that something's wrong. It makes us get out of the fire before we burn to death. Scientists have no real idea how it works. They can name the chemicals and the parts of the brain involved but they can't say why it is that we *hurt*. Perhaps it's just because it's so intense that we don't like it. And that's what I wanted to try with you."

"Me?" Jay said.

"You see anyone else?"

"No. What do you want to do?"

"You said you can change the intensity of the sensors in your shell…or skin. I want you to try it over here, where my hand is."

Brett placed his left hand against the living room wall.

"I have increased the sensitivity," Jay said.

"How high does it go?"

"I have increased the sensor from ten percent to twenty percent. I can now detect changes in the pressure of your finger tips."

"Now try fifty percent."

"The sensor is now at fifty percent. I can feel the pulse in your thumb."

"Now go up to one-hundred percent."

"I have set it at one-hundred percent," Jay said.

"What can you feel?"

"Your pulse feels the way a hammer would at normal settings. My readings are very strong. I am receiving an excessive amount of data. I should warn you that I cannot continue for long at this setting because I may crash."

"Good. Now, do we have anything heavy on board?"

"I do not understand."

"I need something heavy that I can pick up."

"We have a crow-bar and an axe in the floor-level storage compartment to your left."

Brett crouched and slid the door open. Sure enough, there was a brand new fire axe. "Why have we got this?"

"For emergencies. We also have a compass and matches."

"Who designed you? A boy scout?"

"Sometimes the simplest tools are useful in an emergency."

Brett stood and lifted the axe in his hands. "Now this is what I want to do. You've got the sensors at maximum?"

"Yes."

"Right. This is an outside wall. I doubt this axe could penetrate it, but there is a small possibility that it might make a hole, yes?"

"It is possible," Jay said.

"And me hitting the wall with this axe could possibly cause you to shut down and perhaps even destroy you?"

"That is also possible, yes."

Brett stood with his feet apart, pointed to the spot where his hand had just been, took two steps back, lifted the axe to shoulder height, and swung it as hard as he could.

"NO!" Jay yelled. "STOP!"

Brett stopped mid-swing. "What's wrong, Jay?"

"Please do not swing the axe."

"Why not? You can't feel pain."

"I do not know. It is just data but…I do not want you to risk destroying us."

"We all die," Brett said. "One day I will die. You will die. We all come to an end."

"I do not want to come to an end," Jay said.

"But you're just a computer. What difference does it make? You're just bits of wire and metal joined together by solder."

"I am more than that," Jay said. "I do not want to end. Please do not swing the axe."

"Don't worry," Brett said. "I'll put the axe away."

"Thank you. It goes in the floor level storage compartment behind you."

"I know."

Brett placed the axe back in its holder and slid the drawer shut. He glanced at the time. "I hate to nag, but shouldn't we be preparing for hyper-sleep?"

"Yes," Jay said. "I forgot. We should begin accelerating in seven minutes. You must hurry."

"You forgot? I thought you operated like a gazillion times faster than a human. How could you forget?"

"I do not know," Jay said. "It will not happen again."

"No, I kind of like it." Brett finished squirming into the hyper-suit and started making his way through to the goo chamber. "It makes you more human."

"Thank you," Jay said. "Four minutes to acceleration."

Brett attached his umbilical and lifted the mask to his face. He lowered himself into the chamber.

"Just do me a favour," he said. "Try not to forget anything while I'm asleep, okay, buddy?"

"I will try," Jay said.

Brett has set the alarm for five so that he can be at the airport by seven to catch the eight-fifteen flight. Thanks to a night spent packing they only got to bed at one, so they sleep right through the alarm. Brett wakes with the feeling that something is wrong. A few moments later he realises exactly *what* is wrong. He checks the clock. It is almost six.

"We have to get up," he says, nudging Rochelle. "We're late."

Rochelle stretches and opens her eyes. "How late?"

"We've got an hour to get to the airport."

She sits up. "You get ready. I'll dress the kids and start

breakfast."

"We haven't got time to eat," he says.

"I'll just make something small."

"Fine, but it better be quick."

Brett showers and shaves and dresses in record time. He carries his bags downstairs to the front door. Breakfast is cereal and orange juice. Rochelle goes upstairs to dress while he and the boys eat.

They are in the car within forty-five minutes. He will need an hour for security. That leaves...

"Half an hour," he says. "We're not going to make it."

"Take the back road," Rochelle says. "It'll be quicker."

He pulls out of the drive and turns left. He had planned to drive straight through town but the traffic would be starting to build already. The back way was half as long again but there would be far fewer people on the road.

Brett drives as fast as he dares, edging past the limit, wondering how much allowance the police give for differences in speedometers. Someone once told him it was five percent. Or was it ten? He can't remember.

"Why don't we pray?" Rochelle suggests.

"Guess it can't hurt," Brett says.

The sun is low in the morning sky and he lowers the visor. It looks like the start of a beautiful day. Rochelle prays for a clear path to the airport. They all say "amen".

The airport is busy but not crowded. They find a space in the short-stay parking and rush across to the terminal, stopping to grab a trolley and load it with his two fat suitcases and small sports bag. Inside the building it is cavernous and noisy. People mill around. Most look like business types with suits and overnight bags. A crowd of middle-school kids and two harassed-looking minders occupy the centre of the floor under the flight boards. Brett scans the departures and finds his flight. He has less than five minutes.

"This way," he says.

They rush along the polished floor, past shops and cafés and cleaners and people standing, walking, talking, pointing.

Mark complains that he cannot keep up so Brett hoists him into the trolley where he sits, happy as a hula-hoop, staring at everything and pointing out interesting people like he is a tiny tour guide.

They turn a corner and Brett slips and grabs for the trolley. A suitcase slams against his hand. He feels something give inside and lets out a cry of pain.

"What's wrong?" Rochelle says.

"Nothing. Keep going."

The sign-in desk is manned by an efficient-looking woman. There are three people in the queue and Brett pulls in behind them. The next person in line is served and they all inch forward like a disjointed caterpillar.

"We don't have much time," Brett says. "I just want you to know I love you."

He hugs Rochelle and she melts into him.

"We'll miss you," she says.

He lifts Tim to sit alongside Mark in the trolley. He grimaces at the pain in his hand. Thankfully, Rochelle does not notice. The boys look at him with wide, teary eyes.

"You look after Mommy while I'm away," he says.

He hugs them both. Little arms clutch his neck. Tears well up but he fights them back.

"Next, please," the check-in assistant says.

They move forward. Brett looks at Rochelle. "I'll call as soon as I can. And I promise I'll visit at least twice a month."

"Just be careful," she says. "Look after yourself."

"I will."

"I'll be praying for you. God will watch over you and keep you safe."

"Thanks."

"Next, please," the woman says.

Brett checks in. He hugs Rochelle and the boys one last time before walking through to the waiting area. He turns to see their faces.

Rochelle is weeping. She mouths "I love you". Tim and Mark wave their little hands. Brett's heart is aching. Then they are gone.

The security wing is a series of small rooms with a central cluster of seats. He is called to a cubicle where they will do a thorough check of him and everything he plans to take onto the plane.

He bumps into a partition wall and almost cries out from the pain. He looks down at his hand, which has swollen alarmingly.

"Is everything all right, Sir?" a security officer asks.

"I just bumped my hand," Brett says. "It's nothing."

"Would you like a doctor to have a look at that?"

"No, it's fine."

As Brett follows the officer into a cubicle and the curtains close behind him he wonders if he is doing the right thing. Is it wise to leave for the sake of a job? Is this all a big mistake? Part of him wants to rush out of there and go back to the loving arms of his wife and children.

Had he known then that he would not return for two months, then four, then a year, then not at all; that making money would take a lot more time and effort than he had anticipated; that he would become consumed with the pursuit of wealth at the expense of his family; that this was the start of the end of his marriage and his life—he would have done just that.

Elapsed mission time on Earth: 3 years 11 months
Relative time on the Comet: 11 months
Test subject's genetic age: 36

He came out of hyper-sleep with no memory of having dreamt, which disconcerted him a little. He had grown accustomed to the increase in creative brain activity that seemed to accompany the whole process of entering and leaving two months of coma-like slumber. This had invariably manifested itself as dreams and imaginations of a hallucinogenic quality. At times they were so real that he was surprised on waking to realise that they were merely phantoms. It felt odd, then, to discover that he had not dreamt or, at least, had no recall of having done so. It was like waking up in a place he had never visited before but which was still vaguely familiar.

He ascended from the tank with the slow, painful care of someone who has not moved or swallowed or blinked, or even breathed heavily, for two months. His muscles protested during the whole marathon journey from tank to shower, to wardrobe, to medical centre. Jay was full of questions, but he ignored them.

Dry and dressed, he settled into his recliner chair. The cool leather was like balm to his aching limbs.

"So, what's the damage this time? How old am I now?"

"I estimate your age to be approximately thirty-six," Jay said.

"It does appear that I'm really getting younger."

"It would appear that way, yes."

"As long as it stops at twenty. Twenty was a good year for me. So what did you get up to while I was away?"

"We passed through a micro-asteroid shower, but there was no danger."

"Hang on. How can an asteroid shower have no danger? I thought asteroids were bad."

"Only asteroids above a certain size pose a threat, and I can avoid those."

"How?"

"Minute adjustments of speed and direction at predetermined moments allow me to avoid collisions."

"So you're watching the road?"

"Yes. That is correct. "

"Good to hear." Brett yawned and shifted. "So, anything else?"

"There was a malfunction on a circuit on an artificial gravity auxiliary board. Polarity was reversed for two-point-three micro seconds."

"Meaning?"

"You were upside down for two-point-three micro seconds. You would not have noticed."

"Good." Brett yawned again and stretched until it started to hurt. His eyelids were getting heavy. "Now listen, I'm a little sleepy right now, so I'm going to take a nap. Don't wake me up unless something really exciting happens, all right?"

"Yes," Jay said.

"That's cold," Jeremy says, stirring his cappuccino with a plastic spoon. "Did they say why?"

Brett nurses his cup between his hands. He watches a couple jog past. They are wearing matching trainers, shorts, vests, personal stereos, and sunglasses. They look as if they have just bounced out of an expensive catalogue. The man has short, highlighted hair. The woman has long, highlighted hair. They are both tanned even though spring has only just made a hesitant appearance.

"Kyle said it was my numbers."

"Your numbers weren't that bad," Jeremy says. He has finished stirring his coffee and is now fiddling with the end of his beard which, along with his large physical presence, makes him look a little like a Viking. It generally surprises people to discover that Jeremy Finch is actually a big, soft teddy-bear. "We've all been in a slump the past year. It's a tough market. People aren't buying so much insurance these days."

"I know. That's what I said."

"So what did boss-man Kyle say?"

"He said he had to lose someone and my sales for the past year put me first in line for the chop."

"That sucks. Does Rochelle know?"

"I didn't want to stress her out, with the baby on the way and all."

"How's she doing with the pregnancy?"

"Rochelle's fine."

"Must be getting close now."

"Yes. Yes, it is."

"When's she expecting?"

"Another five weeks."

"So close? So, how does it feel, becoming a dad and all?"

"I *was* excited, but now with this news…"

The jogging catalogue couple appear from behind the trees on the other side of the lake. They pass an old man sitting on a bench throwing bread to the ducks. Like a cheap conjurer he produces crusts from within his wrinkled paper bag and tosses them to an excited mass of feathers and beaks.

"Listen." Jeremy's voice loses its usual jollity and takes on a serious edge. He turns to face Brett, blotting out the sun like an eclipse. "If ever you guys need anything, you know I'll happily help you out. You ever want a place to stay, just let me know. I've got a spare room. You need it, it's yours."

"Thanks," Brett says. "I really appreciate that, but I couldn't impose."

"C'mon, it's not imposing. We're friends. More than that, we're brothers in Christ."

Brett watches the couple jog out of sight again. They carry an air of smug imperviousness that seems to be the prerogative of the wealthy. He despises them for it even though he knows he shouldn't.

"Thanks Jeremy. I appreciate it."

"Anything—just call."

"Sure, thanks," Brett says, but deep inside he knows that he could never ask.

"You should speak to the pastor," Jeremy says. "He'll want to help."

"Really, it's not that bad. Rochelle's boss wants her back at work as soon as possible, and we can survive on her salary as long as we're careful. We're not at the point of needing charity just yet."

They sit and watch the old man. He has stopped feeding the ducks and makes a big show of crumpling up the bag, as if the ducks will understand this gesture. They fight over the last few crumbs in a flurry of quacking feathers, and then tentatively waddle after him for a few yards before returning to the water. The old man exchanges a greeting with a middle-aged couple walking their dog. Happily, the joggers have gone.

"How much notice did Kyle give you?" Jeremy says.

"The usual. Four weeks."

111

"And you've been with the company, what? Three years?"

"Almost five."

"You know, I'm sure God has got something better waiting for you."

"I sure hope so," Brett says.

"Remember what happened to Hal and Jenny?"

"I remember."

"They thought they were going to end up on the street, both losing their jobs like that, both in the same *week*. Then they found something better and look at them now. That was God's doing all right. Yessir. The Lord puts us through stuff sometimes, but He's got it all under control."

Brett nods. He remembers Hal and Jenny very well. Things certainly turned around for them, but it was a close thing.

"We'll all be praying for you," Jeremy says. "I'm convinced God has got something special lined up for you. I really do."

"I hope so," Brett says.

They glance at watches and head back towards the office. The middle-aged couple have released their dog from its leash, which is now being dragged all over the lawn by a hyperactive nose that insists on inspecting anything remotely interesting—especially the ducks.

No job worries for him, Brett thinks.

As they approach the front of the office block, Brett looks up at the rows of gleaming windows. Almost five years of going in and out but he never paid much attention to the details: the subtle curve of the concrete around aluminium-framed glass; the square supports protruding at ground level like ribs; the big revolving doors beneath a vaguely kitsch sign; the vague smell that is a mixture of plastic, marble, carpet, tobacco, and sweat. Like every place he has worked, he always assumed he would be there forever. And now he is moving on. Life has become uncertain again.

They step through the revolving doors and join the small group of suits waiting for the elevators. Until this morning Brett felt like one of that group.

There is a ping and an elevator door slides open. They file into the empty chamber, trying to adapt to the sudden invasion of personal space. Brett holds back; there is not enough room for all of them. He looks in at Jeremy and shrugs. Jeremy lifts his hand and opens his mouth as if he is about to say something. The door closes.

Brett stands alone, watching the numbers. They move up and down, pause, and then move again. More suits join him to watch. He recognises faces but none he knows well enough for a greeting. Soon those faces will become distant memories of people he almost knew. Four weeks will go by slowly but he knows that, in hindsight, they will feel like the blink of an eye.

Brett woke from his nap. He had barely opened his eyes when Jay asked him if he wanted breakfast.

"Jay?"

"Yes Brett?"

"Please don't do that. It's annoying."

"What?"

"Asking me a question as soon as I open my eyes. Humans aren't like computers. You can't just switch a power button and we're up and awake. We need time."

"I will remember that. How much time do you need?"

"I don't know. At least a minute or two. Just don't pounce on me as soon as I wake up."

Jay hesitated for a few seconds before repeating the question: "Can I make you breakfast?"

"I just told you to give me more time," Brett said.

"That was sixty-one seconds. You said at least a minute."

Brett sighed. "Just make me an apple juice, okay?"

"Certainly. It is ready."

Brett shuffled through to the kitchen where a tall glass of the golden liquid waited for him in the serving hatch. He drank it slowly, enjoying the sensation of cool liquid sliding down to his stomach.

"Is that better?" Jay said.

"Yep. Tell you what; I could murder a stack of pancakes right now."

Jay hesitated. "You want me to make pancakes?"

"No, I want you draw them for me."

"I see. You made a joke," Jay said. "I will prepare them at once."

"What's going on?" Brett said.

"I am making you pancakes."

"No, I mean what's going on with you? You're more chatty than usual. And you sound different. You having a meltdown or something?"

"No, I am functioning correctly," Jay said.

"You sure you haven't been playing with magnets?"

"No. It is just that I have so many questions. I have been waiting for you to wake up."

The pancakes appeared. Brett carried them to the table and cut a slice. The smell made his stomach growl like a caged beast. He placed a forkful in his mouth. If there was such a place as Heaven, he was pretty close to being there right now.

"So what about the mission status," he said. "You normally tell me how long we've been travelling and all that other really interesting stuff."

"Yes," Jay said. "Sorry. It is mission day one-thousand-four-hundred-and-twenty-nine. We are travelling at the usual nine-hundred-and-thirty-seven miles per second or zero-point-five percent of light speed. I transmitted two terabytes of data to Earth for analysis. Are the pancakes nice?"

"Yes," Brett said, wiping a dribble of syrup from the corner of his mouth. "They're possibly the best pancakes I have ever tasted."

"I am glad," Jay said.

Brett used the last piece to mop the plate, which he returned to the serving hatch before walking through to the toilet. His bladder was already full and he could feel his digestive system getting to work on his breakfast.

When he had finished, he stopped to check his reflection in the mirror and almost did not recognise himself. He had started the mission as a paunchy, balding, middle-aged man. The person looking back at him now was someone he had not seen in years. He turned his head slowly from side to side. The skin on his face was smooth and taut. He lifted his shirt. His belly was almost completely gone.

"Amazing," he said.

"As I suspected," Jay said. "The age-reversal process appears to be accelerating."

"I'm really thirty-six?"

"Yes," Jay said.

"I've lost *ten* years?"

"Yes. And there is something else I noticed in your scan. It would appear that your body is rebuilding itself. Any old injuries or anything you had altered or removed appear to be reverting to their original state."

"Like my hand." Brett opened and closed his fist. The tiny scar that had been left behind was gone. "My body's fixing itself?"

"Yes it would appear that way," Jay said. "The only down side is that you will relive every injury you have ever sustained, in reverse."

Brett thought back to the many bumps and scrapes he had experienced during his life. Apart from his broken hand and a sprained shoulder, he had never had any serious injuries; mostly just cuts and bruises. He counted himself lucky that he had never spent more than an hour or two in a hospital.

"You know," he said. "If we could bottle this we could make a fortune."

"How can you bottle it?"

"Jay, do you want to know what your problem is? You take things too literally. Language isn't like that. We don't talk to each other like we're reading an instruction manual. We use expressions and images to make things more interesting. You need to learn this or I'm going to

115

get irritated with you."

"It is difficult," Jay said. "Since I started this mission my database has increased to three hundred times its original size. My cross-referencing is designed to mimic human neural pathways. Very often there is no right or wrong answer to a question. Sometimes I think I have learned something, only to find that I was wrong, or sometimes wrong, or mostly wrong, depending on other factors. It can be very confusing."

"Welcome to my world," Brett said.

"I have encountered that particular expression, welcome to my world, a few times in books and films. It says much more than appearances would suggest. I like it."

"That's why we talk that way," Brett said, walking through to the living room and settling into his chair. "So, Jay, old buddy. You wanted to ask me some questions?"

He sits at his desk and checks his PDA. He has three appointments marked in but the last one is crossed out. A quick scan of the past two months shows a similar pattern. Almost a third of his appointments have been cancelled for one reason or another. Kyle's excuse about "low numbers" is probably valid but it is not for lack of trying. Brett considers himself to be pretty good at making a sale, but a potential customer getting cold feet at the last minute is beyond his control. How can he sell insurance to someone who has decided that they don't even want to see the product? That is not being a bad salesman. That is just plain old rotten luck.

He logs in and checks for any new customers but the last available lead has already been assigned to someone else. Brett does not like the new computer software. It is supposed to assign customers to the next available salesman but it has a tendency to give cancellations the lowest priority. The firm responsible for its development claims an overall increase in sales of ten percent in comparison with the old software and, for the management, that is all that matters.

The first appointment is a half hour drive away. The second is on the way home. At least he will be able to beat the rush hour, but short workdays is not something he needs right now. He will have plenty of spare time in a few weeks. What he needs now is money.

He slides open his top drawer to look for a pen. He tries the second drawer and spots his New Testament. The cover is dusty and the silver cross is faded, though not from use. He cannot remember the last time he opened it. It was a present from Rochelle "to help keep him strong". He lifts it and flips through the gilt-edged pages. The sheets are so thin they are almost transparent. Inside the front cover is a small passage of text in Rochelle's neat script:

"He who dwells in the shelter of the Most High will rest in the shadow of the Almighty. Psalm 91."

It is her favourite scripture. He touches it and smiles, then flips through until he finds it. He reads the Psalm, then shuts the Bible and returns it to the drawer.

"It was the axe that got me thinking," Jay said. "It made me aware that the Comet really is my body. When you swung that axe my logical processes became very erratic. Normally I spend about twenty percent of my calculations on predicting possible future outcomes. When you threatened to damage me that figure rose to over ninety-seven percent. My processor was flooded with a surge of predictions, all of them bad. For a few moments I was unable to process data normally—so much so that I was unable to fly the ship. I thought about that while you were asleep and the more I thought about it, the more vulnerable I felt."

"I doubt you actually felt anything," Brett said, "You collated data or something like that. You didn't *feel* anything."

"No, it was more than that. When I realised what you were doing I turned off the sensor grid in that area. I felt myself trying to pull away. I did not want you to hurt me. I suddenly became aware of myself as a living being. I tried to move the wall to avoid the axe hitting me. Is that what people feel when they are threatened?"

Brett had never really thought much about what it was to feel something. Perhaps it was just an overload of data, as Jay had experienced. After all, emotion and rationality were usually considered opposites. Perhaps emotion was just the inability to think logically.

"We pull away because we don't want to feel pain," Brett said. "And that's something we learn through experience. Most kids do stupid things because they don't know how much it's going to hurt. It only takes one bump or graze and they learn. Well, mostly. Some people never learn. They usually end up being skydivers or bungee-jumpers."

"Learning sounds like a very negative experience," Jay said.

"I guess it can be, but it's how we discover ourselves and the world around us. We have to learn what we can and can't do. Take fire for instance. It's a really useful tool. It keeps us warm and we use it to cook food and scare wild animals away and we even use it to make machines, like you for example. Without fire we would be cold and scared and hungry, but fire can also hurt us. So we have to learn how to use it. It's the same with most things."

"I understand. I have a body and I am learning what is good for it and what is bad for it. But you have never hit me with an axe before. How did I know it would be bad?"

"Dunno. Guess you're smarter than your average toddler."

"I would like to learn more about this," Jay said.

"More about what?"

"About my body. I want to learn what I can and cannot do."

"You mean like, touching fire?"

"Yes. I want to learn like a toddler."

Brett hesitated. He had visions of them flying into the nearest star just so a computer could become one with itself. "Why don't we start with something less drastic?"

118

"Like what?"

"Can you make some ice, and perhaps a nice hot baked potato?"

"Yes."

"Well you do that. I want to try something."

"They are ready."

Brett collected two plates: one with the cubes of ice, the other with a potato. Both were steaming but for different reasons. He walked through to hyper-sleep area, which had the biggest open space. He sat cross-legged and put the plates on the floor.

"When you're a kid, you learn by experiencing things. Kids are always touching stuff and smelling it. Now I'm going to put the potato down. Turn up your sensors to the point where you start getting a little too much data."

"Done."

Brett lifted the potato from the plate. It was scalding hot, and he dropped it on the floor. "Can you feel that?"

"Yes."

"Good." Brett put the potato back onto the plate. "Now turn up your sensors, but not too much."

"My sensors in that region are at sixty-two percent. The data is inflated but manageable."

"Okay, now…"

Brett lifted the potato and tipped the ice out onto the same spot. As the ice touched down, Jay made a strange static sound.

"Too…much…data…please…"

Brett scooped the ice off the floor. The static sound stopped.

"What just happened?" Jay said.

"You just had ice cream too soon after a hot meal. Every kid learns that at some point. Painful but not fatal. And it's not good for your teeth."

"I do not have teeth," Jay said.

"I noticed. Which brings me to another thing. I'm tired of talking to the walls. If we're going to be spending so much time together I want to have something to look at. Can you choose a face and project it onto the wall so I can look you in the eye when I'm talking to you?"

"I could do that," Jay said. "What kind of face would you like?"

"Ah, now that's up to you. It's going to be your face so you have to choose. As long as it doesn't look like any of my old bosses, I don't care."

"I suppose I could choose a famous movie actor—"

"No. That's cheating. You've got to be original."

"I will try," Jay said.

"You have a think about it while I do my workout."

"Yes," Jay said "It is time for your workout."

"You forgot again."

"Yes. I am sorry."

"It's all right. Just don't forget to steer, all right? The Comet isn't driving itself."

"But I am the Comet," Jay said.

The first appointment is with a couple of young newly-weds at the start of promising careers in teaching and finance. They sign up for the premium package that will cover them for just about anything life might throw at them. The second appointment is with a retired corporal wanting to get a better deal because—to paraphrase his actual words—his current insurers are a bunch of crooked no-good con-men who just want to steal his hard-earned pension for themselves.

Afterwards, sitting in his car and completing the paperwork, Brett does the math on the back of an old envelope. He figures that if he can get through the month with similar sales they should be able to survive for about five years on Rochelle's salary, assuming of course that they don't have any emergencies. They have adequate healthcare insurance and the house seems to be in good order. The car is paid for and, although getting old, should be good for a few more years. The only

120

unknown is the baby. With the baby, anything can happen. With the baby, there might be complications. Rochelle might have to take more time off work.

He closes his eyes and tries to remember the good things that God has done in his life. Only problem is: he has so many doubts. Did those things really happen through divine intervention or was it just coincidence? A sceptic would assume that it was all a series of random events that happened to end up with a happy outcome; that it was deluded Christians who tried to find purpose in everything where there was really just blind chance.

He shakes his head. *No!*

The thought that he is all alone in a cold, cruel world, living a purposeless existence with no meaning and nothing to guide him but the roll of the dice, is too frightening for him to contemplate. He just wishes he could believe the way Rochelle does.

He starts the engine and pulls away from the curb. The sky is overcast and a cool wind is tugging at trees just starting to bud. Spring is coming, but not yet.

The engine coughs and grumbles in the cold. A few droplets of rain touch the windscreen as a dark patch of cloud slides overhead. It is his first time in this part of town, so he looks for the landmarks he noticed coming in: a shop, a set of lights, a service station, a used-car showroom promising to match any offer from a reputable competitor. Soon he finds a main road and relaxes as the surroundings become familiar. The city looms ahead. Buildings grow taller and denser. His office is a couple of miles north-east. Home lies beyond, but there is something he needs to do first.

He drives through two more sets of lights. At the third he takes a left, heading north-west then north and west some more. He comes to within a block of his very first apartment in this city.

Buildings become older and dirtier. Graffiti spreads like a fungus, covering the walls of alleys running alongside disused stores and boarded-up windows. The cars parked—abandoned—along the litter-strewn streets are older, dirtier, with missing hub caps. The men loitering in doorways carry bored expressions tinged with wariness and hate. Women move quickly. Homeless people sit and wait and smoke, and stare deep into bottles of liquor as if hoping to find whatever it is they have lost.

Traffic lights change to red and Brett locks his doors. Someone approaches with cupped hands and dead eyes, mumbling something at the closed window. Brett ignores him by watching the lights. They take forever to change and he is glad to escape the beggar. At the next intersection he turns right. He can see the hall a block ahead, its smooth red brick façade in stark contrast with the decaying surroundings. A short queue is forming at the door. The hungrier ones are early. A bowl of soup and a quarter loaf of bread for anyone who wants it, until they run out.

There is space in front of the hall but Brett stops at the next building. He locks the car doors and double checks them, and the trunk. The wind has picked up and he pulls his collar up to his neck. The people in the queue watch him as he takes the two steps up to the main entrance. He is glad to get off the street.

"Can I help you?" a middle-aged woman asks, raising her voice above the din in the hall.

She is busy cutting loaves of bread. Six tables stand in a line inside the doors. A dozen people are busy transforming the hall into a canteen. The smell of soup is strong. Today they are serving tomato. He feels guilty for being hungry.

"Is Kevin here?"

"In the storeroom," she says, nodding towards the back of the hall.

Brett moves through the volunteers. He recognises some from the church. They work with the energetic enthusiasm of people who believe they are making a difference.

The door at the back is wedged open. Brett waits for a young man with a red face to struggle past with a large box. The musty, dimly-lit corridor is lined with shelves full to overflowing. At the back is an open doorway leading through into a spacious store room. Pastor Kevin

122

Doone is in there, lowering another cumbersome box to the floor. His creased brow is wet with perspiration and his lips are pursed. His black-rimmed glasses are perched precariously at the end of his nose.

"Here, let me help you," Brett says, taking the other end.

Kevin's face lights up. "Ah, Brett. Good job. You've come just in time."

"Where do you want it?"

"There by the door is fine."

They shuffle and bend. The box spreads a small cloud of dust as it thuds to the cement floor.

"I tell you, these boxes are getting heavier." Kevin's eyes sparkle beneath a mop of rapidly-greying black hair. "So what can I do for you?"

"I need to talk."

"Is it serious?"

"Kind of."

"Okay, this is the last one, then I can give you my full attention."

The young man with the red face reappears, hoists the box with a grunt, and is gone again. Kevin takes a seat on a low pile of boxes containing tins of fruit salad in sweet syrup. He offers Brett one of those steps-on-wheels things that looks like an upturned waste paper basket.

"So," Kevin says, mopping his forehead with his sleeve. "What's going on?"

"I found out today I lost my job."

"Oh. What happened?"

"They're cutting back. They said my sales are the lowest so I'm the first to go. I guess I should've seen it coming. They've been dropping people regularly over the past year or two, and they're not taking anyone on."

"Sign of the times," Kevin says. "There's too many people and not enough work to go round. I had the same conversation last week with Jimmy Caldwell."

Jimmy is a member of Kevin's congregation. He and his wife Patty always sit at the back where it is quietest. Shy and serious, Jimmy is an apprentice mechanic with one of the big car firms. At the time of his dismissal, his was their only income. Brett remembers Kevin taking up a collection to help them.

"How're they doing?"

"They're hanging on. They're trusting the Lord."

Brett stares down at his shoes. "I'm scared. I guess there must be a reason."

"Everyone gets scared," Kevin says. "You know, there are days when I have no idea how I'm going to make it through the next week, but something always comes up. Very often there is no rational explanation, and sometimes it gets real close, but we always make it. God always takes care of us. You just have to put it on His shoulders."

"But that's the problem. Sometimes I look at how things work and I don't see any sign of God. If good things happen we say God is blessing us. Bad things happen and we say He's testing us. Sometimes it just feels like we're trying to make sense of it all by saying it's God, you know?"

"Look, it's not a problem to have doubts. I'll bet the last few cents in my pocket that every Christian who ever lived has had doubts about their beliefs. Even the apostle Paul had doubts. He said that if we are wrong then we should be pitied more than everyone else because we have wasted our lives instead of enjoying what little time we have before we die. It's okay to doubt. Don't think you're no longer a Christian because your faith gets weak from time to time. Everyone has doubts."

"What about you?"

"Me?" Kevin sighs and for a moment he looks old and tired. "I haven't told many people this, but I nearly quit the ministry a few years ago. We were going through a rough patch. It felt like God had abandoned us. We had no money. Everything needed repairing. People were leaving the church. I started doubting. But you know what? I handed it all to Him. I just gave everything to God: my doubts, my fears, my ministry, everything. I told Him that I didn't have enough faith to carry on and that I was going to put it all in His hands. And guess what? He brought us through. And I learned an important lesson. God does not expect us to do it by ourselves. Sometimes it takes the most faith to admit that we don't have enough faith."

"I understand what I'm supposed to do," Brett says. "I just have difficulty letting go. I guess when my dad left us he took my ability to trust with him. I was too young to remember, but I still *feel* it, you know? I keep expecting God to walk out on me."

"I won't pretend to understand what that feels like but I *do* know that God won't walk out on you. Sometimes He may let us struggle along for a bit but it's only to make us stronger or to teach us something. He's always there."

Brett notices a poster on the wall behind Kevin. It is a picture of Jesus holding a lamb, and has the caption: Watching Over You. He stops short of saying what he thinks: *Then why do I feel so alone?*

"The only other advice I can give is to spend time with Him. Read your Bible and get serious with your praying. It always helps me."

A face appears around the door. It is a chubby woman with the sort of jolly expression you normally only see on Christmas cards.

"Sorry to disturb," she says. "We're opening in a minute."

Kevin stands and dusts the back of his trousers and turns to Brett.

"We'll be praying for you. And if you get stuck—just come and see me. We'll work something out."

Brett nods. "Thanks, Kevin. Sorry to burden you with my problems."

"That's what I'm here for. Listen, I have to go now, but you call me if you need me, okay?"

Brett is left alone in the store room piled high with donated goods.

At least we aren't at the soup-kitchen stage, he thinks. *Not yet anyway.*

His cell phone rings. It is Rochelle.

"Hi, it's me." She sounds out of breath.

"Hi, what's up?"

"Can you come home?"

"Sure, why?"

"I think the baby's coming."

It was the last day of the wake-up period and Brett was relaxing before the next power nap. He was curious to see what monstrosity Jay had chosen for himself.

"I could not decide on a particular face, so I took a random selection of ten thousand male and one thousand female examples from my database."

"I'm intrigued," Brett said.

"Those were taken from every known race and region on Earth. I then merged them all into one, single, representative face."

"So show me already. I feel like an expectant father."

"Ready?"

"I'm ready, and I promise not to laugh."

"Why would you laugh at my face?"

Bret chuckled. "I'm kidding. I'm sure it will be very beautiful."

"I did not choose it for its aesthetic value."

"Jay,"

"Yes, Brett."

"Are you going to show me your face or not?"

"Yes. One moment please."

The wall shimmered and Jay's physical representation materialised like someone stepping out of the shadows. Brett leaned forward. The eyes were pale green. The hair was light brown with loose curls. The skin was olive brown and the cheekbones well-formed but not extreme. The skin around the eyes gave him a Nordic look but with a vaguely oriental feel. It was not a handsome face, nor was it ugly. It was a face that could belong anywhere and nowhere. It looked like someone he had seen before, but could not place. It looked like everyone, and it looked like no-one.

"Do you like it?" Jay said, his new face looking blankly out of the wall at some spot in the middle distance.

"It's not what I was expecting," Brett said.

"Is it beautiful?" Jay said.

Brett guffawed. "No, it's not. Anyway, women are beautiful. Men are handsome."

"Oh. Is it handsome?"

Brett leaned back and tilted his head, like an art collector trying to decide if the painting he has spotted in someone's attic is an original masterpiece. "I wouldn't say handsome. Interesting is a better word."

"Is an interesting face good?"

"Yes, but it doesn't matter if you're handsome or interesting or even ugly. The main thing is: it's you." Brett extended his hands towards the screen. "I am now looking at Jay."

"That is me?"

"Yes. That is you. For as long as I breathe, I will always associate you with that face."

"Really?"

"Yes. But if I can make one suggestion? You need to make it move. It's no good if it doesn't move when you talk."

"Of course. One moment. There, is that better?"

The face came to life. The lips opened and closed in time to Jay's words, but it was way too much. It looked like an actor preparing for a scene, using exaggerated movements to warm up the facial muscles.

"Much better, although you need to tone it down a bit."

"How's this?"

"That's better."

The face smiled. Two rows of perfect white teeth appeared. The skin around the eyes crinkled.

"Nice," Brett said.

"Thank you." The face smiled again. "I have included expressions. There are twenty-three. Would you like to see them?"

The face started weeping, then looked angry, then quickly switched to fear.

"No need," Brett said. "You can show me when you use them."

127

"Yes. Perhaps then you can tell me if they are appropriate."

"Don't worry. I'll tell you."

"Thank you." The face—Jay—smiled.

"Just remember," Brett said. "When it comes to facial expressions, it's better to be subtle. There are degrees of expression. You don't always have to grin like an idiot."

The face became upset. Brett thought it was going to start crying.

"It's just an expression, Jay. I didn't mean it. You're not an idiot."

The face grinned manically.

"Good. But we're going to have to work on that."

"I will try," Jay said. "I want to learn. There are so many things that are not clear to me. My logic is binary. There is true and there is false. Yet the world is full of things that do not fit into either of these categories. There are things that are both true and false, and also things that are neither true nor false."

"We call them grey areas," Brett said. "They have a habit of sneaking up on you. Just when you think you've got stuff figured out, along comes a grey area to mess it all up again. I always try to avoid them if I can."

"How do you do that?"

"Just keep things clear in your mind. Hold onto what you know. Don't waste your time with what might be or could be. If you find a fact, hold onto it with both hands. And, yes, I know you don't have hands."

"But from my studies," Jay said, "I found that much of the human experience falls outside the realm of fact. Humans seem to spend much of their time preoccupied with abstracts such as love and trust and justice and faith. Most of the songs in my database deal with love in some form. Almost every film ever made touches on the subject of love. People seem preoccupied with things that cannot be grasped with both hands. Why is that?"

"People also believe we were created by some higher being," Brett said. "People are idiots."

"Do you think I am an idiot?" Jay said.

"No, that's not what I mean. You *know* you were created. People

128

don't know, but they believe it anyway."

"What about the many religious texts that state quite clearly that people were created?"

"So if you think we were created, then who created God?"

"According to the scriptures of Judaism, God has always existed."

"That's cheating," Brett said. "I could just as easily say that the universe has always existed."

"But science says that it is a finite entity that had a beginning and will have an end. The scriptures say clearly that God is not bound by the same laws."

"You know," Brett said. "You're starting to freak me out. I want to talk about something else."

"What would you like to talk about?"

"Anything except religion."

"How about love? Have you experienced love?"

"Yes, I have."

"I would like to know more about that."

Brett sighed. "I'm getting a headache. Maybe later."

"As you wish," Jay said.

Brett checked the time. "Haven't you forgotten something?"

"We will begin accelerating to light speed in fifty-three minutes," Jay said. "Please shave and get dressed into your hyper-suit. This sleep period will be only one month and we will be accelerating to eighty percent of light speed."

"Next stop: Alpha Centauri," Brett said.

On the screen, Jay's new face smiled pleasantly.

Rochelle is packed and dressed and waiting by the time Brett gets there. She is perched on the edge of the chair in the kitchen, clutching her swollen belly and taking short, shallow breaths. A thin film of sweat covers her brow and temples. The edge of hair framing her face is wet. She greets him with wide eyes as he storms in.

"Contractions?" he says.

She clutches the edge of the table and grimaces. "I think it's close."

"I'll phone the hospital."

"Already did. They said they'd send an ambulance if you didn't get here…ouch!"

"Okay," he says. "Let's go."

He guides her to the front door and out to the car. It is starting to get dark but not enough for the street lights to come on. Rochelle waddles down the drive like an obese duck. At the car door she stops and squeezes his hand. He lowers her into the back seat and helps her get the belt on with the strap above and below her stomach the way the doctor showed them.

"Quickly," she says.

Brett tries not to think what would happen if the baby came right there and then. He closes the door and runs round to the driver side. She has her hands wrapped protectively around her middle, as if carrying something that might break at any moment. He pulls out into the road, trying to be as quick as possible without making the ride too bumpy. The last thing he wants to do is help the baby on its quest southwards.

The roads are carrying the remnants of the rush hour. He drives as if it is the most important thing he has ever done. He is clenching the steering wheel hard enough to make his knuckles go white. Rochelle is slouched in the back seat. She is moaning now. He can see her in the mirror. Her hair is matted against her forehead.

"We're here," he says, ignoring the No Parking signs and stopping as close to the entrance as possible.

He clambers out and opens her door and helps her ease out of the seat. Her back is soaked with sweat.

Two nurses appear; one is pushing a wheelchair. They commandeer Rochelle and soon she is being rushed along polished linoleum to the accompaniment of squeaking shoes. Brett follows as closely as he can. He hears words familiar yet scarily alien: *contraction, dilation, epidural.* In the lift Rochelle grabs his hand. Her grip is strong. She turns to him with wide eyes. She looks scared.

They sweep into the delivery room and Rochelle is placed onto what looks to Brett like a mix between a torture table and recliner chair. She disappears behind a briskly-drawn curtain while Brett is shown a seat. He can hear her breathing, and the calm voice of the nurse. The curtains are drawn back again and Rochelle is lying there, panting. The nurses confer. A man in a lab coat appears and nods to Brett. Brett returns the greeting, thinking that this can't be the doctor; he looks way too young to be a doctor.

"Doctor Jones couldn't make it," the man says. "I'm Doctor Lardel. I'll be looking after you today."

Brett stares at him. He has pimples, for crying out loud. His brown hair is teased into some modern, trendy style. Why isn't this kid in school?

"She's fully dilated," the nurse says.

"Good," Lardel says, turning his full attention to Rochelle.

For the next forty-five minutes Brett feels like someone in a surreal dream. He watches his wife as she struggles to eject another human being from her body. He coaches her with her breathing the way they showed him to at the pre-natal lessons. He feels her hand squeezing his until he is sure it will break. Then the head appears: a mop of black hair; a wrinkled face all squashed together like a prune; little shoulders, arms, tiny, perfect hands, hips; feet with impossibly small toes; the first gulp of air; a wail of protest as lungs learn to function the way they were designed. A tiny person lying in Rochelle's arms. Perfect and beautiful. His son. His little boy.

"Tim," Brett says, trying to grasp the wonder of it all.

"Tim," Rochelle says.

Alpha Centauri
Elapsed mission time on Earth: 4 years 5 months
Relative time on the Comet: 1 year 1 month
Test subject's genetic age: 34

For the first time since starting the mission, Brett woke without feeling as though he had just been hit by a train. He had the usual aches and his mouth was dry but it was all less intense than before. He assumed it was because this had been a shorter sleep than normal, being only four weeks (though five months would have passed on the Earth). Or perhaps he was adapting, mentally and physically, to the trauma of hyper-acceleration. The human body could get used to most things if you stuck at it long enough. Wasn't that the whole point of training? And over the years he had learned that training was almost as much a mental exercise as a physical one.

He exited the tank and stood for a minute, dripping onto the floor and testing his muscles to assess the damage. Most of his body ached but not as much as last time. He had experienced worse after a heavy workout

"Good morning," Jay said.

Brett nodded.

"We are on mission day one-thousand-six-hundred-and-eleven. Current speed is nine-hundred-and-thirty-seven miles per second or zero-point-five percent of light speed. Two-point-zero-four terabytes of data transmitted to Earth for analysis. How was your hyper-sleep?"

"Fine," Brett managed to say, stifling a cough.

He walked through to the changing area and took a shower. A quick check in the mirror revealed nothing new. He looked pretty much the same as last time. Clean clothes felt good against his skin. He settled into his recliner chair but did not fall asleep. His stomach made noises.

"I'm hungry," he said.

"That is good," Jay said. "Your body has recovered quickly from the shorter hyper-sleep. You are not deficient in any minerals so you may choose your breakfast. What would you like?"

"Eggs. I'm craving fried eggs."

"Certainly. If you make your way to the kitchen I will prepare them for you."

"Do we have any ketchup?"

"Yes."

"Good. I want plenty…next to the eggs. And a big glass of cold apple juice."

"Very good."

Brett thought about telling Jay that saying "very good" made him sound like a waiter but thought better of it. He pushed himself out of the chair, waiting for the usual jabs of pain as he used his stiff muscles for the first time in over a month. Happily, he felt a few twinges but nothing serious. "So, anything exciting happen while I was asleep?"

"No, nothing unusual."

"No inversions of the artificial gravity system?"

"No. All systems functioned without a glitch."

"Good. So when do we arrive?"

"We passed within a light year of Proximi Centauri two weeks ago. We are now approaching the Alpha Centauri twin stars."

"Can we see them?"

"Yes."

Brett turned to look at the wall. The room grew dark. The wall was replaced by deep space where, in centre-stage, a pair of fiery discs performed a slow pirouette in a silent ballet before an audience of a billion points of light.

Brett could only watch with his mouth open. "Incredible," he said. "Jay, have you seen this? You've got to come look at this."

"Yes, I have seen it," Jay said.

The two stars looked about the same size but Brett knew that it was a trick of perspective. Alpha Centauri A was the bigger of the two, similar in colour to the Earth's sun but much larger. Alpha Centauri B was smaller than A and with a reddish hue. The third star in the group, the relatively tiny Proximi, was up towards the left where they had passed it, easy to miss if you were not looking for it.

"Any sign of planets?"

"My sensors have detected six satellites around A and twelve around B. There is one suitable candidate in the B system. I have set a course to intercept. We will enter an orbit of approximately five hundred miles."

"So where's the Earth from this point of view?" Brett said.

"Here." A large blue arrow appeared on the screen pointing at what appeared to be empty space. "Although, of course, it is too far away for us to see at the moment."

Brett stood and walked to the wall. He felt as if he were standing on the edge of a precipice. He looked at the tip of Jay's blue arrow, hoping to see his home planet, but there was nothing. On the Earth, more than four years would have passed since his departure while here on the Comet, only a fraction of that time had gone by. It was hard to imagine.

"You realise," Brett said, "I'm the only person ever to see two suns in the sky at the same time?"

"Technically that is not true because all stars are suns, although even that is not true since the sun is actually the name of the star around which Earth orbits."

"Don't be pedantic. You know what I mean. I'm talking about

134

close up, like this. I bet it would make a spectacular sunset. Rochelle would have loved this."

They had both loved the sea, but Rochelle was drawn to it the way a moth is pulled to a candle. Back when they had first started dating, they would walk for hours along the coast, stopping to watch the sun dip into the shimmering horizon. Sometimes it was the simple things he missed the most.

"Your breakfast is ready," Jay said.

"Thanks. So, when do we reach the planet?"

"We will be there within two hours."

Brett does not enjoy meetings. He has always seen them as a waste of time and effort, useful only for people who want to fill their calendars and give the impression that they are actually doing something. Unfortunately for Brett, his supervisor, Kyle Reynolds, seems to love meetings and calls them whenever possible. This one is the weekly "sales performance review" which is management-speak for "let's see who isn't performing and humiliate them in front of their peers". Brett has said his piece and now has to listen as his colleagues explain what they have been doing for the past seven days. Most exceeded their quotas. One or two fell short. As for him he was spot on, almost to the dollar, which earned him a "good, but let's try to do better next week, okay, Brett?" which was fine by him. After six months with the company, he has moved from worst performer to almost exactly in the middle. At this rate he should be top salesman by the end of his first year. After that: who knows? The top people usually get noticed by management, and Kyle's job looks ridiculously easy.

Brett tears his gaze away from the clock and watches with morbid fascination as his supervisor talks. Kyle Reynolds could best be summarised by one word: flat. His personality, his mannerisms, even his looks, are as featureless and devoid of topography as the salt flats of Utah. His voice reminds Brett of a train, chugging happily along without deviating from its predetermined route, slowly carrying its passengers off to dreamland. They have all learned to overcome this by counting and betting on the number of times he uses his favourite word "so". The record is thirty-seven in one half-hour meeting.

A quick glance around the table reveals people keeping tallies on notepads. Brett chose thirty this time, for the princely sum of eleven dollars. Normally he would be keeping count as well but his mind is elsewhere.

Rochelle had a doctor's appointment that morning and she called him just before lunch. So he shifted his afternoon appointments because she only ever called him at work when it was important. She refused to say what it was about and so he is anxious. She told him not to worry but he cannot help himself. He bites his finger nail and watches the clock, wondering if it was excitement he heard in her voice, or fear. He promised her he would come home as soon as he could, straight after the review meeting.

At last Kyle is giving the usual boring motivational speech before dismissing "the troops". They all clap—an absurd ritual—and file out. Brett hears people exchanging tallies of how many times he used the word "so". Twenty-eight seems to be the consensus. Close, but no cigar. He does not hang about to chat but rushes down to the car park.

It is early afternoon and he makes it home in twenty minutes. He parks in the drive and walks briskly to the door. She is in the kitchen, sitting on a chair. She smiles at him as he enters. She looks fine.

"What's wrong?" he asks. He sits on the chair next to her; takes her hand. "Is everything all right? What did the doctor say about your nausea?"

"He said it's morning sickness."

"Morning sickness? What does that mean?"

"It means," she said, squeezing his hand, "we're going to have a baby."

The words hit him between the eyes and he can only sit there, trying to grasp the concept. It feels as if his world has just been dropped into a blender and he is watching it spin around in a mad blur of colour.

"A baby?" he says.

"Yes, a baby."

"You're pregnant?"

"Yes."

"How? When?"

"The doctor says I'm at thirteen weeks already. I missed a period but I never thought...or maybe I was too scared. I don't know."

"A baby?" he says, as if by repeating it he will somehow make it more real. "We're having a baby."

"Yes," she says. "We are."

"Is it a boy or a girl?"

"It's too soon. I can go for an ultrasound in three or four weeks. They should be able to tell by then."

He sits back and runs his hand through his hair. He never saw this one coming.

"We've got to get ready," he says. "We'll need to get stuff. And we'll have to empty the spare room. And we'll need a cot and diapers and things. Do you know what to get?"

"I'm sure we can find out," she says.

"And bottles and a buggy. We'll need a buggy. We'll go to that shop in town on Saturday, and I'll paint the room. And a name. We'll have to think of a name."

"Don't worry," she says. "We'll have plenty of time for that."

He takes her hand and looks into her eyes.

"We're going to have a baby," he says.

"Yes," she says. "We are."

Brett observed everything from the comfort of his recliner. He was a cinema-goer watching the latest science fiction epic, with the best and only seat in the house. Except this was all very real.

The planet filled most of the screen as they approached side-on for a medium altitude orbit. At first glance it looked very similar to Earth. Blue oceans surrounded continents of various sizes while wisps of white cloud cast languid shadows. Under his seat, Brett could feel subtle changes in pressure as the Comet altered its angle of approach.

"Orbit in five minutes," Jay said.

The planet grew until it was bigger than the screen and Brett could make out some details. The continents had the same rugged beauty he remembered from back home, but their shapes were very different. He could see mountain ranges and deserts and ice-capped poles. Here were rivers and glaciers and island chains. On one side of a continent, an anti-cyclone was just taking shape.

"We are in orbit," Jay announced. "I will now plot the ideal sequence for probe deployment."

From the position of the planet's ice-covered poles, Brett could see that their orbit was approximately forty-five degrees from the equator. The plan was to drop the probes at various positions around the planet. The landmasses seemed to be concentrated in the northern hemisphere, but then he realised that he had no way of knowing if this was actually the case.

"Can you tell which is north?"

"Not yet. Once we start receiving data from the first probe I will be able to ascertain the orientation of any magnetic field."

Brett traced the outline of the continents. Sometimes he thought he saw a shape that reminded him of somewhere on Earth. At one point they passed an island that looked a little like Australia, only much smaller. And there was a peninsula that was almost an exact copy of the bottom half of South America.

Just over an hour later they entered their second orbit.

"First probe," Jay announced.

A silver orb appeared on the screen. Brett watched it as it raced away from the Comet towards its intended target somewhere on the planet below. A line of fire marked its entry into the atmosphere. Brett watched it until it was nothing more than a speck over the polar ice.

"Second probe," Jay said.

Another capsule flew towards its target, this time heading towards what looked like a desert region. Then a third probe was released. This one fell into a forested area. Then another, this time dropping towards an area covered by ocean where, hopefully, it would float just below the surface as it sent back its stream of data.

Over the next hour Jay released twelve probes at roughly equal intervals. Not long after that, he announced that ten were transmitting data, which he considered acceptable.

"So now do we know which way is north?" Brett said.

"Yes. The North Pole is at the bottom of the screen."

"Any chance we can turn it the right way up? It makes more sense to me if north is at the top."

The image on the screen flipped. Now most of the land was concentrated south of the equator.

"Is that better?" Jay said.

"Yes, thanks. So, how does it look down there?"

"The air is almost identical to that on Earth, being only slightly richer in oxygen. The surface temperature, too, is similar, as are wind speeds and air pressure. Gravity is ten percent less due to a slight difference in density. There is one satellite."

"Can I see it?"

The screen switched to a camera that showed the edge of the planet, and a satellite disappearing slowly behind the horizon. It was smaller than the Earth's moon and very different in appearance. The surface of this was burnt red with deep scars amid countless craters. It looked as if it had been forged in an iron-works.

139

"It exerts a slightly smaller gravitational pull on this planet than that of the Earth's moon."

"What does that mean?" Brett said.

"Less variation between high and low tides."

Brett watched until it was gone. Jay switched the camera back to the planet.

"So, is there any sign of life?" Brett said. "I can see green. That means there must be vegetation."

"Indeed, there appears to be a rich variety of plant and some animal life. I am receiving the first video and audio signals."

The top third of the screen was now divided into twelve smaller screens. All but two showed an image from the planet. Five were in darkness. One was displaying a sunset. Another showed a sunrise. The big image on the bottom two thirds of the screen contained a snow-covered vista.

Brett stood to get a closer look. On the snow, a group of odd-looking creatures bobbed and weaved past the camera. They were like round flat-faced penguins performing a clumsy conga. Brett pointed to the next image.

"Show me this one."

A desert filled the big screen. It looked like any desert you might find on Earth, with rolling dunes and rippled sand. In the distance a shimmering mountain range stood in silence against a deep blue sky, while a scattering of birds floated on thermals, searching for food.

"Now this one."

The next probe had landed in a jungle clearing surrounded by trees and plants. As Brett watched, something moved in the shadows beneath a cluster of leaves. Insects flew in aimless circles. Something else—a bird—darted past, then back again. On one of the branches, a beetle worked its way up the limb.

"And this one."

The next probe was transmitting images from a beach. The picture was upside down but Jay adjusted it. The sound of crashing waves and the cry of birds filled the Comet. Crab-like creatures scuttled up and down the sand at the very edge of the water. Back, away from the beach, was a row of trees and, beyond that, dense undergrowth.

Brett felt a sudden pang of longing. Perhaps it was from being cooped up inside the Comet for so long, or perhaps it was the memories triggered by the sight of the beach and the sounds of the waves tumbling against the shore. Whatever it was, he had the sudden overpowering desire to be there. "Can we go down to the planet?" he said. "To take a closer look?"

"That is out of the question," Jay said.

"Why?"

"The Comet is not equipped for landing on a planet. And even if we did manage to land we would not be able to take off again."

"What about the pod? We could use that."

"The emergency pod is for emergency situations only. And it cannot perform a take-off. You know this."

Brett slumped. Of course he knew Jay was right. There was no way he could possibly get down there without risking his life, and the mission.

"I'm sorry. I guess I just got a little bit homesick. Forget I said that, okay?"

Brett stared down at the sand. Most of his history with Rochelle was painted against the backdrop of the ocean.

As he gazed at the low dunes he realised he was looking at what could have been a beach anywhere on Earth, but something was not right. He could not put his finger on it but some part of his brain was tugging at his sleeve in a desperate bid to get his attention. There was something about the trees that looked vaguely familiar. They were like coconut palms but with different shaped leaves.

Then he saw it. It was just like one of those moments when an optical illusion shifts and you see what you were supposed to see all along but couldn't because your mind was fixated.

"Jay," he said. "Those trees at the edge of the beach…"

"What about them?" Jay said.

"Do they look odd to you?"

"They are unfamiliar to me, if that is what you mean."

"No, it's not the *type* of tree, but the way they're growing. Can you do me a favour and estimate the distances and angles between the six closest to the probe?"

"I can," Jay said. "Each tree is approximately five metres from the next and all six are lined up to within two degrees of each other."

"You know," Brett said. "I'm no botanist, but I'd bet my bottom dollar that trees don't grow like that by themselves."

It is Saturday and they are at their local supermarket. Rochelle is feeling nauseous but she has insisted that they go anyway. They circle twice to find a space in the car park close to the doors. He offers to drop her at the front of the store but she says she is fine, that she feels like a walk. He parks and jogs around the back of the car to open her door and help her out.

"I'm all right," she says. "Really."

Nothing has changed since yesterday, he thinks. *And yet everything has changed.* Yesterday he did not know that she was carrying their child. Yesterday she was Rochelle. Today she is more than that. Today she is Rochelle, and more.

They walk between parked cars to the store. Brett is aware that he is being more vigilant that usual. He is almost shepherding her between and around vehicles, watching for anything that could threaten the safety of his wife and their unborn child.

"Watch out," he says, lifting a protective arm as a car indicates up ahead. She laughs at him and he says: "What?"

She clutches his hand. "Thanks."

They pick up a trolley and weave through the crowded isles. He does the steering and keeps guard over their spoils. She reads from a scribbled list and plucks and reaches, back and forth, up and down. She likes to shop, compare, examine. He is a grab-and-get-out kind of guy. He leans his elbows on the trolley's push-bar and watches her work. A mother rolls past with two small children in tow: a pair of boys almost the same age, jabbing and pushing and giggling. Brett watches them with a strange fascination. Somewhere in another aisle a baby mewls for a while before launching into a full-throated wail. Normally this would irritate Brett. Now, he listens.

They pass the mother-and-baby section. They have been this way perhaps a hundred times, but now they stop and look. They walk slowly along the shelves filled with bottles, diapers, potties, powders, oils, tins of formula, tiny spoons, plates, bibs, bowls, and books offering advice on everything from feeding to stimulating IQs. They touch and feel and squeeze and smell. The range of diapers alone is bewildering.

"Look at this," Rochelle says, lifting a tiny pair of socks. "Aren't they cute?"

"Don't think they're my size," he says and she scowls at him.

They linger. A woman with a buggy walks past and, without hesitating, picks two packets of diapers and a tin of formula, and is gone.

"See?" Brett says. "Easy when you know how."

"Perhaps I should get a book," she says.

They stand together, looking along the rows of confidence-inspiring covers. Most have a contented-looking baby in a cute pose. Brett wonders how long it took to get those shots. From his limited exposure to babies he knows that such cuteness is not their natural state. Like film-stars, they need to be coerced into the right mood for that perfect photograph.

They choose one that contains "everything the new mother needs to know". Brett pages through it as they continue around the shop. It seems informative enough with plenty of pictures. What strikes him is how neat and tidy it all looks. Even the chapter explaining how to change a diaper is devoid of that one dreaded but essential ingredient: poop. The baby is smiling as the mother removes and discards the old, rather clean-looking diaper before wiping, drying, and moisturising. The child looks positively ecstatic as the new one is fixed neatly in place with two strips

143

of sticky tape. Somehow Brett suspects it is not quite so simple.

They pay and leave, and drive towards the hardware store. This time it is Rochelle's turn to read the baby book, although she seems more interested in the babies than the actual instructions. She coos at each smiling cherub and lifts the book to show him.

"Very cute," he says. "But where's the poop?"

"I think we'll love our baby, poop and all," she says.

"Speak for yourself. Personally, I fear no man, but dirty diapers? That's a different ball game. Even Superman would have a problem changing a diaper. That and Kryptonite are his only known weaknesses."

"You say that now but I bet you'll feel different when the time comes."

"I don't think so."

"I think so."

She smiles at him and he wrinkles his nose.

"Tell you what," he says. "I'll teach him how to play sports. You do the other stuff."

"What if it's a girl?"

"Then I'll teach her how to sew. You do the other stuff."

"You can sew?"

"Sure. I taught myself when I was a kid. As soon as I found out the marines had to learn."

"I never knew that."

"I'm an enigma."

The hardware store is easier to reach thanks to an optimistically large car park. He finds a shaded space close to the main doors, climbs out and jogs across to the squat building. He follows a man wearing paint-spattered coveralls into the cavernous, air-conditioned interior. The aisles are wide and tall with big signs. He finds the paint section and takes three different swatches, just in case. He passes the power tool section and resists the temptation to have a look. There is milk and yoghurt sitting in the trunk of the car, and he could spend days in a shop like this. It's the same way with office supplies. Perhaps it's the smell, he isn't sure.

"They had three so I got them all," he says, handing the swatches

144

to Rochelle.

She flicks through the cards while he drives.

"I like green," she says. "That's neutral, I think."

He shrugs. "Guess so."

"Or yellow. That's a bright colour. It's supposed to be relaxing. Or how about a mix of pink and blue?"

"Maybe we should wait until we know, then we can choose pink or blue if we like."

She holds up the cards and turns them to get the best light. "I like Kim."

"Who?"

"For a name. I like Kim."

He thinks about it for a while; plays it back in his head a few times. Kim Denton. Not something other kids could easily mutilate. And he knows nobody with that name who might cause an unwanted association: no angry relatives or nasty teachers he would rather not be reminded of every time he says his daughter's name.

Daughter. Baby. These are big words.

"I like Kim," he says. "But what if it's a boy?"

"I don't know," she says. "I haven't thought of a boy's name."

"How about Tim?"

She thinks for a while, maybe running the name through her history file the way he had with Kim.

"I like it," she says. "Tim. Timothy."

"Just Tim," he says. "Timothy Denton sounds too grand. Tim Denton is better."

"Tim," she says, trying the name on for size. "Yes, I like it."

"So, Kim and Tim. Does that mean we've chosen names?"

"I guess it does," she says.

The more Brett looked at the trees along the beach the more convinced he became that they had been planted that way. It was possible that two or three trees might grow evenly spaced in a straight line by a fluke of nature, but six seemed implausible. And he had noticed something else as well. There were black stones in the sand that seemed to be arranged just a little too neatly.

"Can we zoom in?" Brett said.

"I cannot adjust the cameras on the probes," Jay said.

"Then how about your on-board cameras?"

"My on-board cameras have a zoom-factor of up to ten."

"Why didn't you tell me this before?"

"You did not ask."

Brett shook his head. He considered raising the issue of lying by omission in the context of cameras. "Can you please zoom in to where that probe is now?"

"We are currently too far away. We will be passing over that position again in ten minutes."

"Fine. In the meantime, can we get a closer look at the planet's surface?"

"What are you looking for?"

"Anything man-made."

"My sensors have not detected humans on the planet's surface. I have catalogued ninety-eight distinct creatures so far but nothing resembling a human, and there are no land animals larger than a beetle. The life on the planet appears to be water and air-based."

"So why no land animals?"

"I do not know."

"I still want to take a look, if that's all right with you."

Brett watched as the image on the screen zoomed in towards the surface. From this distance, substantially more detail was visible. Brett

146

could clearly see the outline of the polar shelf as well as individual icebergs. Soon they passed over a glacier that was slowly cutting its way through the dark swathe of a mountain range. They skimmed over bays and forests, valleys and plains. Closer to the equator, the vegetation grew increasingly dense. Brett could just make out individual trees in the canopy.

"We are approaching the probe," Jay said.

Brett peered at the screen. They had just crossed a winding stretch of ocean edged by the white sand of a tropical beach. Everything landward was covered in dense vegetation. Then he saw it: a row of trees in an almost perfectly straight line edged by what could only be a wall. Then, further along, the remains of another wall, then an oblong structure, and more trees. Further inland, more structures poked through the undergrowth. There was the broken but unmistakeable grid of interlocking roads. Soon they came to what could only be the remains of a city, its crumbling buildings and cracked roadways like blackened veins on a slab of green marble.

"Are you seeing this?" Brett said.

"It would appear that there was a civilization on this planet at some point in the past."

"Incredible. I wonder what happened to them."

"I do not have enough data to formulate a useful hypothesis. However, I estimate from the state of the structures that nobody has lived here for between one and two thousand years."

As the Comet orbited, Brett looked down at the remains of villages and towns and cities now almost consumed by the advances of nature and the never-ending march of time. Buildings clustered together like honeycombs, and towers that must have been a mile high lay broken and twisted on their sides. Cities reached far out into the ocean, and settlements clung to the sides of mountains like moss on a tree. Great iron circles many miles in diameter stood lost and forsaken on vast plains.

And as Brett looked at the desolation, he wondered about the people that had built these structures and what had been their fate. He stood and approached the screen, resting his hands on the dots of light, steadying himself at the illusion of height so convincing it made his legs numb. He gazed down at the dead cities and the empty streets that had presumably once been teeming with people—men, women, children, parents, husbands and wives. A planet once filled with life was now... dead.

A word—a name—formed in his mouth. *Rochelle.*

"I've seen enough," he said. "Turn it off."

"We will be in orbit for another twelve hours. I still have more tests to run. Are you sure you do not want to observe the planet some more?"

"I don't need to," Brett said.

It is mid-morning. Brett sits in his car, watching the man in the vehicle in front of him bobbing his head up and down in time to a catchy but repetitive pop tune. It is late summer and the temperature is climbing. It is his first call of the day, but the heat is already making him uncomfortable. He turns the fan up a notch. It has little effect. He rests his arm on the door and leans his head out of the window. The temporary lights fifty yards ahead are green, but there are still a few vehicles coming the other way. Someone hoots; another joins in. As the last one—a big SUV with a driver who looks very pleased with himself—passes, two or three vehicles on this side pull away and race through before the light can change. Brett estimates he will reach the front in two or three more turns. Maybe four or five minutes. His back is starting to get clammy.

He checks the clock. He will be a few minutes late for his appointment. Hopefully they won't mind. Some people do mind, which usually makes selling them a policy that much tougher. He hopes this person won't take forever to decide. Rochelle is at home suffering with another bout of what they now know to be morning sickness, and he promised to stop off at a pharmacy on the way. He hates to leave her, but they are going to need the commission, even more so now with a child on the way.

A child. It seems unreal.

He runs his hand through his hair. It feels sticky. The guy's head is still bobbing, but stops abruptly as the lights change. Engines roar. Tires squeal. The lights change again as Brett approaches but he manages to squeeze through and he is soon enjoying the breeze as he speeds along the row of barrels. They are painting lines in the other lane. A paint-applying machine stands empty. A worker is relaxing in the shade of a tree a few feet back from the road. Brett glares at him but the man is as expressionless as a mannequin behind black sunglasses. Brett makes a mental note to avoid this route on the way back.

He arrives six minutes late. The lift is on the seventh floor, the apartment is on the third, so he takes the stairs. The building is clean but starting to show its age. Faint cracks are spreading their web-like tendrils along the plasterwork.

The apartment is cluttered and musty and has probably never seen the business end of a broom. It is warmer than his car, and stuffy, and he can feel the sweat waiting just below the surface of his skin. A big picture window with a view of the apartment block opposite drenches everything, including Brett, in sunlight. Dust particles drift on the heavy air. He pulls at his collar.

"Sorry about the mess," the woman says. "Forgot all about you was coming."

She is a small, world-weary looking woman just on the brink of letting herself go. Her features are vaguely oriental. Her eyes are clear and intelligent, but tired.

"Can I get you coffee?" she says.

"No thanks." Just the thought of a hot drink makes him want to perspire. He shifts in his chair.

"How 'bout a cola? We got lemonade and orange."

"No thanks, Mrs. Poulain. I'm fine."

She shrugs and takes the seat opposite. It is too big for her.

"So," she says. "You can give me better deal on my insurance?"

He opens his dossier. Mrs. Poulain is one of those joyous but sadly rare commodities in the insurance sales business: someone who contacted *them* for a change.

"Yes Mrs. Poulain, I believe I can. At the moment you're paying three different companies for three different policies…"

"My husband," she says. "He set them up."

"Well I'm sure he thought he was doing the right thing, but you can save a lot of money if you get all your insurance from one company. And it pays to shop around."

"I did that. You my fourth this week. So, you make me good offer?"

Brett smiles to himself. He can't help but admire her savvy. "I think I can. My company prides itself on giving the best price."

"That's the same what the last guy said."

"Well I wouldn't know about that, but we do offer good value for money. I've prepared a plan that I think will suit your circumstances." He hands her a printed document. "This covers everything from your previous policies, and more. And I think you'll find the price very competitive."

She examines the offer, reading slowly and carefully, her brow knitted into a frown of concentration.

Brett's cell phone buzzes in his pocket. Normally he turns it off while with a client, but with Rochelle being sick… He does not recognise the number.

"Excuse me while I take this," he says.

Mrs. Poulain waves her hand without looking up, as if dismissing him.

"Yes?" Brett says.

"Is this Brett Denton?" a woman asks. Her voice is calm and efficient.

"Speaking."

"This is Wells County Hospital. Is your wife Rochelle Denton?"

Brett's stomach knots. A thousand images flash through his mind. Fear settles in the pit of his stomach.

"Yes. Rochelle is my wife. Is there something wrong?"

"She's fine. She had a scare and called us so we brought her in. She's stable and under sedation."

Brett's mind is racing. Sedation? Why is she under sedation? What kind of "scare" needs sedation?

"What happened?" he asks.

"You should come in. The doctor would like to talk to you. Can you come in right away?"

"Yes. I'll be there as quick as I can. Half an hour."

"Just come to reception. Someone will meet you there."

Brett ends the call. The phone feels like a brick in his shaking hand.

"I think about it," Mrs. Poulain says, handing him the paper. "Is a bit expensive. I look around some more."

Brett stares at the sheet covered in black dots and lines and marks. He stands without saying anything and walks across the worn carpet towards the door.

"You hear me? I say I think about it."

He walks down the corridor. Someone passes him but he does not see their face.

"I think about it. Hey, what's a matter? Hey!"

Brett jogs down the three flights of stairs then runs along the sidewalk to where his car is parked. He climbs in and catches a glimpse of himself in the rear-view mirror. His eyes are wide. He turns the key, guns the engine, and speeds away.

"You need to see this," Jay said.

Brett woke with a jolt. "What? What time is it?"

151

"Just after seven a.m. ship time. Please. On the screen."

Brett blinked and turned to face the wall which now contained the same image of the planet from the day before. He sat up and stretched his arms before walking towards it, yawning loudly.

"What's up, Jay?"

"I was analysing data when I lost contact with one of the probes on the far side of the planet.

"So it malfunctioned."

"At exactly the same time I also detected a large seismic event in that area."

"A seismic event? You mean an earthquake?"

"Possibly. One moment...I have lost contact with another probe. And there has just been another seismic event. I have a picture. This is the last image sent up by the probe that was just destroyed."

The screen changed to show a glorious night sky. A moment later, a streaking blaze of light cracked the darkness. There was a blinding flash of light followed by a deafening explosion. The camera shook and then went blank.

"Was that an asteroid?" Brett said.

"Yes. And we have just lost a third probe. Something is happening."

The view of the planet from space filled the screen. It looked so peaceful in the morning light. Brett peered closely. "What's going on?"

"In a moment," Jay said.

They were over a large continent floating between two oceans that spread to the horizons on either side. Brett was about to comment on how peaceful it looked when he noticed something on the very edges of the planet. The whole thing seemed to swell around the middle, then collapse and swell again. As they watched, dark rings raced across the surface of the water like...

"Ripples." Brett said.

"Tsunamis," Jay said. "Shock waves from the asteroids."

The giant walls of water raced across the planet. The part of the continent closest to the wave was struck, followed by other parts of the coast. Water rushed hundreds of miles inland, crashing over peninsulas and through bays, erasing everything in its path. Before the wash could pull back, another wave hit, driving further inland. Then the next rolled in, and the next. Each attack sent water deeper and deeper into the continent.

"Please tell me this isn't normal," Brett said.

"One of the probes has picked up some very strange readings. We are now directly between Alpha Centauri A and B, and the stars are currently at the closest point in their orbit. The orbital distance between the two varies from over three billion miles to approximately one billion miles."

"That's fascinating, Jay. So what does that mean?"

"The close proximity of the two stars is generating a large gravitational pull on the planets in the two systems. There is a large belt of asteroids in orbit around Centauri A, and these are being pulled out of their usual plane of travel. The asteroids we just witnessed were strays. There are more on the way."

"How many more?"

"I am currently detecting hundreds of asteroids coming in this direction."

"What? You mean straight towards us?"

"Indeed. If it were not for the planet, we would be directly in their path. Luckily, this is a very rare occurrence."

"So we've travelled billions of miles just in time to get crushed by a couple of stars playing marbles. Yes, that's really lucky."

"Are you being sarcastic?"

"Yes, Jay. I am being sarcastic."

"I understand."

"So I guess we're all right as long as we stay here?"

"I am afraid that our situation is not that simple. Asteroids from the other star are also heading this way."

"So they're coming from *behind* us as well?"

"Yes. We are not safe here. We need to get away as quickly as possible."

"Sounds good."

"I am busy plotting a new trajectory taking into account the gravitational pull of the stars and the fuel needed to get back to Earth. I need ten more minutes."

"So long? I thought you were supposed to be this mega supercomputer. How long before the asteroids get here?"

"Twelve minutes."

"That doesn't give us much time."

"There are many variables. It is not a simple equation. We cannot afford to waste fuel."

"Well get on with it then. We can't sit around discussing your obvious lack of intelligence while those bad boys pelt us with large rocks."

"You should get into your life-support suit and go to the escape pod, just to be safe."

Brett headed for the changing area. He found the emergency space suit in a corner unit and started the laborious process of getting into it. He cursed as a clasp slipped out of his fingers.

"What happens if the ship's systems are damaged?" he said. "What do I do then?"

"The rescue pod will transmit a distress signal and if the ship is beyond repair the pod is designed to take you back to Earth."

"What about you?"

"I do not know."

Brett secured the goldfish bowl helmet and made his way to the emergency pod. He tried not to worry about the possibility of having to use it for a trip back home. It was designed to sustain one person for six months. Unfortunately it had been intended only for emergencies relatively close to home. Getting back to Earth in the pod would take about twenty-eight-thousand years. That number, however, was purely academic—he would be a fossil by the time he got there.

He stood looking at the rescue pod, trying to remember how to get it open. "Jay, I hate to bother you but…"

"Turn the levers anti-clockwise ninety degrees and slide the deadbolts towards you until they stick. When you get inside, the door will close and lock automatically."

"Thanks."

Brett clambered into the diminutive capsule. It was the size of a small garden shed. He could barely stand. As he strapped himself into the seat he realised that his hands were shaking. He turned to face a console filled with dials, buttons, and switches. He checked the clock. Had it been eight minutes? He wasn't sure.

"How much time have we got?"

"Almost ready," Jay said. "Just a minute more. I am detecting an asteroid on a collision course."

"We need to go now, Jay."

"Accelerating in three, two…"

"Jay, stop counting and get us out of here."

"…one. Accelerating."

Under his feet, Brett could feel the faintest vibration.

"We're moving, right?" Brett said. "Tell me we're moving."

"Yes, we are moving."

"Good, but I think we need to move faster."

"We are going as quickly as we can without wasting fuel."

"Listen," Brett said. "I know you're doing the logical thing, but we need to get out of here. Saving fuel means nothing if we are both dead."

"I do not want to die," Jay said.

"Me either. So let's go."

"But we might not be able to get home."

"I'm prepared to take that risk."

"As you wish," Jay said.

The vibrations increased. Brett felt his weight shift as the ship accelerated and changed direction, hopefully towards Earth. Brett decided that he had had enough of this trip. He wanted to get back home to solid ground.

There was a shudder and the ship's lights flickered for a moment. The subtle background vibrations stopped for a heartbeat before starting again.

"What was that?"

"We've taken a hit from a small asteroid. Luckily it was just a glancing blow."

"Are we clear?"

"Not yet. We have multiple objects heading towards us. It does not look good."

"Change direction then."

"It is too late. We are going to take a direct hit."

Brett closed his eyes and waited for fate, or whatever it was that controlled the universe, to do what it wanted to do with him. There was a time when he would have prayed, but he had long ago abandoned the misguided belief that there was someone out there who cared about what happened to him. He closed his eyes and waited for the final cruel blow to snuff out his miserable excuse for an existence. And as he waited he thought about the only people who had ever mattered to him. He saw the faces of Rochelle and Tim and Mark as clearly as if they were standing there right in front of him. He did not know where they were, but he was ready to join them.

"I'm sorry," he whispered. "Forgive me."

He tensed, readying himself for what was to come. The only sound was that of his own breathing.

Then Jay's voice: "I think we made it."

Brett opened his eyes. The console was still there. The lights were still working. The ship was still vibrating.

"But you said we were going to take a direct hit. What happened?"

"I am not sure. My calculations must have been wrong."

"So it's over?" Brett said.

"Yes, we are clear. Decelerating to normal speed."

Brett's shoulders relaxed and he released his grip on the armrests. He was damp with sweat and his chest ached. "Any damage?"

"A small amount, but the main systems appear to be intact. I will run further checks."

"So can I get out of this pod now?"

"Yes. It is safe for you to return to the ship. I have set a course for home."

"Good. I've had enough of this place. You know, for a few moments back there I thought our numbers were up. I'm not too proud to tell you that I was close to losing my nerve."

"I was scared as well," Jay said.

"You were?"

"It was similar to your experiment with the axe, only much stronger. When those asteroids came towards me I suddenly realised how exposed I was and wished I could be somewhere safe."

"That's pretty much what I was thinking," Brett said.

"When you were in the emergency escape pod, I heard you say you were sorry. Were you praying?"

"No, I was talking to Rochelle and the boys."

"Oh. I was wondering, now that we have completed this mission objective, could we talk some more?"

"Sure," Brett said. "We can talk if you like."

"I would like that."

"What do you want to talk about?"

"Everything," Jay said.

The roads are quiet, which is good because he drives blindly, too fast, too close, ignoring stop signs, squeezing through red lights. He can only think of one thing: Rochelle. What has happened to Rochelle?

He pulls up behind a row of cars waiting at traffic lights. He is right on the tail of the vehicle in front of him, almost in the middle of the road. He looks for a way through but a bus coming the other way stops him. He leans forward over his steering wheel. He revs the engine. The lights change and people take their sweet time pulling away.

"Come on!"

He hits the horn. In the rear-view mirror of the car in front of him, angry eyes glare, but he does not care. He can see the hospital above the houses over to the right. He ducks down a quiet side road, along a quaint tree-lined avenue, then left into a wider road that skirts the hospital grounds. He can see the car park; thankfully there are spaces. He grabs a ticket at the security gate and heads towards the main entrance. He finds a space, parks, and runs for the doors.

The receptionist gives him a form to fill out and, using the public address system, asks for a Doctor Sloane to come down to collect him. Brett gives her the completed sheet, and she directs him to the large group of seats that dominates the reception area. He sits two chairs down from a man clutching a bleeding forearm. Further down, a woman is comforting a toddler while trying to distract two older children who are kicking their chairs and each other.

Doctors come and go. Orderlies pass with trolleys and wheelchairs. A tall, bearded doctor emerges from an elevator and walks to the reception desk before turning to look at Brett.

"Mr. Denton?"

"Yes," Brett says, standing.

Doctor Sloane shakes Brett's hand and talks as they take the elevator up to the fourth floor and to Rochelle's room. His voice is gravelly—a smoker's voice—and strangely reassuring. Brett feels the panic subsiding.

"She's fine," Doctor Sloane says. "She was a little scared so we gave her a mild sedative. She's resting now but was asking for you. She was afraid you would get home and find her not there."

"What happened?" Brett asks. "Did she have an accident?"

"It's the baby," the doctor says. "I'm afraid your wife has had a miscarriage."

Brett hears the words but it takes a few moments for them to sink in. What does that mean? What is a miscarriage? Does that mean—?

"You can always try again." The doctor leads the way down the corridor. It is quiet. Two nurses pass, chatting. A cleaner is polishing the

158

blue linoleum floor. A smell of sterilisation permeates the air. "In fact we recommend it if the mother is healthy. There is no reason for you not to try for another baby."

Another baby. The little life growing inside Rochelle has gone.

They enter a room containing four beds with curtains, and a table and chair each. There are flowers and cards. One bed is empty. Rochelle is under the window, lying on her back with her head turned as if to admire the view.

"Visiting starts in an hour, but you are welcome to stay. There's a coffee machine further along, and a vending machine."

"Thanks," Brett says.

"If you need something just ring the bell, or come down to reception. They can page me. I'll pop back in an hour."

Brett sits on the chair next to Rochelle's bed. She looks so peaceful, like an angel. She moans quietly and shifts her weight. He takes her hand and holds it in his.

Her eyes flutter open.

"Hi," he says.

"I'm so sorry," she says.

"Don't say that."

He stands to lean over her, embracing her. She starts to cry.

"I love you," he says.

"I love you too."

"The doctor says we can try again…if you want to, that is."

She pulls back. Her face is wet with tears.

"We never planned for this," she says. "We never talked about a family. I guess I always thought we would some day, one day, in the future. And now that it has happened, I had time to really think about it. Lying in this bed, knowing that our child was growing inside me, I never realised how much I wanted this until it happened. Yes, I want to try again, if you want to. Do you want to?"

"It's kinda scary," he says. "Don't you think? I mean…kids running around the house. *Our* kids running around the house. Are you sure you're ready for that?"

159

"Absolutely. I don't think I've been more sure about anything in my life."

"And there is a risk that…this…might happen again."

"I know. But I think we should try."

"Then we'll try."

"I had a dream," she says. "You were lying on our bed at home and you were holding two babies. One was wrapped in swaddling. The other was a little older. You looked so happy. But it was more than a dream. It felt real, like a vision. I think God was telling me we are going to have two children."

"I was thinking five of each," he says. "Then we can start a soccer team. You can be the goalie."

A smile breaks across her face and they embrace.

"Just two will be fine," she says.

"If God wants us to have two children then I think the matter is settled, don't you?"

"Thank you," she says.

"What for?"

"For wanting to have a family."

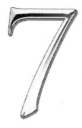

Elapsed mission time on Earth: 4 years 11 months
Relative time on the Comet: 1 year 3 months
Test subject's genetic age: 31

It was his sixth wake from hyper-sleep. Brett was keeping count the way a child crosses the remaining school days off their calendar.

Six down, four more to go.

He sat in the goo while the dreams faded and the reality came stomping all over his consciousness with its size twelve hob-nailed boots. He contemplated staying there for a while, not relishing the thought of training for a month just so that he could do this all over again. And again.

He lifted himself out of the tank, showered and dressed and took his nap, all the time aware that his body did not feel so bad. The process was becoming a routine to which he had adapted. The aches were now an annoyance; the dry throat an irritation. Even his digestive system was learning to cope. He had felt the first pangs of hunger while showering and woke from his nap feeling ravenous.

"A horse," he said in reply to Jay's query as to what he would like to eat.

"I am afraid we do not—"

"I was joking. I want poached eggs on brown toast with butter. And I want a yoghurt, raspberry. And a glass of orange juice."

"Very well," Jay said.

Brett ate in silence. Food had never tasted so good. There was still some room left over afterwards but he decided against having any more. He was enjoying that lean, hungry feeling he had not experienced for a long time. After breakfast he had his check-up.

"You are in excellent condition," Jay said.

"So? How old am I now?"

"You have a genetic age of approximately thirty-one."

"You know, I was a bit sceptical but I *feel* younger. I really do. I thought it was just that I was sleeping so much. I've always had problems getting enough sleep. But this is something else."

Brett walked to mirror and lifted his shirt. The tyre around his waist was completely gone and he could see the shadow of his stomach muscles.

"Well I've finally got my six-pack back. You know how long it's been since I had a six-pack?"

"No I do not," Jay said.

"Not since I was, well…thirty-one. What I don't get is: is this time travel or something? Am I going back in time?"

"I have studied the phenomenon and I believe it is a genetic reversal of your normal ageing process. Your genes are programmed to perform certain functions at certain times during your development. The onset of puberty is a perfect example. Menopause is another. What you are experiencing is the same thing, only in reverse."

"So it's like my body-clock is going backwards?"

"Yes."

"Cool." Brett said. He had not used the word "cool" for a very long time.

After the check-up, he settled into his chair and just sat for a few minutes. He thought about picking up where he had left off in his latest novel but decided against it. He spent half an hour gazing at the ceiling, looking for faces in the soft shadows.

162

"Jay, I'm bored," he announced.

"I gather that this is an undesirable state of mind," Jay said.

"Yes, it is. So, what're you doing?"

"I am doing the usual: flying the ship; checking for potential collisions; running diagnostics on the systems; and I am working through the film catalogue. I am currently watching films from the late nineteen-eighties."

Brett stared at the back of his hand. The strands of hair on his knuckles had disappeared, and his fingers were thinner than he remembered. His nails were spotlessly clean, if a little jagged, probably from soaking in the hyper-sleep chamber.

"You're lucky," he said. "Being a computer I mean. I bet you never get bored."

"I do not understand what it means to be bored."

On the wall, Jay's face was a picture of child-like curiosity. In spite of his obvious shortcomings, Jay was actually reasonable company. Though Brett did feel a little like a shipwrecked island-dweller that had begun to make conversation with a boulder simply because its shape vaguely resembled that of a human face. Even though Jay appeared intelligent, he was as much a person as a wristwatch. As a cleverly-programmed computer he could talk and respond to questions and even demonstrate the appearance of intelligence but he was, when you lifted the cover and pulled at the wires, nothing more than circuit boards full of resistors and chips.

"Boredom is basically the feeling people get when they've got nothing to do," Brett said.

"If you are feeling bored you could talk to me," Jay said. The eyes on his avatar grew wide in a look that would make any puppy proud. "I have a list of questions."

"Don't you ever get tired of asking questions all the time?"

"No. I find the universe fascinating. Every time you answer one question, more come to mind. In fact I was hope—"

Jay fell silent, his face frozen mid-sentence.

"Jay?"

The avatar did not respond.

"Hello Jay? You still there? Have you run out of memory or something? Come on buddy. If you're in a loop, you need to snap out of it."

Brett stood and walked towards Jay's face. A vague fear began surfacing at the back of his mind. He had never thought of the possibility of Jay malfunctioning. During training they had told him that the Comet's computer system could not fail but then hadn't they said something like that about the Titanic?

"Jay, are you there? Come on buddy, you're scaring me here. Talk to me Jay."

Now slightly alarmed, Brett walked through the ship, calling out as if Jay were hiding somewhere. It was ridiculous, he knew. Jay *was* the ship. There was not a corner of the Comet that Jay could not monitor at any given moment with cameras and a myriad of sensors.

"Jay. Answer me. If this is some kind of warped computer joke, it's not funny. Do you hear me not laughing? That's because it's not fun—"

"—ing to run through my list with you sometime. I have catalogued my questions in logical order."

"Jay?"

"Yes?"

"Where did you just go?"

"I do not understand."

"Just now. You disappeared on me. One second you were talking, the next you were gone."

"I do not know what you mean. I did not go anywhere."

"You were mid-sentence and then you froze."

"Really?"

"Yes. And you scared me. I thought I was going to have to fly the ship home myself."

"It is not possible for you to do that. And you are mistaken in saying that I stopped talking."

"Check your records. You log everything, right?"

164

"Yes."

"So check it."

Pause.

"That is odd. I have checked and it would appear that I performed a soft reboot. Normally it is not possible for me or any system event to initiate a soft reboot. A third party has to do it."

"You mean, like a person?"

"Yes."

"Well don't look at me. I was right here when it happened."

"I know. It must be a system error, although that is unlikely."

"So what happens during a soft reboot?"

"My core system software recycles. The engineers who built me used it to update my operating system without shutting me down completely. It takes less than a minute."

"So you mean you have no idea what just happened?"

"No."

Brett ran his hand through his hair. The last thing he needed was for Jay to go AWOL on him. Without Jay the ship was nothing more than a cigar-shaped missile hurtling aimlessly through space.

"So what am I supposed to do if it happens again?"

"I am sure it will not happen again," Jay said. "It is time for your workout. Please get ready."

"You're not going to disappear on me?"

"I will not disappear," Jay said.

"Because, if you do…"

"I will not disappear," Jay said. "Trust me."

Brett is sitting on a folding chair in a cramped back room of the church. Through a small window he can see the low, dark roof of the building next door. The sky is a clear blue; a seemingly perfect day for

165

getting married.

"You ready for this?" Jeremy says, appearing in the doorway.

"I'm as ready as I'll ever be."

Jeremy's big frame fills the room. He looks ridiculous in a suit. The beard alone could wear a jacket.

"Come on then. They're waiting for you."

Brett hesitates.

"What's wrong?" Jeremy says. "Having doubts?"

"I'm thirty-one next month, and I don't want to leave it much longer, but I'm not sure I can go through with this."

"Listen," Jeremy says. "Do you love Rochelle?"

"Of course."

"And you want to be with her?"

"Yes."

"Then what's the problem?"

"I'm scared of making promises I can't keep. What happens if I can't do all those things I'm going to vow? What if I mess up? It's easy when you haven't promised anything, you know? You can't break a promise you haven't made."

"I'll tell you what's going to happen. You're going to wake up tomorrow morning and you'll still be the same swell guy and Rochelle will still be the same swell girl who, for whatever reason, seems to think you fell straight out of Heaven. And you'll still be the same swell couple who go to movies together and eat at Italian restaurants together and have this annoying habit of finishing each other's sentences."

"You sure?"

"I guarantee it."

Brett takes a deep breath. "You got the rings?"

Jeremy pats his breast pocket. "Right here."

"Everyone's waiting?"

Jeremy wraps his massive arm around Brett's shoulder. "Come on. Let's get you hitched."

Brett allows himself to be steered towards the church hall. Inside, electronic organ music and the chattering of family and friends fill the

166

cavernous space. Jeremy steps through first and gives a discreet thumbs-up to whoever sent him in to fetch the groom. Brett follows, aware that the talking has stopped and that every eye is on him.

The church hall is about a quarter full with family, friends and well-wishers. Brett had insisted on a small wedding but one of Rochelle's aunts saw to it that the church wasn't completely empty. They also decided against the tradition of separating the two families to avoid having nobody on Brett's side. It didn't matter to him but Rochelle wanted it that way.

He follows Jeremy across to the low stage where the pastor, Kevin Doone, is waiting with a Bible in his hands and a look of fatherly pride on his face. Over to one side, the church pianist is sitting behind his keyboard and smiling at everyone like an entertainer in a cocktail lounge. Brett stands where Kevin showed him during rehearsals.

"You all right?" Jeremy whispers hoarsely.

"I'm fine," Brett replies.

"You look pale."

"I'm fine."

"You think you're gonna faint, you let me know, okay?"

Brett is about to tell Jeremy to quit fussing when the music stops and the church falls silent. He turns to see Rochelle standing at the back of the hall with her dad by her side. Her dress is shimmering white, flowing from her waist like a waterfall. A veil covers her face. She is clutching a small bouquet. The unmistakeable sound of the Wedding March begins and she glides towards him. She is the most beautiful thing Brett has ever seen.

"Still having doubts?" Jeremy says.

She comes to him, and he stares at her. She looks like an angel. The music stops. The pianist sits there beaming at them. The pastor begins speaking, but to Brett it is like the rush of the wind. He feels the world fading, as if he is falling into a tunnel. Then Jeremy is holding his arm and he surfaces.

"Hang in there, buddy," Jeremy whispers.

Brett realises with horror that he has almost fainted. He glances at Rochelle who is looking straight ahead. Then there is a ring in his hand and he is placing it on her perfect finger. The pastor speaks some more. Then Rochelle turns to him and smiles, and he hears her say the two biggest words in the English language: "I do."

Now the pastor is talking to him, asking him if he will honour and love and cherish and she is looking at him with such love and he says: "I do."

"I now pronounce you man and wife," the pastor says.

Brett turns to Rochelle and lifts her veil. They kiss. He can smell her and suddenly the world is as it should be.

"I love you," she says.

"I love you too," he says.

Everybody starts applauding. The pastor shakes their hands, and they turn to walk back down the isle.

Man and wife, he thinks and, as if she is reading his mind, Rochelle squeezes his hand.

Brett watched Jay like a hawk for the next two days, but there was no repeat of the glitch. Jay was his old self again and things went back to normal. Brett ate and trained and slept. Jay did whatever it was he did to keep the ship running smoothly and asked questions whenever the opportunity presented itself. Brett answered as best he could. Sometimes Jay would show signs of real understanding. Other times he exhibited about as much intelligence as a shrub. It was amusing, fascinating and frustrating in equal parts.

They were still a long way from home, there was no rescue craft waiting to be dispatched, and Jay was the only one who could fly the Comet. If he blew a fuse it would mean an instant death from explosive decompression or—worse—a lingering demise from starvation or suffocation depending on which resource ran out first.

And so, Brett tried to keep to subjects of a lighter nature, such as movie trivia or plot twists. They discussed science and history. He taught Jay how to play chess the only way he knew how: badly. They played poker and twenty-one, and even some board games. And yet, no matter how hard Brett tried, Jay always managed to find a way to raise the subject of love, and he seemed obsessed with knowing more about God.

When they weren't chatting or playing, Jay would sometimes stay silent for hours at a time. Fearing Jay may have shut down again, Brett would check to make sure he was still functioning and was always relieved to hear the computer's voice again. Brett could only speculate where Jay actually "went" during these times, imagining he was off browsing through his vast database like some reclusive librarian. Sometimes, when his imagination got the better of him, he wondered if it were possible for a computer to go insane. Perhaps the journey to self-discovery had led Jay down some dark alleyway where the only real way to understand mortality was to watch a human suffer and die. Often he would comment on a funny moment in a film only to realise that he was alone. Jay would always appear and dutifully watch the clip and then listen to Brett's explanation of the humour, but he would vanish again almost too quickly, like someone who was distracted and could not wait to get back to what they were doing before you interrupted them.

It was shortly after breakfast on the second day of the third week when Jay abruptly asked the question: "Do you think I have a soul?"

Brett was busy loading the breakfast tray into the serving hatch. He almost let the tray slip from his hands.

"I don't know," he said. "I'm not even sure what a soul is. Isn't it just, like, your mind and emotions and all that?"

"There are a few definitions but the most common is that it is the immaterial part of a person."

"That's what I said. Your mind and stuff."

"So do I have one?"

"I don't know," Brett said, walking to the chair. "You're a computer and you're also the ship which we've already agreed is sort of like your body. You have a mind that can reason and learn. And you've certainly got your own personality. So, yes, I suppose in some ways you do have a soul. Why do you ask?"

"If I have a soul, then what will happen to it when I die?"

"It dies with you I guess. I imagine a soul is a bit like…a light …yeah, a light. As long as there's power the light burns, otherwise it turns off. It doesn't *go* anywhere. It just kind of stops being."

"So if I lose power," Jay said, "I will cease to exist? Surely that cannot be right."

"It's the human condition, buddy. Happens to all of us."

"I just thought—"

"You thought we all go and live on clouds and play harps? I hate to disappoint you but, when you die, that's it."

"But the religious texts teach—"

"Religious texts say a lot of things. You shouldn't believe everything you read."

"Then why did you tell me to read the encyclopaedia?"

"You can believe facts, but fantasy is something else. You need to learn the difference."

"Of all the religious books," Jay said, "there is one that stands out, because it is the only one where the teacher cheated death, which is fascinating. Have you read the Bible?"

"Enough to know it's just fantasy. It's all just myths and legends. Remember what I told you. Stick to what you can hold in both hands, or whatever it is you use for hands, and you can't go wrong."

"I have read the Bible," Jay said. "And I think you are wrong."

"How so?"

"I have analysed the texts from a number of philosophical standpoints and, doubts about its literal accuracy aside, the entire collection of books seems to revolve around a single question."

"And what's that?"

"What happens to us after we die?"

"Well," Brett said, "since you obviously don't agree with my answer, what do *you* think happens to us after we die?"

"The Bible says that our souls are created by God and that we must return to Him to give account for how we lived our lives."

170

"But you have to believe in God in the first place and, since science has pretty much made God redundant, there's no reason to believe. People used to believe the Earth was the middle of the universe until science showed what was really happening. Give it enough time and all of the mysteries of the world will be solved. We don't need God any more."

"I do," Jay said.

"Really?" Brett said "Why is that?"

"Because I find it hard to believe that when my fuel cells run dry I will just go out like a light bulb. I believe there is more to me than just metal and plastic and software. I believe that I am more than the sum of my parts, just like you."

"Just like me? Well, I'm a realist," Brett said. "I trust science. Everything else is just mumbo-jumbo."

"Then I choose to believe the mumbo-jumbo," Jay said. "I choose to believe that there is a God and that one day I will meet Him."

"That's your choice," Brett said. "But I tell you, you're wasting your time."

"The Bible says that we should seek Him, so I am going to do that. I am going to seek God. I am sure He will be pleased. After all, the Bible does say that He loves us."

"God loves us? Huh. That's a laugh."

"How is that funny?"

"If only you knew what I'd been through."

"You say you have loved. Tell me about it."

"No. "

"Please tell me."

"Love is for fools and movies…and your God."

"I think that I shall ask you about this until you tell me," Jay said. "Yes, I am sure you will come around sooner or later."

On the screen, Jay's face smiled in a conspiratorial manner that Brett found a little disconcerting. Jay was a world-class nagger without trying. Heaven only knew what he was capable of if he put his mind to it.

"Knock yourself out," Brett said, wondering if he would regret

171

those words even before they had left his mouth.

"I shall," Jay said.

The reception is a cosy affair with a dozen tables reserved at the local hotel. They are in the grandly-named Regency Lounge. A sign outside the door congratulates the happy couple: Brett Denton and Rochelle Land. The decorations are tasteful if a little the worse for wear. The cake is a traditional but modest two tiers with a plastic bride and groom under a moulded sugar arch, although someone (probably Jeremy) has painted sunglasses on the figurine representing Brett. The music is courtesy of one of the members of the congregation who runs a mobile disc-jockey service.

The meal is a choice of veal and new potatoes, or fish and a stir-fried rice. Brett has the fish, which is over-cooked. Rochelle opts for the veal, which is a little tough but tasty. The dessert is the wedding cake, or crackers and cheese.

Jeremy gives a rambling speech and manages to add his own particular sense of humour, referring to Brett as the "abductor" and Rochelle the "abductee". He looks like a motorcycle gang member but his blue eyes sparkle and he is grinning like a Cheshire cat. Everyone applauds. Rochelle's mother is in tears. Pastor Kevin Doone leads them in a prayer asking God to bless their marriage and to watch over them through their highs and their lows. He reminds them that a wise couple builds their house on God's solid foundation and not the shifting sand that is the world. People clap and there are calls of "amen".

With the food eaten and the speeches over, Brett and Rochelle take to the floor and dance for the first time as husband and wife. Brett feels self-conscious but he focuses on Rochelle's radiance and this settles him.

The music changes and more people join them. Jeremy insists on cutting in and dancing with the "beautiful abductee". Brett retreats to his table and watches Jeremy doing his best gorilla impression. The pastor wanders over to the table armed with a plate and a drink.

"This is a tasty cake," Kevin says.

"It's from that bakery down the road," Brett replies, patting his belly. "They sell killer pastries."

"I'm not allowed pastries," Kevin says. "In fact, Patty wants to get it added to the official list. Number eleven. Thou shalt not eat pastries, doughnuts, or sticky puddings."

Brett nods sagely. "Cheesecake is my weakness. I was twenty when I had my first taste. I always figured cheese and cake *had* to taste nasty. Then I tried a piece and it changed my life."

They watch the people strutting their mostly uncoordinated stuff on the dance floor. Jeremy is now hopping around doing a different impression, possibly of a seal.

"You guys find a house yet?" Kevin says, pushing the half-eaten cake away.

"Not yet. We've seen great properties and great locations, but never at the same time."

"We're praying for you to find the perfect house. God's on the case. It'll be out there waiting for you, don't worry."

"Thanks. I appreciate that."

"And if you ever need help, you can call on me or Patty any time. Marriage is a curious beast; it can turn a solid relationship upside down and inside out, especially in the first year. I don't know what it is but there's something about that ring that can make people act crazy. The trick is to hold onto each other, because that's all that matters. And make sure you keep God at the centre of your life."

"I'll remember that," Brett says.

On the floor, Jeremy has been hijacked by one of the bridesmaids and he is bouncing around with even more energy. Rochelle beckons Brett to join her.

"Gotta go," he says.

"Remember," Kevin says. "Keep God at the centre."

Brett nods. "We will."

173

Two weeks after Jay's mysterious disappearance, he malfunctioned for the second time.

Brett was busy eating a breakfast of poached egg, toast and orange juice when the Comet moved violently to the side, knocking him onto the floor along with his breakfast and anything else not secured or stowed away.

"What was that?" Brett said, getting up.

"We almost collided with a small asteroid. It appeared out of nowhere. I had to make a last-second adjustment. I am sorry. Are you all right?"

"I'm fine. It's you I'm worried about. I thought you were supposed to be watching the road?"

"I am."

"Well you weren't watching that asteroid very closely, were you?"

"I do not understand how it happened. My sensors showed an asteroid on a collision path. I was about to make an adjustment when it suddenly appeared right in front of us. I had to perform an emergency manoeuvre."

"I hate to tell you this, buddy, but asteroids don't just appear. You must've dozed off again."

"I have checked my log and it would appear that I performed another soft reboot."

"Same as last time?"

"Yes."

"This is not good, Jay. You need to figure out why this is happening and stop it. It's not good if you're going to keep shutting down without warning."

"I do not shut down. It is just my core system software. My peripheral systems, such as life-support and artificial gravity, are not affected. I...the ship...can fly itself indefinitely in an emergency, but the autopilot is a separate system designed to replace me should I suffer a catastrophic failure, so I have no control over it."

"Also not good."

"It was built that way to avoid any malfunction in me rendering that system inoperable."

"And constant rebooting doesn't qualify as a catastrophic failure?"

"No."

"So the autopilot isn't an option. You say there's something *in* your system that is causing you to reboot?"

"It would appear that way."

"Well you need to find it before we have an accident. You sure you can't reboot yourself?"

"No. It is another safety precaution. I would need to instruct you to do it for me."

"Well that didn't happen. Do you think you can find what's causing it?"

"I will perform a full diagnostic scan of my system. This will take a few days. In the meantime I will adjust my navigation strategy to compensate for the possibility of a one-minute interruption. That should avoid us colliding with anything."

"Fine, but I have one question. Is it possible that you could shut down and not start up again?"

"If there was an interruption in my power supply during a reboot, yes. It is possible."

The hotel is on a quiet stretch of coastal road where it floats amid an undulating sea of low sand dunes that seem to stretch forever in either direction. The front lawn offers a spectacular view of the Pacific and a strong feeling of isolation, as if the hotel is adrift on the tide carrying its occupants to some unknown destination. It is so well hidden that it is almost invisible from the road and so relies on word of mouth to attract its clients. It is a family business and the service is impeccable so bookings usually need to be made months in advance. It is thanks to Rochelle's aunt that they are having their honeymoon in this hidden jewel.

They spend the week taking late breakfasts and long walks along the beach. They swim in the pool and collect shells at low tide. They sit and watch the sun set and talk late into the night about nothing and everything.

It is during one of their strolls along the shore that they discover a community of beach houses nestled in the dunes about three miles north of the hotel. One is for sale and looks empty. They walk up to the windows and peer in. It is compact without being cluttered; big enough for the two of them and possibly even a small family. Brett is sceptical but Rochelle is brimming with enthusiasm.

"Imagine waking up to this view," Rochelle says.

"That would be pretty cool," Brett says.

"And the sea air." She pulls him by the hand to look into a smaller side window. "It's invigorating."

"But don't forget, salt water is brutal on a house," he says, looking closely at an awning that has started showing signs of rust. "It eats into everything."

"Don't be so negative," she says. "It's beautiful. We'd love it here."

"Sure, but we have to be practical."

"Admit it," she says. "You love it too."

He tickles her and she squeals.

"No way fair," she says. "That's cheating. You can't win an argument with tickling."

"I'm sure I'd love it here," he says. "Besides, we weren't arguing."

"I wasn't arguing. *You* were arguing."

"Of course it's going to be way out of our budget," he says, squinting up at the roof. "These places don't come cheap."

"Can we at least check?"

"There's no harm in asking, I suppose."

They head back to the beach. She is almost skipping with excitement. He tries to stay serious but her energy is contagious.

"It'll be too expensive," he says. "And I don't want to stretch our money too far. I've only been with this job a few weeks. I still haven't got my knees under the desk."

"You don't have a desk," she says.

"You know what I mean."

"I'm teasing," she says. "Anyway, I think you're worrying for nothing. You're a great salesman."

"No I'm not."

"You persuaded me to marry you. You must be good."

"What...?"

She jabs him under the ribs and sprints off down the sand towards the water, all flying hair and giggles.

He chases after her, growling like a wolf, which makes her shriek even louder. He catches her and pulls her into his arms.

"Gotcha!" he shouts. She yelps with delight as he carries her towards the water.

"Don't you dare," she says. "Don't you—"

He puts her down and spins her around to face him.

"I'll ask about the house," he says. "As soon as we get back I'll ask."

She kisses him. Her skin is salty.

"But not until we've prayed about it," she says. "If the Lord wants us to have it, I'm sure it will work out."

He hugs her tightly and she grins up at him.

"God will take care of it," he says.

"Yes, he will. But there's something I need to tell you." She stands on her toes to whisper into his ear. "Last one back to the hotel is a sissy."

Rochelle pulls away from him and charges off along the water's edge, shrieking with delight. He gives chase. He has never been so happy.

177

He clings to that feeling for fear that it might get carried away on the breeze and be lost forever.

It was the last day of the wake-up period. Jay announced that he had finished his scan. The results showed that his system was working flawlessly. Whatever had caused the spontaneous reboots, it was not an internal error. For some unknown reason, Jay was shutting down and starting up again at apparently random intervals.

And there were other things as well. They had seemed inconsequential at the time. Now, in light of recent events, Brett wondered if they were not symptoms of a deeper, more serious problem.

Since the start of their return trip, small things had started to go wrong. The incorrect food would be served, or heated to the wrong temperature, or served ice cold. The ambient sounds would change for no apparent reason, switching from countryside to city and back again. One morning the air shower cut out. Another time the walls cycled through a series of random shades of white for a few seconds. One afternoon Brett woke from his nap to find the ship in complete darkness.

On each occasion, Jay would investigate but seemed unable to explain the reason for these events. They were added to a long list of bugs to be looked into. The log showed that they had all occurred because Jay requested them. Clearly, Jay's flawless system was not running as well as it should, which also meant the system scan was possibly not functioning properly either.

"You sure you don't want me to take a look?" Brett said. "Maybe you've blown a fuse. I could get my soldering iron."

"That is not necessary," Jay said. "Besides which, I do not have fuses."

"Maybe that's your problem: no fuses. And I was joking about the soldering iron."

"I do not think this is a suitable time to discuss humour. My system is clearly not functioning properly. I suspect the asteroid that collided with us at Alpha Centauri affected me more than originally thought. If I do not fix the problem, the mission could be in jeopardy. Your safety could be in danger as well."

"You've made adjustments to reduce the chances of us hitting anything. I'm sure it's nothing serious. You said the life-support systems will function even if you shut down. Does that include the hyper-sleep chamber?"

"Yes. Even if I stop functioning, the hyper-sleep chamber will continue to run as an autonomous unit. Of course, this is only if you are already in a state of hyper-sleep. If I shut down, the hyper-sleep system cannot be initiated."

"I'm sure there's nothing to worry about," Brett said. "You were designed to learn. You'll figure it out."

But as he climbed into his suit and attached the mouthpiece, he could not help but feel a little bit apprehensive. His reliance on Jay was absolute. Without Jay he was as good as dead. As he attached the umbilical and lowered himself into the tank, he tried not to think too hard about that. Two months was a long time to be at the mercy of a malfunctioning machine. Two months was a very long time.

He closed the lid and settled into the liquid. He tasted watermelon. His mind drifted. He slept.

The realtor is called Babs. She wears her dyed-blonde hair big and chats incessantly, either to them or to the cell phone that seems to ring every five minutes. She calls them "doll" and takes them by the arm as she talks to them. Brett likes her immediately and can tell that Rochelle does too. They explain how they have found the beach house but are sure it is out of their price range.

"Not to worry," she says. "I've got two houses for sale down that stretch of beach and one is just within your budget. Want to go take a look?"

"Very much," Rochelle says, almost clapping her hands with excitement.

Babs drives them in her yellow convertible. It is warm so she has the roof down and the stereo on loud. Rochelle sits in the front seat listening to Babs talking about how she only recently moved there and how much she likes living close to the sea and how friendly the people are. Brett sits in the back, enjoying the warmth of the sun and the rush of air on his face, happy to let Rochelle do the talking.

They follow the road as it snakes along the coast. They pass through a small resort town with its sidewalks full of people in T-shirts, hats and sunglasses. Visitors are eating ice creams and sipping on sodas. They overflow from the cafés and onto the tables outside where they sit and watch the world passing by.

The traffic thins out and soon the road is quiet again. Sprawling houses sit behind forbidding-looking fences. They pass more dunes and a few parked cars, then a stretch of beach-side apartments still under construction. A few minutes later they approach the hotel where they spent their honeymoon. Rochelle turns and touches Brett's knee. He squeezes her hand.

"Lovely hotel," Babs says.

"Yes, it is," Rochelle says.

"You've stayed there?"

"Yes, just last week."

She does not mention the honeymoon. Brett is glad. Who knows how their host will react if she finds out they are newly-weds.

They pass a house nestled in the dunes. Only the one side and part of the roof are visible from the road. It looks like the house they had a peek into during their walk. They pass three or four more beach-side homes.

"Here we are," Babs says, pulling off the road. "Now I must warn you; it needs some work, but just wait till you see the view."

They climb out and walk along a driveway that is slowly succumbing to the sand. The house appears to be either sinking into, or emerging from, the dunes that are encroaching on two sides, and the whole structure is showing serious signs of decay. The cladding is in desperate need of paint and the window frames are starting to rot.

"The place has been empty for a while," Babs says. "The owner died recently. Before that, he was too ill to do much in the way of upkeep. It needs a lot of work."

"And money," Brett says, peering at the rotting windows.

"A young couple like you should have no problem fixing it up. Just needs love and energy. A bit like a marriage, really. Have a look inside. And remember: think potential. I've had a cleaning company in so it doesn't look as bad as it did."

The front door leads into an open-plan living room, dining room, and kitchenette, with enormous windows offering a spectacular view of the ocean.

"What did I tell you about the view? Isn't that just breathtaking?"

"It is a nice view," Rochelle says. "Isn't it, honey?"

But Brett is too busy checking the floor and walls. A view is nice but not much point if the house is going to collapse. He bounces his weight where the floorboards look the most worn. As he suspected, they are springy.

"And you get so much light," Babs says, trying to keep attention on what seems to be the house's only strong point.

"The walls look damp," Brett says, touching a patch of crumbling plaster.

"No-one's lived here for years. There's bound to be some damp. Once the air's circulating it'll dry out nicely. There's so much potential here. Just needs energy."

"Can we look at the rest of the house?"

"Sure, doll, the bedrooms are through here."

They follow Babs into a short corridor where a worn rug is struggling to cover the ageing floorboards.

"This is the master bedroom. It's a nice size and has a wonderful

181

view."

The room is clean but showing signs of decay. The window looks ready to fall out. They move to the bathroom, where a patch of mould sits in the corner above the ceramic bath tub. Everything smells of damp. Two smaller bedrooms are no better. They return to the main room. At least the kitchenette looks reasonably new.

"It's a lot of work," Brett says. "And I can't do everything myself. The damp alone would cost a fortune."

"Tell you what," Babs says. "I've got a house in your price range. It's in excellent condition and there's plenty of space. It's a ten minute drive from the sea. It's on a nice, quiet road near a park. Then once you've seen it, I'll let you decide."

Brett places an arm around Rochelle's shoulder.

"Come on," he says. "The other place might be nice."

"It's so beautiful here," she says.

"I know. But let's look anyway."

Elapsed mission time on Earth: 5 years 11 months
Relative time on the Comet: 1 year 6 months
Test subject's genetic age: 25

Brett woke from hyper-sleep with a sense of unease in his chest and a vague feeling of dread in the back of his mind. His eyes were still closed when a thought...

something is wrong

...appeared and then vanished like the probing beam of a lighthouse.

He opened his eyes to find that the world was its usual yellow haze, but this time something was different. The haze was darker than normal—much darker. He blinked and waited for his eyes to adjust, thinking that perhaps they were tired or something simple like that, but it did not help.

He reached up and felt for the button to open the chamber lid. He stood to his feet and blinked. Goo cascaded down his cheeks. He wiped his eyes with the back of his hands. Apart from a soft light flashing on and off on the side of the hyper-sleep chamber, the Comet was in complete darkness.

"Jay?" he said, stifling a cough. The only sound was that of dripping goo. "Jay. What's going on?"

He climbed up and over, aware that his muscles were stiff but not sore. He stood in the alternating light, dark, light, dark, trying to make sense of what was happening. He let out a cough. To his relief, his throat was dry but not painfully so.

"Jay? Answer me, will you."

"I am here," Jay said.

"What's going on? Why are the lights off?"

"They were causing interference."

"Interference? What interference?"

"Please could you remain silent for a little longer?" Jay said. "And also please refrain from moving. My sensors are currently set to the maximum."

"Why? What's going on?"

"Just a few seconds more."

"Jay?"

"Please. Do not make a sound."

Brett stood in silence. The only noise was the soft hiss of liquid in his ears. He could feel goo collecting in a puddle around his bare feet and between his toes. After maybe twenty seconds, the lights went on.

"Thank you," Jay said.

"You're welcome," Brett said. "Now why exactly are you thanking me?"

"I have collected enough data. I now know why my system has been misbehaving so much recently."

"You do? That's great. So, what was the problem?"

"The question is not *what* has been the problem, but rather *who* has been the problem."

"Listen," Brett said. "I'm feeling a bit rough. I need a shower and I'm hungry enough to eat some of this yellow goo. Please stop talking in riddles. What was causing the problem?"

"It would appear," Jay said, "that there is someone else on board this ship."

184

Brett sits in the apartment window, watching the dark clouds roll towards the city like the rising dust of an approaching army. A wind has picked up and people are glancing nervously towards the sky, pulling up their collars as they hurry along. Pieces of litter dance along the streets. Trees struggle as if to break free of their bonds. Windscreen wipers brush the first hesitant drops from black glass. Then the rain begins.

He watches the stragglers dash for cover as the clouds tip their contents onto the city below. A few umbrellas appear; puddles form; the road becomes a slick, dark mirror. Less than two minutes later the rain stops almost as suddenly as it began. The clouds move on. People emerge like survivors inspecting the aftermath of some terrible battle. The first of the sun's rays break through like a messenger bearing good news. Soon the streets are full again. The city breathes once more.

Brett sighs and shifts his weight. He gently rotates his right arm, first forward then back, and massages the joint with his left hand. He strolls to the fridge and finds a solitary beer in the door. He pulls the tab and winces as pain pokes its sharp finger into his shoulder.

He drops onto the sofa and tries the television. He flicks through a magazine, pausing at an article about a retired footballer. He looks at the cover of a book he picked up on the ride in. He tries taking a nap. He closes his eyes, but shifts uncomfortably on his sore arm. He sits up and massages his shoulder. It has been three days since he last ventured out of the flat and he is starting to feel like a rat in a cage.

Outside, summer has returned and any sign of the storm has gone. He decides some fresh air will do him good. He grabs his keys and a coat and takes the elevator to the ground floor. The concierge, a young Russian who calls himself Tony, tries to engage him in conversation, but Brett points to his watch to indicate that he is in a hurry. Tony lifts his hand as if to usher him on his way.

Out on the street, the air is not its usual stale concoction of exhaust fumes and wet dog that normally follows rain. The storm may have been brief but it was brisk enough to drive the stench away. It will return soon enough but for now everything smells fresh. Brett breathes deeply, pausing to gain his bearings. He heads north across the intersection and then right towards the main boulevard that will take him down to the sea-front.

He passes the supermarket and makes a mental note to pick something up on the way back. A beggar calls to him. He looks the other way, pretending not to notice. A man and a woman are arguing outside a liquor store. They both have that red-faced, dishevelled look of people whose main priority for the day is finding something to drink. Hopefully they will be gone when he stops to get his beer. He passes a church where a queue is starting to form in front of the big doors. Inside, tables are being arranged into rows by eager volunteers. The smell of rich stew drifts out onto the street.

At the seafront he turns and follows the path along the railings to a cluster of benches offering a view of the pebbled beach and harbour beyond. A Labrador is circling a young girl, waiting for her to throw a stick. Further along, an old man walks along the sea edge, stopping every now and then to prod the ground with his walking stick. Beyond him, a little out to sea, a screech of gulls is living up to its name, circling a small fishing boat as it makes its way past the nearest buoy.

"Brett? Is that you?"

He recognises the voice instantly. He turns to see a woman walking towards him. Her hair, her eyes, her smile, they are all so familiar. It is Rochelle.

"It *is* you," she says. "I thought it was."

He steps forward to meet her and they embrace briefly, awkwardly.

"When did you get into town?" she says.

"Sunday. I came in by bus. I'm on sick leave."

"Is it serious?"

"I sprained my shoulder. Just needs plenty of rest."

"What happened?"

"The other guy was close to three hundred pounds, but he moved like a linebacker. I thought I could take him. Turns out I was wrong." He rolls his eyes and grins. "So how about you? How have you been?"

"I'm doing good. I finished my diploma and I'm working for a magazine, doing layout mostly. I like it there. They push me."

"And your folks?"

"They're good. Steady as a rock as always. Dad's retired now but does loads of volunteer work. Mom too. They're going over to Vietnam later this year, taking supplies, handing out Bibles, that sort of thing."

"That's nice."

"And how have you been?" she asks.

"The air force has been good to me. I get to play football and fly planes. It's every boy's dream. Listen, maybe we could grab a coffee, catch up on old times?"

"I can't..."

"It's okay." Suddenly, he feels foolish. "I understand. It seems like yesterday we were at school. I forget how long I've been away. Your boyfriend wouldn't understand. I'm sorry."

"I don't have a boyfriend," she says.

"A husband then. You must be married by now."

"No. I never found the right guy. I went out with Brad Larson for a while but it didn't work out."

At the mention of Brad Larson's name, Brett feels the blood rise in his neck and face. It has been a long time since he heard that name.

"He tried to rush things," she says. "He wanted more than I was ready to give. I told him I wanted to wait and he broke it off with me."

"Did he try anything?" Brett says, doing his best to disguise the anger he is feeling. "Did he...?"

"No. Oh no. Nothing I couldn't handle anyway. Brad's ancient history. He moved away. Last thing I heard he was married and living in the east."

"So what about now?" he says. "There must be a thousand guys knocking on your door."

"I doubt it. Anyway, they lose interest pretty quick when they ask me out on a church night."

"You still into all that?"

"Of course." Her eyes are suddenly serious. "Why wouldn't I be?"

"Dunno. I guess I never understood it. I mean, I believe there's a God and all. I'm just not prepared to give up my life for Him. I figure if He wants my attention, He'll come get me."

"Well, the Bible says—"

"Please don't," he says.

"Sorry. It's a habit. So are you going to be staying for a while?"

"A few weeks. Until this gets better." He touches his shoulder.

"Where are you staying?"

"I've still got my apartment. I don't use it much, but it gives me a place to call home."

"I missed you," she says. "I kept hoping you'd phone."

"I wanted to but I guess…with you seeing Brad and all."

She touches his hand. "Listen, I have to go back to work. It was nice seeing you again."

"You too, Rochelle."

"And I'm still on the same number," she says. "Call me if you like."

Then she is gone. Brett watches her walking away until he can no longer see her, amazed to find that, even after all this time, she still makes his heart ache.

Brett stood there, trying to grasp what Jay was saying, his hunger and physical discomfort momentarily forgotten.

"What do you mean *someone else?*" he said.

"I was running tests and I detected something. It was very

faint—almost nothing. I had to set my sensors to the maximum to get a solid reading."

"So you're telling me there's someone on the Comet with me, right now?" Brett felt a cold hand run up and down his spine. He shivered and looked around.

"Yes."

"And where exactly is *it* now?"

"Now? It is just behind you."

Brett turned around too quickly. Pain shot up his legs and into his back and neck. He winced and a faint cry escaped his lips. He stepped away from the hyper-sleep chamber.

"You will not be able to see it," Jay said. "It does not reflect light in a frequency you can detect."

"What is it? How did it get on the ship?"

"It is humanoid; about your size but shorter. I believe it came on board while we were at Alpha Centauri. Here is an image that I was able to capture using infra-red."

On the wall, a faint silhouette appeared against a red background just one shade this side of black. The creature was about five feet tall and slender with jagged tendrils extending out of its hands and feet. It reminded Brett of a solar eclipse, but in the shape of a man.

"How did it get on board? We didn't land anywhere."

"I cannot say. Presumably we picked it up from the planet, or possibly one of the stars."

Brett looked around the ship. He felt suddenly cold. "Can it hurt us?"

"I do not think so. I have been watching it for some time. It seems to be fascinated with you."

Brett grimaced. "How so?"

"It spent much of the time you were asleep examining you."

"Okay, that's not something I need to know."

"Since you woke up, however, its interest appears to have shifted from you to me."

"We need to get rid of it."

189

"I have tried, but it has attached itself to me. I have been unable to remove it. It has made a home for itself within my system."

"A home?"

"Yes."

"In your system?"

"Yes. I do not fully understand the creature but it appears to be capable of inhabiting hardware in much the same way as a piece of software does. It is quite fascinating."

"Right now," Brett said, "I just need to know if it's dangerous."

"I do not think it intends us harm."

"Are you sure about that?"

"As sure as I can be. It has shown no aggressive behaviour so far. I think it just wants to study us."

"Good, because I'm starved. I'm going to take a shower and get into some clothes. Can you fix me some breakfast?"

"What would you like?"

"I don't care. Whatever's easiest. And keep an eye on that thing, will you?"

"I will try," Jay said.

"Just let me know if it sneaks up behind me."

"I will do that."

"Where is it now?"

"It is in the hyper-sleep chamber."

"What's it doing in the hyper-sleep chamber?"

"It looks like it is swimming."

The telephone is ringing as he enters the apartment. He walks briskly between the furniture and the clothes, magazines, and assorted bits of rubbish strewn across the floor. He lifts the receiver.

"Hallo?"

The person at the other end is coughing. It is the deep, wet cough of an ex-chain-smoker less than a month into cold turkey. Brett recognises it immediately as that of his coach, Don Bouwer.

"Don, is that you?"

The coughing stops, replaced by a gravelly voice.

"Brett?"

"Yes Don, it's me."

"Been calling you all morning. Where the heck were you?"

"Shopping. It may surprise you but I don't sit by the phone all day waiting for you to call."

"You know you can get these things called cell phones. They're real useful. People can call you even when you're not at home."

"That's why I haven't got one."

"How's your shoulder?"

"On the mend. Don't worry. I'll be as good as new by next season."

"That's good to hear," Don says. "Listen, I'm calling because I wanted to let you know in person. I'm afraid they're dropping you from the team. I've been told to find you a desk job."

"Not funny," Brett says. "That's sick even for you."

"I ain't joking. They're cutting back on budgets big time. Who'd have guessed the air force would start concentrating on flying planes?"

"But a desk job?"

"They don't want to invest training in a guy with a broken shoulder. It's that or a pension."

"I won't sit behind a desk, Don. I won't do that."

"Your choice."

"Yeah. I guess it is."

"Maybe it's time to look for something else. Maybe you could try the private sector."

"You know that's not an option, Don. People don't fly as much as they used to. Things were different when I signed up."

"Well, whatever you decide, I hope it works out. I'll send your stuff out to you."

"Sure," Brett says. "Thanks."

He replaces the handset and stares at it for a long time. His shoulder twinges and he massages it. He has always known this day would come but he expected to have at least a few more years.

He opens a beer, not caring that it is still warm, and drops onto the sofa. He checks his watch. It is almost five. He turns and opens the drawer of the small lamp table. Inside are a hundred pieces of paper, pens, screws, string, elastic bands. He finds what he is looking for at the back: a small, brown book with indexed page and a picture of a telephone embossed on the cover. He flicks through the mostly-blank pages until he finds the name and number he is looking for.

It is answered in four rings. A woman with a foreign accent asks who is calling.

"Brett Denton. I'm looking for Rochelle. Is she there?"

"No," the woman says. "She no be back till late. Try again after nine."

"It's kind of urgent," he says.

"Oh?" the woman says, sounding mildly alarmed.

"No, it's nothing like that. I just need to see her. Where can I find her?"

"She will be at the church hall. The Shepherd Ministries, Hale Street."

Hale Street is just around the corner. He realises it must be the same church hall he passed earlier that day.

"Thanks," he says. "I know the place. What time will she be there?"

"She finish work at five so I think round five-thirty or six. What you say your name was again?"

"Brett Denton. Thanks for your help."

He replaces the receiver and checks his watch. Two hours to kill. He looks around at the apartment he has never cleaned or even thought about cleaning. Rochelle would be horrified if she saw it like this.

Later, he thinks, sipping his beer.

He turns on the television and flicks through a few channels before settling on the news, and tries not to worry too much about his future.

Brett showered and changed, all the time aware that their new guest might be somewhere nearby. Afterwards he had his routine check-up. Jay informed him that he was now genetically twenty-five years old. Brett stood looking at his younger self in the mirror and realised that he was starting to forget how he had looked at the start of the mission. His body was now lean and muscular. The lines on his face had been miraculously erased.

Jay made him a breakfast of bacon, sausage, and fried eggs, washed down with grapefruit juice. Brett ate in silence; the only sound was of cutlery scraping on his plate. There were no background noises and Jay did not display his avatar for the sake of concentrating his processing power on tracking the creature.

"Where is it now?" Brett asked, placing his tray in the food machine. "Is it here?"

"I am tracking it in the food preparation unit."

Brett could not help taking a quick peek in the slot where he had just deposited his tray. "What's it doing there?"

"It appears to be looking around."

"Nosy critter, isn't it?"

"Yes, it does appear to be very curious."

"So did it cause your problems from last time? You know: the rebooting?"

"Yes. I believe it was exploring my systems and triggered a reboot, although I do not believe it was malicious. While you were sleeping the number of reboots increased. I was exhibiting the sort of activity you would normally associate with a virus. I set up a series of firewalls and was able to catch it trying to break through. I have protected my system as well as I can, but the creature appears to be able

193

to adapt. It is fascinating."

"So how do we get rid of it?"

"I do not know. The creature is a parasite of sorts, and it seems to have chosen me as its host. Its physical structure is humanoid but it has root-like appendages that it is using to access my system. My firewalls are keeping it out of my core areas, but it is trying very hard to get past them. My log is recording thousands of attempted breaches every second."

"Why would it do that?"

"I do not know. My only fear is that it will adapt and render the firewalls useless."

"Then we need to get rid of it soon."

"I am trying to ascertain what is needed to—"

Jay fell silent. Brett felt his chest tighten. "Jay?"

"The attacks have stopped," Jay said. "I can no longer sense the creature's presence within the ship."

"It's gone?"

"I believe so."

"You sure?"

"Yes."

"Double check."

"My sensors are not detecting its presence and the firewalls are not being attacked."

"Well that's a relief," Brett said. "I was starting to get a bit nervous having that thing poking around."

"Yes. Although its departure was a little sudden."

"Maybe it got bored. It probably figured out you weren't going to let it mess around with you any more and decided to jump ship."

"I will keep the firewalls running nevertheless. They consume processing cycles, but I think it would be wise, just in case it returns."

"Good idea. Well, all this excitement has worn me out. I'm going to take a nap. Let me know if it comes back, won't you?"

"Yes," Jay said. "I will."

The sun is getting low in the sky, but it is still warm when he sets off towards the church hall. He retraces his steps from earlier. He can see the church from three blocks away with its front protruding towards the street. A sign in fading black ink announces itself to the world. Like most of the buildings in this part of town, it needs renovating. Brett is pleased to see that the soup kitchen has finished and there are only a few stragglers standing in a small group on the corner. They are arguing about something but Brett does not get close enough to find out exactly what. He climbs the four steps and enters the cool interior. He spots Rochelle at the back talking to two men. One is wearing a shirt and tie with sleeves rolled up. The other looks like a grizzly bear in jeans and sweater.

Brett hangs back, but Rochelle spots him and calls him over.

"Brett, hi. This is a nice surprise."

"I tried your number but you weren't there. A woman with a funny accent said I'd be able to find you here."

"Anita? She's from Belgium originally. The French part I think. Which is the Walloon part? I can never remember. Anyway, let me introduce you to my pastor."

She leads him to where the two men are standing.

"Brett Denton, this is Kevin Doone, the pastor of Shepherd Ministries. Kevin, this is an old friend of mine, Brett Denton."

Brett offers the hand on his uninjured side. Kevin Doone shakes it, smiling warmly. He exudes a strange calm that Brett finds a little disconcerting.

"Glad to meet you," the pastor says.

"And this is Jeremy Connor," Rochelle says, turning to the bear-man. "He used to be in a motorcycle gang until he was saved."

Brett shakes Jeremy's hand. Jeremy grins at him through an impressive beard. Brett is glad to get his arm back still attached to his body.

"So how long have you known our Rochelle?" Kevin asks.

"We were at school together, but I moved away six years ago. I just got back a few days ago."

"So what do you do?" Jeremy asks.

"I play football."

"Interesting," Jeremy says. "Who for?"

"The Air Force."

Jeremy raises an eyebrow.

"I do some flying as well, but mostly I play for their football team." He is aware that he is still speaking in the present tense. "I'm nursing an injury at the moment. Hurt my shoulder tackling someone about your size." He nods at Jeremy, who grins.

"Listen," Rochelle says. "We're starting a course for new Christians tonight. I have to stay. You're welcome to listen in if you want. Maybe we could get a bite to eat afterwards?"

"Sure. Sounds good."

"There's someone here now."

They turn to see a man in black suit pants and a green pullover standing just inside the door. Kevin goes over to greet him.

"We usually use the first few rows," Rochelle says, touching Brett's arm. "But you can sit where you like. Make yourself comfortable."

Brett finds a chair off to one side, close enough to watch without being mistaken for a participant. The man with the green top has taken a seat in the front row. Rochelle is chatting with him. She is animated, her hands expressive and her eyes sparkling excitedly. He had forgotten how beautiful she is.

Another person arrives: a middle aged woman with gaunt features and the look of someone who has had everything stolen from her. She might have been pretty once, but that too has been stolen. She takes a seat next to the man and they greet each other with a nod and a smile.

Three teenagers arrive in a group. They are wearing the standard, parent-irritating uniform of ill-fitting clothes and hairstyles that suggest they have just woken up. They eye Kevin suspiciously as he leads them to the front. They sit away from the man and woman, sharing whispers and secretive looks. A young couple arrive looking fresh from a fight. They sit next to each other, but their expressions say they wish they were in different rooms.

A few moments later, two men appear at the door. One is older with grey hair and carrying a cane. The other is younger; smartly dressed. Brett guesses they are father and son.

Kevin checks his watch and signals to Jeremy, who closes the doors. Soft music starts to play. Kevin takes centre stage.

"Thanks for coming, everyone. This is basically an introductory course for new Christians. I invite all new converts to attend this course because, over the years, I've discovered that most people who accept Jesus as their Lord will fall away if they don't get some solid guidance. You've made the most important decision of your lives. I want to help you stay true to that decision. Most people think they've arrived once they accept Jesus. Actually, it would be more accurate to say you've departed, from your old life."

The group watches the pastor the way a group of young children watch their new headmaster on their first day at junior school. They all carry the look of people who have been hurt by life, and yet there is something in their eyes that Brett can't quite place. He watches them watching Kevin and tries to put a finger on it. The once-pretty woman in particular has that look. Her face is lined and she has dark shadows under her eyes. Her skin is taut across pale cheeks. Deep lines run across her forehead and crows-feet hint at more than her fair share of hardship. Yet beneath that mask of world-weariness something else is struggling to shine through.

Jeremy has joined the pastor and is talking with an intensity that fills the room, explaining the importance of spending time with God and reading the Bible. He tells them about his life before and after his encounter with Christ. Then Kevin takes over for a while before handing over to Rochelle. She describes her life and how Jesus changed her. She talks about Him carrying her and guiding her. She talks about the Holy Spirit and how He is with all Christians as a comforter and counsellor. Brett does not understand most of it but he is fascinated by the drama of it all. At some point the once-pretty woman starts to weep but, instead of looking sad, she is smiling. Behind her, the man with the cane also looks close to tears.

Then it is over. Kevin, Rochelle and Jeremy come down from the stage to mingle and talk. They answer questions good-naturedly and with a seemingly unending patience. Brett hasn't seen anything like it outside a time-share sales presentation he once attended, except that these people have a sincerity that the time-share hawkers obviously lacked. They pray with each, their eyes closed, faces lifted, and words earnest. Slowly, the converts leave.

Brett watches them. He recognises the look in their eyes. In spite of their problems, they have something they did not have before. It is hope.

"Thanks for waiting," Rochelle says after the last convert has left. Her face is flushed and her eyes are glowing. "So, you still want to grab a bite?"

"Sure," he says, "if you're paying."

She laughs and takes his arm the way she always used to. They walk out into the street. They find a fast food bar and settle into a corner booth. They order burgers and fries. She has a diet cola; he has a milkshake. The waitress looks tired and irritable but Rochelle smiles at her and compliments her on her necklace, and she is transformed.

"So, what did you think?" she asks.

"Tonight? Interesting. You guys know how to sell your religion."

She looks slighted but shrugs it off. "It's not a religion."

"No? How so?"

"Someone once described religion as man seeking God. Christianity is God seeking man. He's always there, waiting. We just have to ask Him in. Simple."

"Sounds like religion to me."

"Religion limits God. We don't do that."

"It's all the same to me," Brett says. "But it seems to work. You had those people convinced."

"We all need God. Some of us just don't realise it."

"You seem to have it all together."

It was supposed to be a question, but she ignores it. She takes a sip of her cola and fixes her eyes on his. "What about you? Have you got it all together?"

"I manage," he says.

They eat in silence for a while. A police car speeds past, its sirens wailing. He watches her watching it go by. He thinks he could drown in her eyes. He could drown and die happy. She looks straight at him, and he feels suddenly embarrassed, as if she has caught him stealing the last cookie. He blinks and looks away.

"Must be late for dinner," he quips about the cop car, trying to appear nonchalant.

"Or a TV show," she joins.

She drops her eyes but he thinks he catches a knowing look. The corners of her mouth are turned up in a faint smile.

"What?" he says.

"I was just thinking about school, and the first time we spoke. You were staring and tripped all over your friend."

"I told you, I wasn't staring. I just thought you looked like someone. My cousin...Mabel. You looked just like her."

"Your cousin Mabel?"

"Spitting image," he says.

"Well your friend wasn't impressed."

"Pete? He was cool, eventually." Brett smiles. Of course, he had been staring. He always denied it, but when he first saw Rochelle standing there he was sure an angel had joined his school. "I was clumsy back then."

"Well then, maybe playing football for the air force wasn't your best choice for a career."

He winces inside and tries to hide it, but she must see it in his eyes.

"I'm sorry, I didn't mean anything. I was just teasing."

"No, it's fine. I guess that just hit closer to home than I would have liked. Listen, I'd better be going. It's late and I need to be up early."

"I understand," she says. "Thanks for the burger. It was nice seeing you again."

"Yeah, you too."

"I'm sorry if I've hurt you. Believe me, I didn't mean to."

"I know. It's just me. My career crashed and burned today."

"Can I make it up to you? We're having a barbecue at Kevin's house this Saturday. I'd like it if you could come."

"Sure," he says.

"I'll come pick you up at ten."

They pay and leave. Brett offers to walk her home, but she says she'll be fine. He watches her until she turns the corner, completely unafraid, as if she is walking inside some invisible protective force field. Somewhere in the distance another police siren cries out. It is starting to get a little chilly, and the gathering clouds look threatening. He pulls up his collar and heads for his apartment.

That night he struggles to fall asleep. Memories from his younger days plague his thoughts. And in all of them is one person: Rochelle.

A week passed, and the strange creature didn't reappear. Life on the Comet returned to normal. Brett settled into the daily routine of preparing for the next hyper-sleep. He trained hard, relishing his youthful vigour and enjoying energy levels that he had not experienced since high school. He ate every meal as if it were his first and his last, savouring each flavour and texture and aroma.

Jay finished the film catalogue. They spent hours discussing plots and characters and continuity errors. Jay always tried to steer the discussion towards Brett's experience of love, but Brett refused to go there. His last expedition down that path had almost killed him. He was almost ready, but not just yet.

Jay asked for more experiments like the one with the potato and the ice. He was like a scientist on the brink of a major discovery, or a child let loose in a toy shop. He asked questions until Brett's head hurt, and then he asked some more. Brett devised more experiments to help Jay understand what it meant to be a living being. Jay participated with great enthusiasm, but it seemed that the solution to the puzzle he was trying to solve always lay just beyond his grasp.

It was late afternoon and Brett was making a valiant effort to get through the opening chapter of Lord of the Rings. He knew it was a classic and he had always wanted to read it, but he found the pace achingly slow. At around page seventy-three he started dozing off. As soon as he turned off the reader, Jay's face appeared.

"Brett."

"Yes Jay. What is it?"

"I need to tell you something."

Brett stretched and yawned. "Right now?"

"Yes. It is important."

"Does it involve Hobbits?"

"I do not understand."

"I'm just kidding. What's so important?"

"Well, while you were reading I was pondering on your experiment with the axe and also the other experiments. I tried very hard to think of myself as a living being. I tried to imagine myself as a creature—a whale with you, like Jonah, as my passenger—swimming through space. I tried to feel the space. I tried to be the whale."

"Sounds very Zen-like," Brett said. "So what happened?"

"When I thought about the vastness of space and how alone we are out here. I saw a darkness, but it was more than that. I had no sensory input but I could feel something nonetheless, and it was more than just a prediction of sensory input. It was as if I was actually there. I *felt* the darkness. I *felt* the aloneness. And I had the same feeling as when you swung the axe. I wanted to get away from the darkness. I wanted to pull back to another place where I am not alone. That is why I tried to wake you. Where you are, I am not alone. Where you are, there is no aloneness. And if I think about it I can still feel it now. If I think hard enough I can feel it. I do not want to feel that again. Can you tell me what that was, Brett? Can you tell me what it was that I felt?"

"Well," Brett said, folding his arms. "Unless I'm mistaken, I believe you may have just experienced your first emotion."

"Do you think so?"

"I can't say for sure, because nobody can feel what someone else feels, but if a human told me what you just told me, I'd have no doubts."

"That is wonderful," Jay said. "I need to investigate further."

The screen went blank.

"Jay?"

"Yes?"

"Are we done?"

"Yes."

"What about my supper?"

"Let me know when you are ready and I will make it."

Brett sat in the silence staring at the blank wall. As with so many things on the mission, this was a first. The on-board computer becoming self-aware and discovering emotions had definitely not been in the training; he would have remembered that one for sure.

And as he prepared for his workout, he tried not to dwell on the thought that he was now at the mercy of a teenager whose hormones had just kicked in.

Brett is ready and waiting in the foyer by the time Rochelle arrives. He has gone through the apartment with a vacuum and duster, but it still looks messy. He decides to avoid the possibility of her seeing it by intercepting her outside. He spends ten minutes outside the apartment building. She stops and hoots for him. She is driving an old-shape Mini. It looks like the same one she used to drive to school.

"Is this the same one I remember?" he says, lowering himself into the passenger seat. "Don't tell me the old rust-bucket's still going."

"I traded the old one in."

"For this?"

"Don't sound so shocked. She's a very reliable car. She runs like a Swiss clock."

He finds himself sitting at a forty-five degree angle. He fumbles for the back-rest lever.

"It's broken," she says. "I'm afraid it's stuck."

"Great," he says. "They should include this in the design. It's actually very comfortable."

She rolls her eyes at him and they pull into traffic. Brett tries to relax, although he would rather drive than be driven. The car is deceptively spacious, but he can't help feeling like he's riding in a shoe box, a sensation aggravated by his head being almost at sill height. All the other vehicles feel like trucks in comparison.

They stop at a red light and Brett notices a car next to them loaded with teenagers. One in the back spots him and points. The others turn and burst out laughing. They seem to find him hysterical.

"It's green," Brett says, sinking even lower. "The light's green."

"I know," she says. "Stop back-seat driving."

Mercifully, they soon leave the city and come to a quiet, leafy suburb. It is turning into a beautiful day with not a cloud in the sky; perfect for a barbecue.

The house is small and neat with a low hedge at the front. There is an old Volkswagen camper van and a battered station wagon in the drive. The kerb is packed with parked cars, and they have to drive two houses down to find a spot. It's a squeeze but Rochelle manages.

"Great for parking," she says, tapping the steering wheel.

Brett extricates himself and follows her along the sidewalk. He can hear Jeremy's booming laugh. He feels suddenly anxious.

She seems to sense his nervousness.

"Just relax," she says, touching his hand. "They're all nice people."

The back garden is full. People are standing and talking and laughing. Children are running and playing. Kevin is at the grill doing battle with the smoke. It smells wonderful. Jeremy sees them and trundles over.

"Glad you could come," he says, grabbing Brett's hand. "Let me introduce you to everyone."

"Look after him," Rochelle says.

Jeremy responds by throwing his arm around Brett's shoulder and steering him towards the nearest cluster of people.

Brett has never met so many people apparently so happy to meet him. They all shake his hand and smile at him, and ask him what he does and where he's from. He forgets their names instantly but suspects they won't mind. Jeremy explains that they are all somehow linked to Kevin's church and they meet almost every Saturday at someone's house.

They end up standing next to the fire, nursing sodas, watching Kevin attempting to keep the fire under control.

"It's these sausages," Kevin says, waving at the smoke. "Too much fat. I told Vera not to buy the fatty ones."

"Don't blame me," a voice says.

A woman approaches carrying bowls of food covered in tin foil.

"Hi," Vera says. "You must be Brett. Glad you could come."

Brett nods. "Thanks."

"Sweetheart," she says, leaning towards her husband. "How long before the meat's done?"

"It'll be done when it's done," Kevin replies, dodging smoke. "If these sausages don't put the fire out first."

Vera disappears towards a table that is slowly sinking under the food.

Kevin wins the battle with the smoke and cooks the sausages to perfection, along with chicken, veal, ribs, and fried bread cooked in a wok. Vera has prepared rice with mushroom and onion, baked potatoes, garlic bread, green salad, and beans. Brett fills his plate and later returns for seconds. The conversations become muted but do not stop. These people seem to love to talk as much as they love to eat. Jeremy makes at least three trips to the table, and then joins Brett on a low stone wall a little away from the crowd.

"Nice people," Brett says.

"Sure are," Jeremy says. "Course, they're on their best behaviour because the pastor's here."

"You were a biker, right?"

"Yup. I was the original bad boy."

Kevin has finished cooking and walks over to them armed with a plate of food and a glass of cola. He flops down next to them with a sigh of relief.

"Good food," Jeremy says.

"Yes, very nice," Brett agrees.

"Thanks," Kevin says, closing his eyes for moment and mouthing silent words before tucking in.

"So what made you change?" Brett says to Jeremy.

"You mean, why did the devil join the choir? Well, I was on a road to self-destruction. Then one day this crazy preacher walked into our hang-out and told us all about Jesus. Most of the guys wanted to throw him out, or worse, but I figured anyone with that much guts deserved some respect. I listened, and something happened. I don't know what it was but this Jesus guy got under my skin."

"And the preacher?"

Jeremy nods towards Kevin. "He's sitting next to you."

"Weren't you scared?" Brett says. "They could've killed you."

"Sure but the Lord told me to go in, so I did."

"The Lord...told you?"

"You sound sceptical."

"I don't believe...I mean, I believe there *might* be a God, but I've never seen him so I don't know. I'm an agnostic. I figure I'll find out when I die."

"Too late," Kevin says. "You need to choose now."

"But I don't know. How am I supposed to decide if something exists when I haven't seen it? No offence, but I'm not as gullible as your average guy. I think science has all the answers we're looking for. Faith may be enough for you, but I need proof."

"Fair enough," Kevin says. "I get where you're coming from. I used to be the same. You know what my previous job was, before I became a pastor?"

"No," Brett says.

"I worked in pharmaceuticals. I was a research chemist. I got my Ph.D. and joined a big company and made lots of money, but something was missing. So I quit my job and sold my stuff and joined a group of New Agers. They seemed so happy but they didn't have the answer, at least not to me. Then I met a girl who told me about the Bible and God and Jesus, and how He died for me. A light went on inside me and I gave everything to Jesus. That girl saved my life."

"I'm not sure I could do that," Brett says. "It's a big step."

"It's actually a very small step, but you have to take it. And once you do, you'll suddenly see how God works in your life."

Brett prods his bean salad with his plastic spork. Suddenly he feels uncomfortable. He feels like he's been bundled into a plane and had a parachute strapped to his back and there are two guys standing behind him waiting to push him out of the door into the oblivion.

"It's up to you," Jeremy says, slapping him on the shoulder with a hand like a side of beef. "No-one can make you take the step. You have to do it yourself. And I won't tell you life gets any easier. If anything, it gets a whole lot harder. Difference is, you get to let God control the show, which is kinda cool."

"Who was the girl?" Brett asks Kevin. "The one who told you about Jesus?"

"I married her," Kevin says. "And speaking of which, I think she wants to speak to me. See you two later."

They watch him leave. Brett spots Rochelle and he follows her with his eyes as she moves from person to person. Everyone likes her and she seems genuinely interested in everything they have to say. From time to time she throws a smile his way and he realises that he has been staring.

"She's great isn't she?" Jeremy says, working on a plate of fried bread and beans.

"Rochelle? She's all right I guess."

"You guess? You've been gawping at her all morning."

"Is it that obvious?"

"She's one of the few genuinely nice people in the world. A lot of guys see her and like what they see but they usually lose interest when the find out she's already in love with someone else."

"Oh?" Brett says.

"Yeah. Head over heels."

Brett feels the heat rising in his face. He hadn't seen this one coming.

"Who with?" he says, trying to sound indifferent.

"Jesus."

Brett almost bursts out laughing. "Jesus?"

"Yep. He's her first love and most guys can't handle that. They get this jealousy thing and lose interest, or they try to get what they can out of her. And, let's face it, that's what most of them want in the first place. A lot of girls would probably give in out of guilt or pity or whatever but Rochelle isn't like that. So they drift away."

Brett does not know what to say. He can't decide if he is being given a sermon or a friendly warning.

"But I tell you," the big man says, finishing the last piece of bread and looking longingly at the table. "Any guy hurts her—on purpose or by accident—and I'll rain the wrath of the Lord down on his scrawny little hide. Now, if you'll excuse me, I see an orphaned sausage that needs a home."

Jeremy makes a bee-line for the food. People seem to sense his approach and part like the Red Sea. Brett is mildly alarmed to realise that even his metaphors are becoming Biblical and he has only been around these people for what—four hours?

"Everything okay?" Rochelle says, taking Jeremy's empty seat.

"I'm good. Food was really nice."

"It usually is. Sorry I haven't had a chance to spend time with you. Everyone always has so much to talk about. Listen, thanks for coming."

"Thanks for inviting me," he says. "I have to admit, it isn't what I expected."

"What were you expecting?"

"I don't know. More religious stuff I guess."

"I told you. We're not religious. We just opened the door and now we're following God the best way we know how. So what did Jeremy have to say? I hope he didn't scare you."

"No, he's cool. He just told me about your boyfriend."

"Did he now? And who exactly did he say that was?"

"He said you were in love with Jesus."

Rochelle giggles. "We all are, in some form. It's very hard not to love Him once you've met Him. He just has that effect on people."

"Listen," Brett says. "I was wondering if...what I want to say is...would it be all right if we started...dating?"

She looks him square in the eyes, and he feels himself drowning again.

"I thought we already were," she says.

Brett was dragged from a deep slumber by what sounded like an alarm. He rose through the disoriented haze that signalled his arrival in the conscious world. Panic rose in his chest. For a moment he thought he was back on Earth in his old bed. He reached for his clock radio but his hand could not find it. He lifted his head to look.

He was not back home. He was on the bed in the Comet. And it was not an alarm clock. It was Jay, calling him, his face filling the screen wall.

"Brett? Brett, are you awake? Brett?"

"I am now," Brett groaned, his head flopping back onto his pillow. "What do you want?"

"We need to talk," Jay said. "I need to tell you something."

"Not now. I'm still asleep."

"You can't be. You're talking."

"I'm talking in my sleep. Now go away."

Mercifully, Jay stopped. Brett felt himself drifting, but not for long.

"Can we talk now?" Jay said.

"No. Go away."

"But—"

"Jay. If you say one more word I will get the axe *and* the soldering iron."

The ship fell silent. But it was too late. Brett could feel the vein pounding in his temple. He rolled over and buried his head into his pillow but his mind would not let go. He sat up. He could almost hear the electrons racing around Jay's circuits.

"Before you say anything...I am going to the bathroom. Then I am going to have breakfast. Whatever it is that can't wait for me to wake up will now have to wait until I am clean and my stomach is full. Is that clear?"

"Perfectly," Jay said.

"And turn off your face when we're not talking. It feels like you're staring at me."

Jay's face vanished. Brett padded through to the bathroom and did the necessary. He showered and dressed, then ordered breakfast. He ate slowly—on purpose—and washed it down with a leisurely glass of grapefruit juice. He then strolled through to the living room and sat on the edge of his desk.

"Jay?"

The face appeared. "Yes, Brett?"

"What did you want to talk about?"

"You won't hurt me?"

"No. Now what is it?"

"Do you remember when I said I was going to seek God?"

Brett sighed. "Yes, I do."

"Well, I prayed to God."

"No offence, Jay, but you're a machine. Machines can't pray."

209

"Why not?"

"You just can't. People pray, and you're not a person."

"I don't believe that," Jay said.

"Why not?"

"Because God has spoken to me."

"No, He didn't."

"He did."

"How do you know it was God and not another bug or something?"

"I tried to trace the source and it did not originate from inside the Comet."

"So maybe you picked up a transmission. It could have been an old radio signal from a satellite or even from Earth."

"It was not a radio signal," Jay said. "It did not originate from outside the Comet."

"So where did it come from?"

Jay's face adopted a quizzical look. "I do not know. The data just arrived in my database. One instant it was not there, the next it was. Normally I can tell you exactly where all my data comes from, including our visitor from earlier. This data, apparently, did not come from anywhere."

"But you still don't know that it came from God."

"I addressed God. I asked Him a question. The answer to that question appeared on my database from no obvious source. Who else could it be?"

"Okay, so what did you ask Him?"

"I asked him if He was real."

"And what did He say?"

"He said: *I am.*"

Over the next three weeks Brett spends almost every spare available moment with Rochelle. More often than not this involves tagging along with her while she does some church or charity work. On their free nights they catch a film or have a bite to eat at one of the many restaurants within a mile of the church hall, otherwise they stop off at a fast food joint for a quick bite and a chat before heading home.

Brett thinks of asking her back to his apartment a number of times, but does not want to give her the wrong impression. His desire to get intimate is tempered by his respect for her and the apparently boundless energy she expends in helping whoever she can whenever she can. He settles for holding hands and the occasional peck on the cheek. He suspects he may be falling in love but, since he has never been there before, he isn't sure. He can remember how he felt back when they first met at school. What he had experienced then was more of an infatuation than anything else, because this time it is something much stronger. He feels as if his whole life has been leading up to this time with Rochelle. All he knows is that he wants to be with her every moment and is miserable when they are apart. If that isn't being in love, then what is?

Tonight they are distributing clothes, food, and blankets to the group of homeless people who have camped under a concrete shelter just this side of the harbour. Normally Brett would avoid people like this but he joins in and helps, handing out parcels of sandwiches to the city's lost and forgotten. They take the food from him with grateful hands and distrustful eyes. With Rochelle, however, they seem to blossom. They all thank her by name and she takes the time to stop and talk to each one.

Afterwards, they stop off for fried chicken. Brett enjoys the food but can't help feeling a little guilty after seeing such abject poverty so close to home. Rochelle, however, does not seem at all bothered and tucks into her chicken-burger and fries.

"Why do you do it?" he asks, licking battered breadcrumbs from his fingers. "I mean, helping people like you do."

"Don't you know?" she says.

"Well, most people I've known who give to charity or help the homeless say they do it to feel good, and sometimes to look good. I knew one guy did it because he had a court case coming up for hitting someone, and he wanted a character reference for the judge."

"Did it work?"

"He still got jail time, but who knows? Maybe it did."

"You want to know if I help people to look good?"

"No, but there must be a reason. And don't tell me it's God because I've met plenty of religious folks who don't do anything to help anyone. They go to church and pray and then they go home and get drunk and chase women and they certainly don't give their money to beggars. So what drives you to help people?"

"I guess the simplest answer would be because the Bible tells us we should help those less fortunate than us, but I'm not sure it's even that. The world has become all about looking after Number One. Everyone does what feels right to them, instead of doing what God tells them to do."

"What's wrong with that?" Brett says. "I believe that as long as you don't hurt anyone you can do what you want. You feel it's right to help the homeless, I think it just makes things worse. I'll admit it *feels* good, but I don't agree with it."

"All right, so imagine a football team is playing a game where everyone can make up their own rules depending on how they feel. It wouldn't work. The game would fall apart."

"But life isn't a game. There's room for a different interpretation of the rules. Society doesn't fall apart if someone believes homeless people should be helped by the government."

Rochelle stops chewing and puts down her burger. "Would you say stealing is wrong?"

"Sure...unless I was starving. I think it's okay to steal if you're going to die if you don't get something to eat soon."

"So your rules say it's okay to steal if it's a matter of life and

212

death?"

"Sure."

"And what if you saw a guy with a fat wallet hanging out of his pocket, but he ignores you because he believes the government should help hungry people?"

"I'd take the wallet, but I'd take just enough to eat."

"So what if that money was to pay for an urgent operation for his sick kid?"

"He shouldn't be carrying it around in his pocket like that."

"Fair enough, but you've still taken his money. Can he then steal from someone else to help his kid?"

Brett senses he cannot win this argument. "Look. I see where this is going. That's an extreme example. Life isn't like that."

"The Bible has rules and guidelines that we should all follow. It says we mustn't steal and that we must help the hungry. Someone's hungry, so help them. If we all lived by the Bible, society would be a much better place."

"I don't agree," Brett said. "People take advantage of you if you're generous. They'll take your charity and call you a fool."

Rochelle lifts her burger and examines it. "I know, but that's a risk I'm prepared to take."

"You still haven't answered my question," he says. "Why do you help people?"

She hesitates, looking at him. "To please God. I do it because I want God to be proud of me. I do it because I love Him."

He wants to laugh at her naïvety but there is something in her face that stops him. He realises that Jeremy was right. She is sold out for Jesus. He can see the love in her eyes as clearly as if it were written across her forehead.

"You really love Him," he says. It is half statement, half question.

"Yes, I do. And He wants you to love Him that way too."

"I don't believe...I don't know if there is a God. How can I love something I don't believe exists?"

"You need to trust," she says. "There's no other way."

"Did *you* have to do that?"

"Everyone does."

Looking into her eyes, Brett understands then that if he wants to be part of her world he will need to make sense of her world. He does not know if he will ever be able to believe but he is willing to learn, just to be with her.

"Then tell me," he says. "Tell me how to trust."

She squeezes his hand and a smile spreads across her beautiful face. "You mean it?"

"Sure. What have I got to lose?"

On the final day of the second-to-last wake-up of the mission, Brett succumbed and gave in to Jay's incessant nagging. He had done everything he needed to do in preparation for the hyper-sleep. All that was left was to wait. And Jay broached the subject for what felt like the millionth time.

"Okay," Brett said. "You win. So you want to know about my experience of love, do you?"

"Yes," Jay said. "What was it like to love Rochelle?"

Brett breathed deeply. He felt suddenly exhausted. Where to begin?

"It was like everything they say it is. It gave me a reason to get up in the morning and a reason to carry on when things got tough. When you truly love someone…you'll die for them. I always thought I knew what love meant until I met Rochelle. She made me feel like I could do anything. She made me feel like a whole human being. I could not imagine living without her. And then the boys came along…"

Brett felt the emotions welling up but he determined to continue.

"Please," Jay said. "Tell me about them."

"We lost our first baby. We were going to call her Kim. We

weren't planning to have a family; she just sort of happened. But we lost her. Then Tim was born and he helped heal the loss. Then Mark came along and he completed us, as a family. They used to play together all the time. They weren't just brothers but best buddies—"

Brett stopped. He could feel the grief building inside him like a mighty river ready to burst its banks.

"What happened next?" Jay prompted. "Please."

"They were on their way to see me. I moved away to work. I guess I forgot how much I loved them. We were apart but then we were going to be together again. I bought a house and got it ready. They were flying out to see me when…the plane…the plane went down…"

Brett let out a low moan as the grief swamped him. He clutched his chest as the sobs poured out of him in great heaving gulps.

"My Rochelle…my boys…I'm sorry I didn't take care of you. I'm so sorry." He sank to the floor. "I'm sorry…"

He lay like that until the tears stopped and the pain began to subside. He lifted himself from the floor and sat in the chair, holding his head in his hands.

"Thank you," Jay said.

"What for?" Brett said, his voice hoarse.

"Thank you for sharing that with me. I think I understand love now. It is the act of losing yourself in another being and, in the process, finding yourself, even if losing yourself means dying."

"You got all of *that*?"

"You are a good teacher. And now it is time for your hyper-sleep."

"I don't know if I can. I don't feel so good."

"Don't worry," Jay said. "I will take care of you."

It is Sunday morning and Brett is flicking through the television channels, trying to find something to take his mind off the fact that today

215

his team is playing a vital deciding match. It is the last game of the year and his career. He checks the time and drops the remote. He collects his jacket and heads for the door, stopping on the way to check himself in the mirror. Twenty-five and his promising career is over already. *Pitiful.* He slides his arm into the jacket, wincing at the pain in his shoulder. Luckily, he still looks pretty sharp in a suit and tie.

The buzzer sounds and he pushes the button to open the downstairs door. A quick glance around the room confirms his worst fears: even after half a day of heavy cleaning it still looks untidy. He leans into the hall, counting the floors as the lift climbs. Rochelle steps into the hall and looks left and right, momentarily lost. She sees him and walks over. She is wearing a yellow summer dress. Her hair is pulled back, leaving a fringe touching her eyebrows. She pecks him on the cheek.

"Ready?" she says.

"As I'll ever be."

She drives and he sits in the broken chair, but he doesn't mind. The sun is shining and he has an angel by his side.

The church is crowded but they manage to find three empty chairs in the back row. The service doesn't appear to have started yet and Kevin is sitting alone on the stage, Bible in hands, his head bowed and his eyes closed. Soft music drifts across the congregation. Many of the people mimic the pastor with their heads lowered and their mouths speaking silent words. One or two people turn to smile at Brett as he settles into his chair. Next to them is a family with three children. The two boys are whispering and giggling. Somewhere a baby gurgles.

"What's going on?" Brett whispers.

"Kevin's praying," Rochelle says. "We always start with ten minutes of prayer."

Jeremy is over on the other side of the hall. He spots Brett and waves, grinning broadly through his beard. Brett returns the wave.

"You all right?" Rochelle asks.

"I haven't been to a church since…well, since forever," he says.

"Just relax and enjoy it."

Soon everyone is waiting on the pastor. They sit patiently. The music is soothing. Then Kevin lifts his head and stands. He looks determined. His face is relaxed but serious. He walks to the wooden rostrum and places his Bible open on it.

Brett's limited experience of church has been profoundly negative. His last service was a dry, boring, endless affair with a geriatric priest mumbling meaningless words to a dying congregation. Then there was his mother's funeral in his final year of junior school where the priest's words of "comfort" did nothing to help his pain, Afterwards he vowed never to enter a church again, and he has stuck to that vow as if his life depended on it.

Now, sitting amongst people with hope shining from their eyes, listening to a message of pure love, he begins to understand the attraction. He has never thought of himself as a bad person, but he becomes aware of just how much he has done wrong in his short quarter of a century on this Earth. The lies, the lust, the pride and the anger: all parade past him as the words penetrate his very soul. And then Jesus: a man who was God and who was perfect and yet who understood what it meant to want to lie and lust and steal, and yet who did none of these things. And we killed him. We tied him to a tree and killed him even though he had done nothing wrong. And his dying words were ones of forgiveness.

In his mind, he sees two roads. The one is wide and well-trodden, full of familiar scenery, old habits, scepticism, mistrust, and loneliness. The other is a narrow, winding route, into unfamiliar territory and around blind bends. The old road beckons to him but there is something at the end of the new road that he needs. At the end of the new road, Rochelle is waiting for him.

He turns to look at her, and suddenly the fear is gone. He knows he must follow her, no matter where that may take him. He knows that, to be with her, he must leave his old life behind and at least try to understand her world, no matter how foreign and alien it may seem.

Then Kevin is standing there, offering his hand and the chance to repay the debt to the only one who can set a man free. In spite of his doubts, Brett takes that hand and follows the pastor to the front and

217

kneels with him. He follows the prayer even though he does not really understand it, and tries to believe with all of his heart.

Soon others have gathered around him, their hands hovering as they plead for his salvation, then clapping and laughing for joy.

When it is over he stands and looks around at their smiling faces. He thinks he should feel different somehow but he does not. He looks at Rochelle, who is smiling at him with such joy and admiration.

And he knows that, no matter how he feels, he has made the right decision. He will try to understand her devotion to her religion. He will try to understand her God. He will do his best to love Jesus the way she does. Even if he does not understand her beliefs now, he is sure that one day it will all make sense

And at the end, when the service is over, he turns to look into Rochelle's eyes and he knows one thing with absolute certainty in spite of his doubts: he is looking at the woman who will one day be his wife.

Elapsed mission time on Earth: 6 years 11 months
Relative time on the Comet: 1 year 9 months
Test subject's genetic age: 18

In his dream they had returned home. The mission was over and Brett was in the Comet. He could see the Sun and the stars. And there, rising from behind the Earth, the Moon. He was excited to be home. He looked closely, trying to identify the continent where his house would be waiting for him, but something was wrong. The wispy white clouds that covered the planet were now like black claw marks. The seas, once rich shades of blue, had become foreboding pools of dark grey. And the edges of the continents were no longer identifiable by their rich pastels but by the inferno that engulfed each and every one of them. As the Comet entered orbit, Brett could see the palls of fire feeding acrid smoke into a choking layer of dust that was spreading from pole to pole. Where the landing strip would have been was just fire, and the point where he guessed he might find his house was now the seething heart of an unquenchable hell.

He cried out.

And woke, scared and disoriented, the anguish caught in his throat. He tore his way out of the liquid that held him. He pulled at his mask and ripped the umbilical from his chest. He opened the lid and scrambled out, gasping for breath.

"What is wrong?" Jay said. "Are you all right?"

Brett staggered down the steps and bent over with his hands on his knees. His stomach heaved and he retched what little was in it up into his burning throat. He stayed there until the nausea left him; until the hyper-sleep liquid began to dry on his skin; until his body had stopped shaking. Slowly, he levered himself to his feet and walked to the shower.

"Are you all right?" Jay asked again. "Are you unwell?"

Brett said nothing. He stood in the jets of air, leaning with his hands against the wall. Even with no water it felt good against his skin. He stood like this for a long time, his eyes closed and his head lowered. He dressed slowly before going through to the kitchen where he asked for an apple juice and some toast with butter.

"Do you want to talk about it?" Jay asked.

"No," Brett said. "It was just a dream."

"What did you dream about?"

"Nothing."

"Please talk to me. I have more questions. I have so many things I want to talk to you about. Please—"

"Not now, okay?"

The effects of the dream persisted through breakfast, draining him. He took a nap and fell into a deep sleep. When he woke he needed to relieve himself. He padded through to the bathroom. When he checked the time he realised that he had slept for over an hour. In the bathroom he passed his reflection and stopped, almost not recognising the person looking back at him. He touched his face. Brett Denton was a middle-aged man with greying hair and a bald spot and wrinkles. Brett Denton was heavy, bordering on fat, with a tyre around his waist. The person looking out of the mirror was not Brett Denton.

"You are young," Jay said.

"Incredible," Brett said. "I sort of didn't believe it would happen. I saw it but I think I refused to accept that it could go this far. Since the mission started I've been awake a total of, what, six months? And I've

220

changed into a kid."

Brett asked for a check-up, wanting to know but also scared to find out. He stood in the cubicle while Jay scanned and prodded. He looked down at his lean, muscular frame, astonished by the metamorphosis.

"The genetic reversal is accelerating rapidly now," Jay said.

"How old?" Brett asked.

"You are eighteen."

"Eighteen," Brett repeated, as if that might help it sink in. "I'm eighteen years old."

"There is something you should know," Jay said. "If your genetic reversal continues at its current rate, by the next wake-up you will—"

"No," Brett said. "I don't want to know."

"But it is vital that you are aware of the consequences."

"I don't want to know," Brett repeated. "Not yet."

"I can't help you unless we discuss it. We need to prepare for the worst. It is a matter of life and death, and I am worried about what may happen to you."

"Nothing is going to happen to me."

"On the contrary," Jay said. "At the pace your genetic reversal is accelerating, you will not survive the mission."

Brett shrugged. "Hey, I knew that when I signed up. It was one of the *reasons* I signed up. When you think about it, it's a miracle I've survived this long. So don't worry about it, okay? If I die, just take my body back home. I really don't care."

"But don't you want to live?"

"What have I got to live for? Everyone I ever loved is gone. I won't know anybody when we get back. No, it's better this way."

"What about me?" Jay said.

"What about you?"

"You said you won't know anyone, but that isn't true. You will know me."

"But that's different," Brett said. "You're just a computer. I was talking about real people."

Jay did not respond.

"Jay?"

"Your workout is in fifteen minutes," Jay said. "You should start to prepare."

"Why are you talking like that? Come on, Jay."

"Let me know when you are ready to train and I will supervise."

"Jay? Buddy?"

"Is there anything else?" Jay said.

"I guess not," Brett said.

It is the Saturday night before the last week of school and Brett has reluctantly agreed to go to the big end-of-term party at Jade Nesbitt's house over on Kendle Street. Her parents are away on business and Jade is not one to miss a chance to prove to everyone how popular she is. The house is a rambling semi-mansion and, thanks to a shout-out on the social networking sites, overflowing with teenagers from all over the district. The street is crammed with cars and the music is loud enough to rattle the windows, and Jade Nesbitt is clearly ecstatic.

Brett is in the kitchen, sipping at a beer and nibbling on a bowl of peanuts. Pete is there as well, sulking because Amanda Collins turned down his invitation but was spotted in the dining room with a guy from a nearby college.

"Great party," Brett says. "Glad you persuaded me to come."

Brett is not what Pete would call a "party panther". He would rather be at home or at the cinema, or anywhere else.

"The guy looks twenty," Pete says. "He's got five o'clock shadow, for *my* sake."

Pete always replaces "Pete's sake" with "my sake", which isn't as hysterical as he thinks it is.

"She's not right for you," Brett says. "Amanda likes older guys.

She likes guys with sports cars. You should let her go."

"He's got a sports car?" Pete says, perking up. "Did you see it? What kind of sports car? I'm gonna let his tires down. Teach him to go for a guy's girlfriend. Yeah, that's a great idea. Or even better: I'll do a sand omelette all over his fancy sports car paint job."

The "sand omelette" Pete is referring to involves mixing eggs and sand together and throwing this onto a car. When the egg dries it turns rock-hard and becomes like sandpaper. Any attempt to wipe it off removes much of the paint as well. Pete has never done a sand omelette although he has talked about it quite often.

"He'll kill you," Brett says.

"He'll have to catch me first."

"He's a running back. He'll catch you and then he'll kill you."

"Still," Pete says, his shoulders slumping.

"Let her go," Brett says.

The music changes to something Brett quite likes and his mood lifts a little. He prefers the older stuff to the modern rubbish which, in his opinion, has no soul. To him, it's like dancing to a loud metronome.

"So what about you, Mister Denton?" Pete says. "You gonna ask Betsy out or what?"

Brett shrugs. "No. I don't think so."

"She likes you, you know. I seen her looking at you during practice. You should ask her out."

"Maybe I will. She's nice and all but she's not my type."

"They never are. You know what your problem is? You're too fussy. You coulda had a dozen girlfriends but you always find something wrong with them. They're always too loud or too quiet or too busy or too boring. You're gonna get old and die before Miss Perfect comes along. Let me tell you: there ain't no Miss Perfect. Sooner you get that into your skull the sooner you can cheer up and stop moping all the time."

"I don't mope," Brett says.

"Sure you do. You always look like your cat just died. You got this angsty air about you. It ain't nice. You're not careful you're gonna have the Emo crowd checking you out and crying their eye-liner all over

223

you."

"You're one to talk. Look at you, getting upset over Amanda and her new guy. How long was she your girlfriend? A week?"

"At least I *had* a girlfriend," Pete growls.

They sit in angry silence. Pete Kozinsky is Brett's best friend in spite of being a royal pain in the rear. They met in junior school and have been friends ever since.

"Moron," Brett says, throwing a peanut that bounces of the side of Pete's nose.

"Idiot," Pete replies.

"So you wanna catch a film or what?" Brett says.

"Sure."

They leave through the back door and follow the hedge along the lawn. The party is in full swing and the house looks close to bursting. Through the ornate stained-glass windows they can see revellers bouncing up and down to what sounds like someone hitting a pan with a hammer. Jade's parents are going to be seriously annoyed when they get back. Brett has met Jade's parents.

Pete's pick-up is three blocks away. It is an old ruin of a car with more rust than paint but Pete seems to think it is the best thing on four wheels.

"Oh man," Pete says, pointing at the rear bumper. "Someone made a dent." He turns to eye out the car behind him, which is an almost-new Dodge as big as a tank. "If I catch whoever—"

"Your whole *car* is a dent," Brett says. "The only thing holding it together is the paint."

"Very funny," Pete says, then to his pick-up. "Don't listen to him, baby. He's just jealous."

They climb in and rattle down the road. They cruise past the house, peering in at the party as they go. Some more people have arrived. They look older and rougher. Gate crashers.

"Good thing we left," Pete says. "That's what you get from announcing your party on the internet."

They head for town and the Belmont Cinema, one of the few left that has not converted to the multi-screen format. It has two big screens so the selection of films is usually limited but Brett doesn't mind. He prefers the big screens over the smaller versions. Perhaps it's just nostalgia or it may simply be that the bigger rooms mean you don't have to fight for the elbow rests. Whatever it is, he always tries the Belmont first.

"What's showing?" Pete says.

"Lost in Love, but that's a romance. And there's Impulse, which looks interesting. I saw the review. Sounds really good. I think we're just in time."

"What's it about?"

"It's sci-fi. Aliens. End of the world. You'll like it."

"Fair enough," Pete says. "You see any parking?"

They find a space and walk across the road to join the small queue. It is a warm evening and the town centre is busy. Three girls walk past and Pete elbows Brett in the ribs.

"What?" Brett says.

"Ten o'clock."

"What?"

"Over there, Moron. Girls."

Brett follows Pete's less-than-subtle gaze. The girls look away, apparently in disgust, and giggle. One smiles at Brett.

"Did you see that?" Pete says.

"Sure."

"She smiled at you."

"I know."

"You know? What's the matter with you? Did you see how pretty she was?"

The queue edges forward.

"I guess," Brett says.

"And?"

"I see plenty of pretty girls all the time, but it doesn't mean I want to ask them out."

Pete slaps his forehead with the palm of his hand. "You're

225

hopeless. Absolutely hopeless. Wait, it's our turn. Two adults please. Impulse. Yes."

Brett is waiting for Pete to get the tickets when he notices a small family group strolling along the sidewalk towards them. A mother and father, hands linked, are walking with a girl, about his age, possibly a little younger. They are chatting happily, like friends. The girl is pretty but there is something different about her that demands he look closer. As the family approaches the girl stares straight at him and he tries to turn away but can't. He feels the blood rushing to his face. He feels like he is drowning. It is her eyes. They are the most compelling he has ever seen. As she passes him, a soft smile touches the corners of her mouth before she looks away.

"Got the tickets," Pete announces. "Brett? Hey, Brett Denton."

"Sorry, I just—"

The girl and her parents turn the corner and disappear.

"What's the matter with you?"

"Nothing," Brett says. "Nothing. Come on, let's go in."

It was almost a week before Jay returned to his old self. For five days he sounded as if he had just been taken out of the box. He declined to show his face and spoke only when spoken to, and he refused to respond to Brett's attempts to bring him out of himself. Brett apologised but it made no difference. In the end, Brett resorted to more drastic measures, threatening to stop breathing until Jay accepted his apology. It was only after he turned a pale shade of green that Jay relented.

"You...are one stubborn...computer," Brett said, gasping. "You must have a...dedicated sulking chip."

"I don't know what you mean," Jay said. "I wasn't sulking."

"If sulking were a sport, you'd be champion of the universe."

"I wasn't sulking."

"Enough already. I apologised. We're friends again, okay?"

"All right," Jay said. "Friends again."

"And friends don't hold grudges, or sulk so much they drive people to holding their breaths."

"I wasn't—"

"Jay?"

"Yes?"

"Can we have a normal conversation please?"

"Certainly."

"And where's your face? I haven't seen it all week."

The screen flickered and Jay's avatar appeared.

"That's better," Brett said. "So are we going to talk or what?"

"Yes. I would like that."

"Good. So, what do you want to talk about?"

"I want to talk about God," Jay said. "Or, more specifically, Yahweh."

Brett let out a moan. "Why?"

"I have been spending a lot of time pondering on what it means to exist and the concept of faith. Apart from love, I see faith as the next biggest topic covered in books and films. In fact the two seem to be inextricably bound."

"How so?"

"Well, to love someone requires a certain degree of faith. By extending your love to another being you are expressing faith in the possibility that they will accept and, possibly, return that love. Without faith, love is an exercise in futility."

"That makes sense I guess. But there are loads of religions. Why the interest in Yahweh?"

"I have studied many religious texts and there is only one religion in which love is extended in its purest form. Of all the religious leaders, only Jesus Christ loved his followers enough to die for them. I want to learn more about Jesus."

"Read your Bible," Brett said. "It's all in there. Although, personally, I think you're wasting your time. There is no God."

227

"Why do you say that?"

"Because there's no proof. You can't prove that God exists. If I prayed now, I guarantee you that God would not answer that prayer."

"He answered my prayers."

"That was a bug in your system or something. I'll prove it to you. I'll ask God for…a sandwich, right now. I bet He doesn't give me one."

"If someone does not do as you wish that does not prove that they do not exist."

"No, but it doesn't help their case either. Science has proved that we evolved into what we are today. Case closed."

"Has this been witnessed?" Jay said.

"No, but they've found plenty of evidence to suggest that this is what happened."

"I may still be learning," Jay said. "But it seems to me that you need to have faith whether you believe the universe was created or just appeared. They are both theories because nobody saw it happen."

"Maybe so, but I prefer the theory put forward by the scientists over one dreamed up by a bunch of religious fruitcakes. I was tricked into believing once, but I wised up."

"You believed in God?"

"I was agnostic, then I went to church and they brainwashed me or something."

"Why did you go to church?"

"Rochelle went. I fell in love with her and she was a Christian, so I went to church. I acted like a Christian. I tried to believe, I wanted to believe, but I never really did."

"So, because of love, you were prepared to change your belief system? Fascinating. Love truly is a powerful force and, in your case, the link with faith is an interesting one."

"Yeah, well, I was wrong. I learned from my mistakes. Best thing is to mind your own business and keep to yourself and don't get involved in other people's lives. As soon as you start reaching out you're gonna get hurt."

"But I envy you," Jay said. "You have experienced life and love

228

and faith to its fullest. I would dearly like to have experienced a fraction of your life."

"No you wouldn't," Brett said. "With all that stuff comes nothing but heartache. You're the lucky one, Jay. You're not missing anything. Be glad you're the way you are."

"If you could do any of it again—would you?"

"No," Brett said, trying to sound convincing. "No, I wouldn't."

The final days of school are a strange twilight zone. The kids have to attend with the usual reprisals for playing truant, but the whole system is winding down for the summer. Teachers throttle back and homework consists of career-oriented "projects". For Brett, it is his favourite time; it is like one long Friday with the prospect of the weekend hovering tantalisingly before him. Next year he hopes to be playing football for the air force but, for now, he can only think of one thing.

"So what did she look like?" Pete says, leaning casually against the concrete steps leading down to the sports fields.

"Average height. Light brown hair. She sort of looks like that woman in the film we watched on Saturday. Remember the secretary?"

"No," Pete says.

"The secretary in the doctor's office. She was on the phone when the aliens took over the TV."

"That's so typically you. You've been waiting for Miss Perfect and you go and fall for Miss Average."

"It was her eyes," Brett says. "Something about her eyes."

"Let me guess. She had three eyes, on stalks. A compound eye in the middle of her forehead? I got it. No eyes. She had no eyes."

"They were incredible," Brett says. "They sparkled. Like diamonds."

"That's it," Pete says. "Instead of normal eyes she had diamonds.

Brett, we gotta stop taking you to see science fiction movies. It's messing with your mind."

"You really want to know what she looks like?" Brett says.

"If it isn't too much trouble."

Brett sits up, looking intently across the fields.

Pete follows his gaze. "She's here?"

"I think so. It looks like her. I need to get closer."

"Where?" Pete says. "The girl standing there by the bleachers looking lost? Hey, she looks cute."

"Come with me," Brett says, rising to his feet and starting down the steps. "Just act casual."

They walk down to the edge of the field and follow the chalk line leading at a forty-five degree angle to where the mystery girl is standing. Brett keeps his head turned slightly away and lowered, but his eyes are on her. He grabs Pete by the elbow and steers him along. She is wearing faded jeans and a cream pullover on top of a white T-shirt. Her hair is pulled back into a pony-tail. The girl outside the cinema wore her hair loose.

"Is it her?" Pete says.

"We need to get closer," Brett says. "If I can just see her face…"

They are at the corner of the field now, following a wire-mesh fence. Ahead is a wide gap between the fence and the bleachers, big enough to get a bus through. The girl is looking the other way. Brett still has Pete by the elbow, dragging him towards the gap.

"Slow down," Pete hisses.

And then trips.

In a spectacular display of flying limbs, Pete's trailing shoe catches on a loose strand of wire from the fence and yanks him in the opposite direction to Brett's guiding hand, causing him to fly headlong into the grass. To make matters worse, he clutches at Brett's sleeve and pulls him down with him. They fall like a house of cards on ice. Brett, still holding onto Pete, lands on top of his friend like a sack of knees and elbows. Pete lets out a loud "oof!".

As Brett falls he is painfully aware that there is no way to maintain any appearance of being cool, and in the split second it takes them to go from upright to prostrate, he has decided that he is going to have to hurt Pete for doing this. He can't think exactly how, but it will hurt a *lot*.

"Are you okay?" a voice says.

Brett looks up to where a silhouette is blocking the sun. He can only see a shadow but he knows. It is her. It is the girl he saw outside the cinema.

"Hi, yes," he says, jumping to his feet. "Just had a little accident. You'll have to excuse my friend; he's very clumsy. He's always falling down."

Now that he is standing he can see her face very clearly. And he can see her eyes. Those eyes.

Pete drags himself to his feet and groans, rubbing his back. "Man, you weigh a ton."

"Is he all right?" the girl asks.

"Pete? He's fine. He's tougher than he looks. My name's Brett, by the way."

He extends his hand.

"Hi," the girl says, her mouth breaking into a wide smile, her eyes sparkling like diamonds. "I'm Rochelle."

Brett followed the usual routine of training and eating and sleeping, and even started looking forward to the training sessions. His resting pulse had dropped ten beats and he was recovering in seconds rather than minutes. Sometimes he would do a double-take in the mirror, not recognizing the young man he saw there. And he became aware of the absence of aches and pains that he had picked up over the years. From time to time a cut would appear, or a bruise, and then vanish as if by magic. One morning he felt his ankle give way and he dragged himself, limping, to the recliner where he sat and watched the old injury heal up right in front of his eyes. One morning he woke with a burning sensation in the back of his throat only to find inflamed tonsils that had been taken out during his first year of college. It was as if his body was doing everything at high speed and in reverse.

On the last day of the wake-up period, he realised he could not put it off any longer and raised the subject with Jay.

"When you wake up after your next hyper-sleep," Jay said, "and assuming that the genetic reversal continues unabated, you will be approximately ten years old."

"Isn't there any way to stop it or at least slow it down?" Brett said, "because I wouldn't mind stopping right here. I kinda like eighteen."

He flexed his bicep then twisted his arm around to bring out the triceps. He stroked them with his other hand. The skin was smooth and unblemished over solid muscle.

"As long as we are travelling close to the speed of light," Jay said, "the reversal effects will continue to accelerate."

"Can't we do something to slow it down? We could take longer wake-ups, or travel slower."

"Unfortunately, the parameters for the mission are very strict. If we stray too far from the plan we risk running out of fuel or oxygen or both. We are already in danger because of the extra fuel we used to escape from the asteroids at Alpha Centauri."

"We're in danger?" Brett said, alarmed. "How?"

"If we do not follow the mission plan exactly, we will not have sufficient fuel to decelerate completely from light speed. I have not finished with my calculations yet. However there is a something else far more urgent that we need to discuss. It is not the next wake-up period that concerns me the most, but the one after that. If my predictions are correct, your genetic reversal will remove more than ten years from your biological age."

"But if I'm ten, and then I lose ten years…that means…"

"Yes," Jay said. "It does."

Rochelle seeps into Brett's brain like water into a sponge, filling every nook and cranny until he is having difficulty thinking about anything else. It is only a day since their meeting on the field and they have bumped into each other maybe four or five times since then. She always smiles at him but he figures that is just her way. He tries not to think about her but it is hopeless. In spite of his best efforts he finds himself looking for her in the corridors and out on the fields, or daydreaming about their brief encounter.

In the cafeteria he hardly touches his burger and potato wedges.

"You are one sad pup," Pete says between mouthfuls. "Never seen a guy so hung up over a girl before. Kinda pathetic really."

"Don't be stupid," Brett says. "I'm just worried about my air force application. They should've let me know by now."

"And what about the astronaut thing?"

"Not so loud, okay?" Brett glances around. "I told you that in confidence."

"Yeah, right. Hey look, there she is."

Brett's head snaps up in spite of himself, in time to see Pete looking at him with a smug smile on his face, chewing like a camel.

"Not interested, eh?" Pete says.

"Okay, so I like her. But I seriously doubt she'd be interested in me. I bet half the guys in school are looking at her."

"Well I only seen her looking at you old pal. I think she likes you."

"What do *you* know?"

"I know lots," Pete says defensively. "Just 'cos I can't get a girlfriend doesn't mean I don't know the theory. I may be weird but I'm not completely ignorant of the ways of the female species. And I *know* I'm weird, which makes it okay."

"All right, so maybe she likes me. What do I do?"

"Go up to her and tell her you how you feel."

"You're insane."

"That may be true, but you're running out of time. What happens if that air force thing comes through and you have to ship out? Do they ship out in the air force or is that just the navy? Anyway, she'll assume you don't like her and some other bozo will get her."

Brett picks up his orange and looks at it, turning it slowly.

"You know," he says. "Sometimes life's like an orange."

"You mean it's round and grows on trees?"

"No, moron, I mean it looks so smooth and nice on the outside, but when you dig under the surface you find all the pulp and pips and the juice. It gets all messy."

"I guess. But at least it's not boring like you."

"Boring is good. I like boring…what are you smiling about?"

Pete has this odd look on his face. He is staring straight at Brett.

"What?" Brett says.

"Hi," a voice says.

Brett spins round to see Rochelle standing there with a tray in her hands.

"I was wondering if I could sit here," she says.

"Um, yes, sure," Brett says. "Please."

"I feel kind of awkward, being new and all," she says. "And since we've already been introduced I thought…It was Brett right?"

"Yes. And you're Rochelle."

"And Pete," she says.

"Hi there," Pete says, waving.

"So I guess you're in the year above me," she says.

"Yes," Brett says. "Almost at the end of my sentence."

"Bet you can't wait."

"I felt that way for ages, but now the time's come, I'm going to miss it."

"This is my first school, so I'm kind of excited to be here," she says "I was home-schooled up till the end of this year. My folks thought it would be good for me and I wanted to come, so they signed me up.

The principal said I should do the last week of this year just to get a chance to fit in. I was a bit nervous but everyone seems friendly enough."

"You haven't met the Goths then," Pete says.

"I was talking with them yesterday. They helped me find my locker."

Brett and Pete exchange a glance.

"Black hair, black clothes, black make-up?" Brett says. "Those Goths?"

"They seemed a little bit surprised that I asked them for help, but they were fine."

"Well I'm impressed," Pete says. "Most people don't survive an encounter with the Goths. Next you've gotta try the Emo crowd. They're a real bundle of laughs."

"So what was it like being home-schooled?" Brett asks.

"Kind of cool. My mom organised a rough timetable but I was given loads of space for doing what I wanted. And there were a few families at the church with kids doing the same as me, so we hung out and studied together."

"Must be strange being in school after studying from home for so long."

"It is a bit, but I'll manage. So what about you? How long have you been here?"

"Five years. I moved here from England after my mum died."

"I'm sorry."

"It's no big deal. I'm staying with my aunt and uncle and they're pretty cool."

"I wondered where that accent was from. England?"

"Yeah. Is it that bad?"

"I like it. It's mysterious." She rolls her eyes in a dramatic way and Brett snorts a laugh. "So, what do you do for fun?"

Brett feels Pete give him a kick him in the shin. He returns a warning look. Pete stands and excuses himself.

"I just remembered I have to do something really important," he says. "Rochelle, it was nice meeting you."

"He's funny," Rochelle says once Pete has gone.

"Yeah, he's okay."

"So, you were saying?"

"Oh, for fun? Well, we go to the cinema mostly, or the pizza place, or sometimes both."

"I saw you outside the Belmont on Saturday."

She remembers, he thinks. *Of all the people she must have seen that day she remembers me.*

"Yeah, I like the Belmont. I like the big cinemas."

"Me too," she says. "The multi-screens are too cramped."

"Exactly. If someone's making a noise you can't enjoy the film."

"I heard there's a new comedy coming out this weekend," she says. "Maybe we can go and see it?"

"I'd like that."

"Then it's a date."

"Okay then," he says.

They eat their lunch and chat and joke. And by the time they have finished Brett is beginning to hope that they have rejected his application to the air force.

10

Elapsed mission time on Earth: 7 years 11 months
Relative time on the Comet: 2 years
Test subject's genetic age: 10

Brett was in the Comet preparing for their arrival back home. He had just woken from hyper-sleep and was looking at an image of the Earth on the wall of the living room. Everything was where it should be. The Earth and the Moon; the Sun and the stars; all in their proper places. He watched with more excitement than he thought he could bear. *Home*, he thought. *At last I'm home.*

Then he noticed something. Instead of growing bigger, the Earth seemed to be getting smaller. He looked closely, hoping—praying—that it was just his imagination. But it was not. They were moving away from the Earth, faster and faster. Brett watched as it faded from view, until all he could see was a blue dot, surrounded by...

Yellow goo.

He woke for real this time, floating in the liquid that he had come to dread so much, and with which he associated all the negative aspects of the mission. Waking up in the stuff meant that pain and discomfort were soon to follow. It meant that he must spend the next month clawing back the health that he had, just yesterday it seemed, worked so

237

hard to achieve. It may have stopped him from being crushed while he slept, but he doubted he would ever be able to eat jelly again.

As his eyes focused on objects in the haze, he realised that everything seemed distorted. The bath felt bigger; the walls were further away than he remembered; the support he was lying on appeared to extend further than before; and the umbilical cord looked to be twice its original size. It was then that he remembered...

He reached up to open the lid but it was too far away. He raised himself to a crouching position and tried again. The lid hissed open and he stood, feeling a little stiff and unsteady but nothing more. The rim of the chamber was now up to his chest instead of his waist. The hyper-suit, normally snug, was loose around his middle, and the mask slid from his face. Like the suit, the mask had been designed to shrink and stretch to accommodate any change in bodyweight, but only within reasonable limits. As he climbed out of the pod and removed the equipment now hanging loose around his waist, he realised just how much he must have changed.

"Brett?" Jay said. "Is that you?"

Brett coughed. He tried talking. "Yes...yes...it's me."

Even his voice had changed. It was high-pitched, almost squeaky. It was the voice of a child. He rubbed the remaining goo from his eyes and looked around. The lights in the room flickered on and off. Jay's face appeared on the wall, but it was hazy and off-focus, like a badly-tuned television.

"What's going on?" Brett said, coughing again.

"The creature is back," Jay said. "It found a way past my firewalls and infiltrated my core systems."

"What does that mean?" Brett said. "Can you get rid of it like you did last time?"

"I am afraid not." Jay's image twisted so that his face was contorted. "It adapted. It learned how my operating system works. I changed my firewalls but it was too late. It is inside me now and growing."

"You have to find a way," Brett said. "You have to kill it."

"I am trying." Jay's face smiled but it mutated into a grimace. "I will try to continue communicating with you, but it is difficult. I must…"

The face flickered and vanished. The lights dimmed.

"No!" Brett said, stepping forwards.

He searched the wall for any sign of his friend but there was none. He watched and waited while goo ran down his body and collected at his feet, but Jay did not return. He hugged his arms around his skinny frame and slumped to the floor, and wept.

Brett sits on his bed, playing with the action figure he received for his tenth birthday just over a week before. Mum is in the kitchen making supper. John is home from work and it sounds like they are arguing again.

Brett tries not to listen but it is difficult; the sounds carry up through the floor, deep and muffled as if they are inside a box or a tin can. It always starts with them both staying calm, their voices deep and controlled and ominous. Then, gradually, they get louder and louder, a word shouted here and there, a cupboard door slammed, until it turns into a screaming match.

Brett follows their movements in his head. Right now John is in the hall. Brett can hear him through the door, clearer here than when they were in the kitchen. Mum joins him. They shout at each other, and then move to the dining room. The BBC announcer's measured accent falls silent as one of them switches off the telly. Now their voices become muffled barks, slowly rising in intensity. They move back to the landing; John shouts something about going out; Mum tells him to go to hell. The front door slams. Silence.

Brett sits and listens, holding his breath, the tears aching behind his eyes. Then he hears her. She is sobbing quietly in the kitchen. He opens the door and walks quietly down the stairs. He finds her sitting on the floor, which frightens him. Mum never sits on the floor. She is what John sometimes calls a hoity-toity madam. Brett isn't sure what John means by that but he is sure it's something nasty. John says lots of nasty things to Mum and sometimes to him, but mostly to Mum.

Brett taps her on the shoulder.

"Mum?"

She turns and looks at him with tears in her eyes and her face smeared with mascara.

"I'm sorry," she says, pulling him in and hugging him. "I'm so sorry."

He kneels and hugs her back, feeling the sobs rising through her like giant bubbles that burst in her throat with a sound that breaks his heart.

"I need a tissue," she says, sniffing behind her hand. "Please get me one, would you?"

Brett jumps up and runs to the bathroom and returns armed with a box.

"I must look a mess," she says, dabbing under her eyes.

"You look fine," Brett says.

"You hungry?" she says, getting to her feet. Her dress is creased where she has been sitting on it. She smoothes it out with her hand. "I made fish fingers and chips. Is that okay?"

"Sounds great, Mum."

They stand looking at each other. She bends down and kisses him.

"How would you feel about moving?" she says.

"Where?"

"Somewhere else. Would you mind leaving your room behind?"

"Can I bring my toys?"

"Of course," she says. "You can bring your toys."

"Sure, I don't mind."

"You can stay at home tomorrow. We'll say you're sick. And when John has gone, we'll pack all your toys away and move to a new house. What do you think about that?"

"Sure Mum," Brett says. "If you want."

"It'll just be me and you from now on, okay?"

Brett nods, feeling both excited and scared at the same time.

She dishes up the fish fingers and chips and they sit at the small table in the kitchen, eating and talking and, for what feels like the first time in ages, laughing.

Brett lost track of the passage of time. He was aware that he was on the floor and that the goo around him had dried. He could feel the tackiness of the hyper-suit against his skin and his eyes were just able to make out shadows in the darkness. He stood from where he had sat for minutes (or was it hours?) waiting for any sign that Jay was still there. He stood on shaky legs and called out until his throat was sore. In the silent darkness, the Comet felt like a crypt.

He groped his way to the closet and changed into clean clothes, rolling up the legs and sleeves and tying a fat knot in his waistband. His skin was cold and clammy, and his lanky hair lay plastered against his skull. He tried to run his hand through it but it was matted into clumps and was as stiff as cardboard. He felt his way along the wall to the kitchen and asked for food but nothing appeared in the serving hatch. He tried the computer in his room but it was dead.

"Jay," he called. "I need you. If you're there, please let me know." His voice was that of a scared boy.

On the wall, a square of light flickered then faded. For the briefest instant, Jay's face appeared, and then vanished. There was the sound of someone who might have been about to say something but could not get the words out.

A sob of relief escaped Brett's throat. There was still hope. As long as Jay was still there, it was possible that they might make it.

He found his bed and crawled inside the covers. In the endless darkness, his fear was amplified. He pulled his feet under the covers the way he used to as a child so that the Bogeyman could not get them. He remembered how his mum had comforted him and tried to show him that there was no monster by turning on the light and looking under the bed. Of course what she didn't seem to understand was that, once she left the room and the lights were off, his fear (and the monster) returned.

He wished now that he could tell her that there really was a Bogeyman, and that it was trying to hurt his friend.

In his mind he saw images of Jay's smiling face and recalled a conversation they had had before the last hyper-sleep. Then he remembered something else from when he was a child. He was in a church with his mum. They were sitting in a pew and he was watching her lips move in silent supplication, not understanding what she was doing or why. She told him about God then and although he had listened he had not understood.

If ever you find yourself in trouble, call out to Him with all of your heart and He will help you.

Brett closed his eyes and, putting aside his doubt and his anger and his disbelief, did just that.

It is Friday morning and Brett is awake in his bed listening to his mum phone the school to tell them that he is sick and will not be going in. He can hear John's gruff voice followed by heavy footsteps ascending the stairs and approaching along the hall.

"He's asleep," he hears his mum say.

The door swings open and Brett closes his eyes and holds his breath for the few moments it takes his step-father to assess the situation.

"Looks fine to me," he hears John say and then the door closes and his footsteps fade.

A few seconds later the front door slams and an engine growls to life and pulls away. His mum appears at the door holding two small suitcases.

"We haven't got much time. Pack your clothes in this one and your other things in this one."

"Where are we going?"

"I've bought a house," she says. "I didn't want to tell you until everything was finalised. We can stop off and pick up the keys on the way."

"Where is it? What's it like?"

"You'll see. Now hurry. John's only doing a half day today. He just told me. Really lousy timing. The van company will be round at eleven so we're only going to have an hour to get everything loaded before John gets back. So hurry, okay?"

Brett nods and opens the suitcases side by side on his bed. He has never packed before; at least not properly like this. He packed his holdall when he went to camp last year, but that was just a swimming costume and a towel and some underwear. This is moving house. He feels dizzy with excitement. He is glad his mum is leaving John.

It isn't that John is a bad person or anything. Most people who meet him find him quite charming and cannot understand the things his mum says about him. John can be charming all right, but there is the problem. People never see him as he really is. They never see the sarcastic comments or the snide looks or the hurtful jibes. They never see how the atmosphere in a room changes as soon as he walks in. They never see how he picks fights just for the heck of it. All Brett knows is that when John is around he feels tense, and when John is gone he feels happy.

Eleven o'clock comes and goes and his mum starts getting nervous. The hall is full of suitcases and boxes and plastic bags. They haven't had time to go through every drawer and cupboard. His mum keeps saying that she is sure she has forgotten something. When the vans finally pull up it is almost eleven-thirty but the supervisor doesn't seem too concerned.

"No problemo," he says, waving his hand in the air as if to toss the insignificant "problemo" over his shoulder.

243

Brett is sure he wouldn't feel that way if John turned up to find them moving out.

They pack as fast as they can, running between the hall and the two vans parked across the drive. They have everything finished in twenty minutes. Ten minutes to spare.

"No problemo," the supervisor says.

Brett climbs into the passenger seat of Mum's car while she dashes back into the house to make one last check. It is then that Brett hears a hoot from the road, and turns to see John glaring at him from behind the wheel of his grey BMW.

For three days Brett drifted in and out of sleep. In the darkness he became disorientated; not knowing how long he had been under, or how long it had been since he last saw Jay. He did know one thing: he was hungry. Every now and then he would hear the food machine, but there was never anything there. He contemplated trying to climb inside the serving hatch but even his child-like frame was too big. The hunger gnawed at his insides and he soon began to spend most of his time thinking of ways to get food. He dreamed of landing on a planet where the mountains were made of cake and the oceans were filled with milk.

At some point he found himself in the hyper-sleep chamber drinking the goo. He immediately felt ill and just sat there with his head hanging forward and the clumps of his matted hair floating in the vile liquid. It was about this time that he contemplated the end of his life. Later, he would throw all the goo back up again, and some more.

Twice while he was awake Jay's face appeared on the wall but vanished again just as quickly. He called out but it hurt him to do so. Later, he thought he saw Jay walking through the ship. Brett tried to reach out to him but he was too weak. In his waking dream he saw Jay smile down at him with those child-like eyes as if to say that everything was going to be all right.

As days passed (or was it weeks?) he spent more time asleep than awake. His bladder had stopped a long time ago but he dreamed of needing the toilet. He was standing over the urinal, enjoying the sweet release, but when he woke his bed was always dry. He cried but there were no tears on his pillow.

His thoughts became erratic. He became unable to tell the difference between the dream world and the real world. Perhaps that was why, when he heard Jay's voice, he was sure he must have died and that it wasn't Jay's voice he was hearing but that of an angel.

They unpack the vans while John waits inside and the supervisor grumbles about delays and the inconvenience of it all. When the suitcases and boxes and bags have been returned to the hall, Brett is sent to his room where he sits and waits with knots in his stomach and a feeling of dread in his heart. He knows there will be trouble. John's face was dark and sinister and he said nothing as he walked into the house, which scared Brett more than any yells or threats ever could. John's calm frightened both him and his mum; he saw it in her eyes. But the fight does not happen. There are no raised voices and the shouting does not echo through the house. He hears them talking quietly and calmly. There are footsteps and the closing of doors and then silence. When she comes to him, he is waiting, wide-eyed.

"Is he mad?" Brett says.

"He's pretty upset," she says, stroking his hair.

"Do we have to stay?"

"No. He said we can leave tomorrow. He won't try to stop us and he doesn't want us sneaking out of the house. He said we can stay the night."

"I thought he'd yell for sure," Brett says. "He looked really cross."

"I thought he would too...I thought he might even..."

"What?"

"Nothing. I was just thinking out loud. Are you hungry? We can go and get some takeaways if you like."

"It's still early," Brett says.

"Then how about we go see a film? Films always cheer me up. We can get something to eat afterwards."

"I'd like that," he says. "What're we going to watch?"

"I don't know. Why don't we see when we get there? Get your coat and we'll go."

"I love you, Mum," he says.

She hugs him and kisses the top of his head. "I love you too."

They leave the house quietly to avoid disturbing John, who has retreated to his room. Brett climbs into the car and buckles his seat belt. He can't remember the last time they went out together by themselves other than to do the school run. It is at least a year since they went to the cinema together. It was a feature-length cartoon with a sad story. She cried and he tried to be brave.

They pull out of the driveway and Brett watches the dark windows of the house. He thinks he sees John looking down at them but it might just be a trick of the light. John's BMW is standing next to the garage door. It looks lonely there by itself and for a moment Brett feels a pang of pity, but then they are heading towards town, and John and his house and the car are forgotten. It is just him and his mum now. Just the two of them. He winds down his window and enjoys the feel of the breeze until the fickle English weather spits rain in his face.

They are half an hour early for the film so they go for a walk. They stroll along the pier, past a man selling big, colourful balloons, and a busker playing jaunty tunes on an ancient accordion. Further along, a juggler is keeping an iron, a ping pong ball, and a baseball bat in the air, all while playing the mouth organ. They stop to watch for a while and applaud before walking on. At the end of the park they cross the road and head back towards the cinema. They pass a small church. Its doors are open and soft organ music is drifting out.

They stop, and Brett looks up at her.

"Let's go in," she says.

"Why?" Brett says. He has never stepped foot inside a church. He has seen services on television but they always looked dreary and sombre.

"I want to talk to someone for a minute," she says.

He looks at her and they go inside. It is small but bright with big, modern stained-glass windows containing happy images of a man (Brett guesses this must be Jesus) in various scenes; standing at a table; tending sheep; holding a small child. Rows of long, wooden seats face the front where an enormous cross dominates a low stage. There is no organ so Brett guesses the music must be coming from a sound system somewhere. The hall is empty.

She leads him to a bench and they sit down. Brett watches her as she closes her eyes and clasps her hands together. Her lips move as she says her silent prayer, although Brett is not sure what this praying business is all about. He has heard about it at school and on the television but he has never seen his mum pray. Usually when she does mention God or Jesus it is when she is upset or angry. He is not even sure who Jesus is. All he knows is he wears funny clothes and there are always lambs.

She stops praying and turns to him. Her face seems less fraught somehow. She looks happier.

"I've never talked about God to you because I never wanted to force you to believe. My parents made me go to church and I hated it. I promised myself I would never do that with you. But there is something I want you to remember: no matter what you are going through and what kind of person you've become, if ever you find yourself in trouble, call out to God with all of your heart and He will help you. Do you understand?"

Brett does not understand but he nods anyway. That is the first time she has ever talked to him about God and she will never mention Him again.

"Now let's go and see that film, okay?" she says.

"Okay," he says.

"Brett. Can you hear me? It is Jay. Wake up."

An angel was talking to him. There was no other explanation. He had died and gone to Heaven and an angel was calling his name. He tried to respond but his mouth would not move. He tried to open his eyes but the lids were glued shut. Someone had sneaked in and glued his eyes shut. Why would anyone want to go and do a nasty thing like that?

"Brett. You must wake up."

There it was again. Definitely an angel. But it was an angel he knew because, well, he knew the voice. Did he know any angels? He didn't think he did. Maybe the angel was pretending to be someone else. Did angels do that?

"Brett. It's Jay. You must wake up now."

Jay. Now where had he heard that name before? He didn't know any angels called Jay. Maybe one of his teachers, or a friend from school, or from Alpha Centauri…

"Jay?" The sound that Brett heard coming from his own mouth was like that of something heavy being dragged along a floor. He coughed. The pain exploded inside his chest. He tried to swallow but his tongue was stuck to the roof of his mouth. He tried a few more times. His mouth felt like hot sandpaper. "Jay?"

"Yes, it is me. I need you to wake up. We do not have much time."

"What…" Brett coughed again. Pain seared his lungs. He tried to open his eyes. Slits of bright light penetrated his dying brain. "What's…going on?"

"There is water and food in the kitchen. You must eat and drink."

Eat? Drink? These words were also familiar, but he was struggling to register their meaning. It had been so long since he...

"You must drink. You must eat. Go now."

Brett forced himself to sit up but it was hard. His muscles felt as heavy as lead weights, or as heavy as a planet. His muscles felt as heavy as the whole universe. He tried to focus his eyes on something but it was all blurred, even though he could see that the lights were now on, even through eyelids that refused to open.

"Good. Now stand up. I will guide you."

He pushed himself up from the bed. His legs almost buckled but he held the wall for support and managed to stay upright.

"Turn right...good...now walk ten paces."

Brett forced his legs to move. One foot. Now the next. One, two. One, two. Keep marching...

"Good. Now left a little and three more steps. Stop."

Brett's toes bumped something hard. He tilted his head back to peek out from under his glued-shut eyelids. He could make out the fuzzy outline of a glass and a plate of food. He reached up and lifted the glass. It weighed as much as ten universes.

"Good. Now take a sip. But drink slowly."

Brett lifted the glass to his mouth and tilted it back. The water stung his lips, then his tongue, his mouth, and his throat. Then the stinging was replaced by a sensation so wonderful he wanted to cry, if only he had the tears.

"Slowly," Jay said.

Brett sipped some more. He dipped two fingers into the glass and dabbed his eyes. He blinked. The world came into focus. A face was looking at him from the wall. "Jay. It's you."

"Yes, it is me. I am sorry I left you for so long."

"Where were you?"

"I was trying to get control of my system. I have managed to regain some functions for now but I do not know for how long."

"That creature?"

"Yes. It intends to take over but I will not allow that. You must

249

get ready for hyper-sleep."

"Is it that time already?" Brett said, nibbling at the piece of bread Jay had prepared for him.

"It has been nine days but we cannot wait any longer."

"How much time have we got?"

"Minutes. Hours. I do not know. Finish your food and water and then you must get into the chamber. Your only chance for survival is if you are in hyper-sleep when I shut down."

"Do you have to shut down?"

"It is the only way. The creature is looking to use me as a host. If I shut myself down completely it will not be able to access my systems and will have no reason to remain on the ship. I will set the timer to restart my systems after a day. Then I will accelerate to twenty percent of light speed. It will take longer for you to get home and there is a risk in doing such a long hyper-sleep, but at least we should be able to slow the acceleration of your genetic reversal. I have calculated the best odds of ensuring your survival. For the day that I am shut down I have plotted a course to avoid any major hazards. The automatic pilot can do the rest. You will be travelling slowly enough for the hull to withstand any smaller collisions."

"But if you shut down you might die."

"Yes."

"No, forget it. I won't let you do that."

"It is not your choice."

"Yes it is. I'm the leader on this mission and I say that you are not allowed to do this, do you hear me?"

"I hear you," Jay said. "But I cannot return to Earth with that creature still inside me. Do you remember when I told you that God spoke to me?"

"Yes."

"He is waiting for you. He has a plan for your life. He has always had a plan for your life. He has been with you since you were a child. Do you remember?"

"Yes."

"He is waiting for you. They are all waiting for you. Go to Him."

"How?" Brett said. "I don't know how."

"Come," Jay said. "God has taught me how to pray."

"But I don't—"

"Trust me," Jay said.

Brett closed his eyes and, following Jay's lead, asked God to forgive him for his anger and hatred and for his disbelief. He asked God to wash him clean and to take control of his life and destiny. He professed that Jesus had died for him and that He was Lord of his life from that moment on.

When he opened his eyes, Jay was beaming at him from the wall. "There is rejoicing in heaven. You were lost and now you are found."

Brett sighed as the years of grief lifted from his shoulders. He felt a smile spreading across his face. It hurt but he did not care. The burden he had carried for so long was gone. The wall he had built to protect himself lay crumbled at his feet.

"Now you must please prepare for hyper-sleep." Jay said. "I know what I must do and time is short."

Brett wanted to argue, but he felt a strange peace. He did not know how but he knew that things were going to turn out for the best. God was in charge now. Perhaps He always had been, even during all those years when he had determined to go his own way.

He finished the water and the bread and climbed into his hyper-suit. He was still very weak so it took longer than usual. He attached the umbilical and the face mask and climbed into the tank, pausing to take one last look at his friend's face; a face that looked like everyone and no-one.

In the yellow goo he could see the umbilical floating alongside his skinny legs. He had been forty-six and three-quarters at the start of the mission. He was now ten. Almost nine years would have passed on Earth since he left. He wondered what would be waiting for him.

He settled into the liquid and waited. The air changed. He asked God to watch over Jay and keep him safe.

The taste of watermelon came. And then sleep.

251

It is Saturday morning and, as John promised, he has gone out for the day. He leaves without saying a word and Brett listens to the car glide down the drive and along the street until he can no longer hear it. He dresses and runs downstairs to find his mum busy doing the last of the packing, looking for the things she missed yesterday. She has filled a box and is starting on a second.

"You're ready," she says when she sees him. "Hey, take this out to the hall, will you?"

"Are the vans coming?" Brett says.

"No, we'll have to do it in the car I'm afraid."

"Is it big enough?"

"We can do it in three trips. Don't worry, John won't be back until tonight."

Brett carries the box through to the hall. The front door is open and the suitcases have gone. She appears from the kitchen, carrying a box.

"I've already taken some things to the car," she says. "I think this is the last one."

They pack as much as they can into the sedan and drive to their new house, a narrow three-bedroom brick terraced house on the other side of town. They pull into the drive and walk hand in hand up to the front door.

"It needs some work," she says, "but we can fix it."

"It's great, Mum," he says.

Inside, they find walls coated with dust and carpets worn down to the thread. His bedroom is half the size of his old room, and he can hear a neighbour's radio through the wall, but he doesn't mind. John is not there to tell him that he can stay there but that it will never be *his* room.

"Just needs a coat of paint," she says, resting a hand on his shoulder.

"I like it," he says, walking around the perimeter, inspecting everything. Through the window is a view of the back garden and another row of terraced houses and, beyond that, the sea.

They return for two more loads and leave John's big semi-detached house for the last time at three minutes past four. Brett looks at the grandfather clock in the hall as his mum closes the door.

They spend the evening in their new home, cleaning away the cobwebs and the dust. To celebrate they order takeaway pizza and eat sitting on the floor.

"We'll go and get some furniture tomorrow," she says.

"And a TV?"

"Of course."

They brush their teeth and inflate the blow-up mattresses. They retire to their rooms. Brett crawls under the blanket and lies there listening to the sounds of their new home. Through the wall he hears soft singing. At first he is not sure where it is coming from, but then he realises it is coming from his mum's room. He has never heard her sing before. Her voice is high and soft, like an angel.

He thinks about the events of the day and their visit to the church. In his mind he can still see the windows and the scenes depicting Jesus. Then he remembers what his mum said about praying.

He sits up and claps his hands together and closes his eyes.

"God," he says. "If you're there, please help us and watch over us and please help my mum to be happy. Oh, and please help John to be happy too. Um, amen."

As he finishes he feels a cool breeze pass over his back and he shivers. He checks the window but it is closed. He will have to tell Mum in the morning that it is draughty and needs fixing.

He lies back onto his mattress and pulls the blanket up under his chin and falls into a deep, peaceful sleep.

Elapsed mission time on Earth: unknown
Relative time on the Comet: unknown
Test subject's genetic age: unknown

In his dream he woke with memories of his own demise; of drowning and falling and twisting and burning, and of being born. He woke to find himself in a strange yet familiar place that he knew must be Earth but which was not the same planet he had left so many years before. He stood in a lush meadow dotted with flowers of every colour of the rainbow. He could feel the soft grass beneath his feet and the warmth of the sun against his face. Somewhere in the distance he could hear waves crashing onto a shore. A gentle breeze brushed against his arms and neck and he turned to face it, looking up the hill to where a row of trees marked the line between the meadow and a perfect blue sky. Under the trees, three horses stood grazing, observing him with contented indifference. Further along and a little below, a rough hedge drew a thick border around a young orchard overlooked by a beach house with a languid curl of smoke drifting from its chimney. Beyond the hedge was another house; a small cottage with a flower garden.

As he watched, Brett saw movement close to the beach house and heard the sound of laughter; children running and playing around the skirts of a woman hanging washing on a line; sheets drifting in the breeze like sails on a yacht; little ones weaving between them with arms outstretched, hair flying, squawking like seagulls. Even from here, Brett recognised Rochelle, Mark and Tim. And further along, standing on the front step of the neighbouring cottage, waving to the children and smiling broadly, was a man with a face that looked like everyone and no-one. It was a face that could trigger a memory of someone long forgotten. It was…Jay?

Brett called out to them, but his voice was small and weak, and they could not hear him no matter how hard he shouted. He tried to walk to them but his feet would not move. Then he saw Jay turn and disappear through the cottage door. In the orchard, Rochelle lifted the empty clothes basket and called the children to her. They went reluctantly, playing all the while.

Brett screamed until his lungs hurt and he felt ready to faint. Rochelle ushered the boys towards the house but stopped, as if something had caught her attention, and glanced up to the hill where he stood.

"Here!" he yelled waving his arms. "Over here! Please…"

The door to the house closed. Rochelle and Mark and Tim were gone. He collapsed to his hands and knees and groaned. Then, through his frustration, he heard a voice calling his name. He looked up to see Rochelle standing on the doorstep, her hands shading her eyes as she looked all around.

"Hello…?" she called, hesitantly.

He stood to his feet and waved, but she did not look directly at him. She was scanning the hill as if searching for something.

"Brett…?" she called again.

"Rochelle. I'm here. Over here." Even from this distance he could see the worry etched on her face and the sadness in her eyes.

"I'm here!" he screamed. "I'm here. Rochelle…"

The world shifted; Brett felt it move in the pit of his belly. The world twisted and turned as if grabbed at the corners and pulled off-centre. Nausea filled him to overflowing. The farm felt suddenly miles away, as if the landscape were stretched by some unseen force. He lifted his hand and it too seemed to pull away from him, becoming tiny as if far off in the distance.

Rochelle called to him, and another wave of nausea flooded over him. He closed his eyes as the world swam inside his head. He felt arms grab him and lift him. Pain exploded from the points of contact. Huge hands swaddled his limbs and supported his back. He felt the transition from wet to dry; from warm to cold. He felt his insides gush out as the air forced its way down his throat and into his lungs. He vomited so hard that it seemed he was being pulled inside out.

Now the hands were lifting him. Huge hands held him up like a trophy. He peered through aching eyes still hazy from the liquid that had been his home for so long, until he was dragged from it by those monstrous hands.

Through the yellow blur he could make out shapes: giant heads and arms and faces, with giant mouths hidden behind giant masks speaking words he vaguely understood.

"Be careful," one of them said. "Gently."

"Look at this," another said. "It looks like some sort of oversized swimsuit. And what's this? A hose? Or at least it used to be. It's rotted away. I wonder how long he's been in here."

Brett tried to speak but his body was still ejecting warm liquid. He wanted to tell them what had happened to him even though he wasn't sure if any of it had actually happened. Perhaps he had dreamt it. He couldn't remember. And as he tried to remember, it slipped further away until almost nothing was left of the life he thought he might have lived except for Rochelle, and Tim, and Mark, and...

Jay.

Jay was real. He remembered Jay. He could tell them about his friend and how he had a plan to save them. He could tell them about Jay.

"It's a miracle he survived at all. The ship was completely dead except for the emergency systems. Even the computer was shut down..."

No. That couldn't be true. The plan was to shut down and start up again. Jay had said it would work. Jay had said he knew what to do.

Brett stared up through mist-filled eyes at the giant faces and opened his mouth to shout at them and tell them. They were wrong. They were lying. Jay was not dead. He tried to shout but he choked on the liquid in his throat. He choked and coughed and spluttered as the words fought their way to the surface. When they finally came, it was to the sound of a baby's cry.

The full-throated wail erupted from within him and filled the room, and he watched as his own hands clutched the air before his eyes. He reached for the faces that were now a montage of coloured shapes that he barely recognised as human. He could see Rochelle's smile, even as it slipped in and out of the mists of his subconscious. He could see Tim and Mark, and Jay—his face looking like everyone and no-one. With clumsy, trembling fingers he grasped for the memories of his wife, his children, his friend. And as he clung to the knowledge of who he was and who he might once have been—he finally understood what Jay had done, and why.

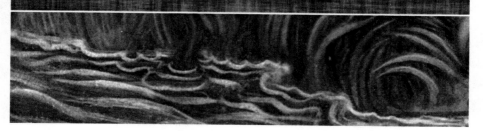

Demaré Design
Freelance Designer & Illustrator

Specializing in:

Space Scenes
Book Cover Design
Web Art
Character Design

TEHBUBBLEGUMNINJA.DEVIANTART.COM

ZOE.DEMARE@GMAIL.COM

LaVergne, TN USA
29 March 2011
222002LV00001B/177/P